T0128526

Tobias Lincoln Hunt

Stephanie M. Captain

authorHOUSE®

AuthorHouse™
1663 Liberty Drive
Bloomington, IN 47403
www.authorhouse.com
Phone: 1-800-839-8640

Published by AuthorHouse 5/29/2012

ISBN: 978-1-4685-9407-2 (sc)
ISBN: 978-1-4685-9406-5 (e)

Dedication

To my God---

The one and only Wise God

To You be dominion and power.

Without you I would be nothing.

Thank you for redeeming me through your Son Jesus Christ.

Special Dedication

To Kaniya---the feistiest almost 2 year old I've ever met

You got your wings

Tinker Bell has nothing on you

Fly high baby, fly high!

Your Mommy, brother, and Shekinah family misses you greatly---

We will see you again though.

Acknowledgements

To my best friend and husband thank you for always supporting and loving me no matter what.

My children ~ Amos, Ashley, & Aaron-Michael

You are the children that I prayed and asked God for—

I love you and am pleased with what God is doing in your lives.

To my new daughter-in-law-- Chantal, welcome to the family,

And to my one and only Simien you are indeed YaYa's baby.

You bring so much joy to my heart.

If I started naming the people that have helped me, believed in me, prayed for my success, and stood by me, this would be too long to print. So I will just say thank you from the bottom of my heart. I have the best:

Mother (Beulah)

Siblings

Friends

God-parents

Pastors and Church family anyone could ever have.

TABLE OF CONTENTS

Chapter 1

Watching her lay there still, lifeless, cold; I wondered about her life. She was a beautiful woman, even in death that was evident. Judging by her mourners she was loved. I watched her children, some grief stricken, screaming for momma that was forever gone. Others' quiet tears trickled down their face, but never saying anything, they sat. Some were caring for the father, the husband that no longer had a friend, a wife, a dance partner. After 42 years, 3 months and 5 days he was alone. His children would go home, his remaining siblings would return to their families, and the mourners would leave one by one and he would "be" not having a choice in the matter. He was no longer a husband, but he was a father and a grandfather. He still had a reason to stay a little longer despite the overwhelming longing to join her; his children, seven good reasons. They had been her heart and song, her pride and joy and they needed him. She would want him to see to their pride.

It was evident they did not want to let her go, these children. I watched them. Listened to them speak of her. Roscoe, not much taller than 4' 10 speaks of the last time they laughed together. He soon becomes overwhelmed with tears, shifts the gum in his mouth and exclaims, as if he just got the news, "Man she's gone! Damnation Momma's dead! Momma!!!!" Making no apologies to the preacher for his lack of religion. After all, it wasn't the preacher's mother laying there. He continues until some gentle hand guides him and his bare feet back to his seat.

Then there was Valerie. If she had switched places in the coffin with her beloved mother no one would have noticed it. For a moment I thought that was exactly what she was going to do. Until she starts running around the

1

casket in an airplane type demonstration. She then stops her tribal ritual, kisses her mother and sits down as abruptly as she had risen.

Sadie was all together different. She was poised, serene, even a bit melancholy. She graciously attended to the guests; far and near, related by blood or just word of mouth. One of the younger siblings, Collier takes the microphone and begins to rant and rave. I couldn't really understand his words, his accent being much heavier than the others. Whatever it was he said it almost incited a riot.

"Sit down and shut up," Kenny says.

"No, you shut up," was Collier's defiant reply.

I suppose that was all Victoria could handle. Maybe it was the Chemo her poor body had been battling or the fear that soon this would be her journey; I don't know, but she snapped. Right before everyone's very eyes. Leaving her pew, leaping over three relatives and a toy poodle she grabs Collier by the neck and proceeds to put him in a headlock while delivering him blows to the chest. Someone in the audience says, "Whip his butt he knows better!" But another voice overrides that one.

"Family meeting!"

Two words and the atmosphere changed, just like that. No one questioned when Graham spoke, no one. It was no question as to who was in charge. All rose and went to a private area that only God and them knows what was said. As they quickly and quietly exited the room I swear I saw their mother point her finger in a scolding manner from her powder blue casket. Grief can do some terrible things, but guilt, guilt had no boundaries. I don't know what was said in that room, but when the tribal meeting was over, the family was a picture of unity and love. Not another outburst, not another insult, they were on Oscar behavior.

By now I was at the point of mental and physical exhaustion. I couldn't watch anymore. I felt sick. A different kind of sick I had never experienced. I had to leave. I hoped my friend could forgive me, but I was far too emotionally drained to be of any comfort to her or anyone else for that matter. Weaving my way through the maze of mourners, some professional, some not, I made my escape.

Chapter 2

The drive home was short. The University was only a 45 minute drive from my friend's family, but our apartment was at the half way point. Those twenty-two minutes were an eternity for me. I do not recall the blue bonnets, the wild flowers or the Auditorium, just the sickness. When I arrived home two words haunted me for the remainder of the night, "Family meeting."

Mommy had been my only family until that car accident. I did not know the man that provided the sperm that brought about my existence nor did I care too. Ms. Ann did not even begin to qualify as family. The court called her "Custodial Guardian," but I had a few other things I preferred to call her. She claimed to work for God but I am sure she is a witch. I had the claw prints all over my soul to prove it. No, she was no family of mine. All through my high school years she threatened me to get good grades. "I'm not paying for your education; you'd better earn a scholarship if you plan on going to college because I don't have any money." What she really should have said was, "My trifling behind has spent every dime your mother left you on my new house, my new Porsche, my fine clothes, and the deacon sneaking in and out several times weekly. You know the one with a wife that lives across town in the big house with the white picket fence." Obviously they forgot I could hear as well as see.

Ms Ann's friends and neighbors were no better. I was at their disposal for humiliation and rejection; their version of hide and seek. You seek me out for the basic necessities of life and I will humiliate you to the point that you will seek to hide who you are from everyone and I still won't give you what you need.

Why had I ever agreed to accompany my friend to her grand ma ma's funeral? I don't believe I ever really mourned my own mother. For the first year after her death I was angry. Angry with her for leaving me with Ms. Ann, for having me in the first place, for not taking me with her, and then for not being able to see that Ms. Ann loved her but hated my guts. I should have been in the car that day. It was hot chocolate Monday. That was as normal as the sun coming up in the morning. She picked me up from school. I did homework and we sat around the fireplace drinking hot chocolate in the winter or in summer lemonade and talking about any and everything. Mondays were her day off and it was our bonding time. Only, this day she didn't come for me. I waited and waited. No one noticed me sitting on the curve waiting alone. A twelve year old that looked more like an eight year old, sitting for hours and no one noticed. When it began to get dark I walked to the next block to the store and asked if I could use the phone to call a cab. Mrs. Washington, the cafeteria lady saw me and said, "Young lady where do you think you are going in a cab?" I proceeded to tell her that I had emergency money for the cab. This was my mother's plan B. She always made me carry emergency food and emergency money. I used to ask her when to use it and she would say, "In an emergency." I would whine back, "But Mom, how do I know?" She always said, "You'll know." Mrs. Washington made me put my money away and told me "Baby, today you get to ride in Mama Washington's Lexus." I wondered how the lunch lady drove a Lexus, but my thoughts were all over the place and that one didn't stay long. When we got to my house a policeman was backing out of our driveway. That's when I knew. I still have that emergency money until this day. I never could bring myself to spend it. All I remember after my mother died was the anger. I realized living with Ms. Ann I must figure out how to survive. If I mourned I would die. Some days that didn't seem like a bad idea.

My prison sentence with Ms. Ann had been four years, five months, and seven days. I worked my fingers to the bone and graduated at sixteen; hatred being my sheer motivation, and had myself declared a legal adult free from the courts system at seventeen. I thought I could get my inheritance, only there wasn't one. It was gone. But as my mother taught me, I used my back up plan. I had a choice of three full scholarships. The first choice in the city with "her," the second choice, a neighboring state, and the third choice was the University of Alms, San Antonio College of Engineering. I chose Texas because it was the farthest away. That's when I met Jane. I think I would have given up on school and life for that matter, if it wasn't for Jane.

Rocking back and forth I laid on the couch balled up in a knot. My head hurt. My stomach hurt and I wanted to throw up, but I couldn't. I wanted to call my only friend, but she was in mourning. This was the one time I should have been there for her. I felt myself begin to shake. My palms and feet were sweating and my vision blurry. My chest felt like I had been kicked by a horse repeatedly. Zombie like, I took my cell phone from my pocket and dialed one. When the voice on the other end said, "Hello", all I could get out was a barely audible, "Help me."

I don't know if I passed out or not. When I opened my eyes initially I figured I must have been dead, but quickly realized that I was not so lucky. I could see Jane in the distance, staying out of the way of the Emergency Medical Technician team. I was uncomfortable and did not know why. Confused I reached up and found the source of my pain and pulled and the entire room erupted.

For the next couple of days I had several tests. Jane never left my side. She sat reading, listening to music or dozing right next to my bed until I walked out of that hospital. Her family was insistent upon me staying with them for a couple of days. All of my excuses were null and void and so with Uncle Jimmy leading the way, Aunt Valerie and Aunt Tracie on either side of me we walked out of the Medical Center.

If anyone can be overdosed on tender loving care, it would happen among this family. You will eat when you are not hungry. Food and a laxative cured anything; to include headaches and heartaches. You were made to sleep when you weren't tired. No matter what you did during the week or how you did it, you still had to meet Jesus on Sunday morning. If by some chance you couldn't go where He was, such as my case, the preacher brought Him to you, free of charge. Not liking rice was the immortal sin and disagreeing with your elders was somewhere up there with throwing rocks at Jesus. Whatever it was they said made you feel better than anything the doctors could ever have the good sense to learn in medical school and what the voodoo man did not know. Two days was all I could take.

Chapter 3

Sleeping was getting harder and harder for me lately. Graduation was on my mind. What to do, where to go, what job to take? I had my Bachelors in Engineering and several opportunities to pursue. I was at the very top of my graduating class. What would I say to all those people feeling so empty and alone inside? Jane's family was all I had but they had no idea about my life. Some secrets are better kept. I knew a lot of people but few knew me. I was known as the sensible one, the stable one, the nice one. Ms. Ann told me my entire childhood with her I was "Nobody's child", some days that was exactly the way I felt. I couldn't tell you if Ms. Ann was dead or alive and I preferred to keep it that way. When I graduated from high school and officially became an adult I chose to add my mother's maiden name; Waiters, for mine so she would no longer have to be a part of my life. I never told her what school I chose, I never even told her I had choices. I just packed my bags and left. She went to her usual gossip session she called support and I left, never looking back. Me, the suitcase I'd come with, the emergency money my mom had given me, and the few hundred dollars I had managed to save over the years without Ms. Ann knowing about it.

Truth be told those weren't the only things bothering me. I had been having these dreams, if that was the right thing to call them. Conversations with my mother and about my mother just seemed to interrupt my life for the past several months. I didn't know what they meant and I didn't have anyone to really talk to about them. Journaling was the only thing that gave me some sense of peace so that is what I did; until recently. I was "feeling" and I hated it. The dreams, the thoughts all made me remember, wish, hope, long, resent, question; and that all lead to one thing, extreme sadness. I had learned to develop certain methods for not thinking about certain things. I went to school full time, worked a full-time job, read hundreds of books, I studied, I made people laugh, and I wrote, up until now it all worked. Now I just stared at the ceiling night after night finally falling asleep briefly because of sheer exhaustion, only to be awakened by these dreams of my mother. It was like she was trying to tell me something but I didn't understand her. She was speaking clearly, at a good tone, but in another language; one I did not speak and could not understand. It was always the same. I am walking up155th place. When I get to the corner of the street where it merges with Main Street and I am not really sure if I should go left or right, so I just stand there. As I am standing there I see this lady from behind. She looks familiar but I can't see her face but I know I must follow her; so that is what I do, follow her. Only she turns and goes right back the way I had just come. I try to catch up with her to tell her no, this is not the right way, "I've been down this road," but she walks faster and I have to almost run to catch up with her. All I can see is the back of the long pink dress she is wearing flowing in the wind. Her hair is in tresses and every now and then she does a half turn but I can only see the profile of her face. She continues up Main Street, down 155th place, to West Avenue and Chamberlin. Finally I get to the bend in the road at Lyndell Court, but I can no longer see her. Frustrated, I sit at the corner on the verge of a panic attack. I'm confused. I'm tired and all I want to do is get back home, but I don't know the way. I am lost. I begin to get angrier and angrier because I was naïve enough to follow her and even to trust her. I get up and begin to throw rocks on the side of the road. One by one I tossed until without warning something changes. I can't really tell you how I know something changed except to say that I felt it, or rather it was a smell; a fragrance that brought me back to my sanity. I knew the smell. It was my mother's favorite perfume. The only kind she ever wore. Soft and subtle with a slight hint of flowers. Then, I lose it and begin to scream. "Mommy, Mommy, Mommy! Why did you leave me! Help me Mommy I'm lost!" Then from the midst of nothing and nowhere I hear her voice, "Baby, you know the way. You already know the way."

Chapter 4

Today was it; Graduation. I was exhausted. Not from partying, not from term papers; but from mental anguish and sleep deprivation. I did not expect an entourage, I had never had one. I don't know what happened to my mother's cousins, her uncles or aunts when she died, but they had certainly forgotten about me. When she died I guess they went with her because I never saw or heard from them again after the funeral. She had been an only child and having come from a small family herself, most of her relatives were older. Maybe it was the fact that I was shipped from Shirlene, Illinois to Kristina, Florida. That was a lot more than a few miles. I had two cousins, twins of my mother's youngest uncle, who had waited late to have children. Twins named Jewel and Jamie; I missed them the most I think. The last time I saw them was at the repast. The three of us were playing on the patio at their house. They loved Uno and I pretended to be having a good time for their sakes. Only I could hear the whispers. "Poor thing." "Humph, Lord have mercy, poor thing." "Such a shame." It was all I could do not to yell, "I hear you, I am not deaf!" But had I done that, they still would not have heard me. I wondered why the twins never wrote. Why didn't anybody write or call, come by or something? I wondered what I had done to make them all hate me. Why did they just let Ms. Ann take me without a fight. I couldn't understand why Ms. Ann felt the way she did about me. Why didn't my mother know how her friend really felt about me? Why couldn't she have given me a choice on where I wanted to stay in the event something happened? Right after my mother's funeral Ms. Ann and her relatives took me and their children to Disney World. When we got back she informed me we were moving to another house. After that, I was her slave, her maid, her meal ticket, and her sob story. Poor Ms. Ann giving up her life for the orphan girl. I always asked her about my mother's family, but she would always say, "They don't want you. If they did they would send you something every now and then. They are all no good just like you are no good. I don't know how you could think someone would want you".

I knew I needed to change my thought pattern. Ms Ann was the last person I wanted to think about today. I had to take a detour before I got in my cap and gown. Driving the short distance was one many of mixed emotions. It's not like mixed emotions were a new thing for me, but the volume had been turned up to the tenth power today. As I drove into the parking lot of the Law offices I tried to gather my thoughts. I didn't see a car yet so I figured traffic had gotten the better of us both. Surprisingly for a Saturday morning downtown was not extremely busy. I decided to take out my speech and drill myself some more. I did not need to be embarrassed, not today. Looking over the words on the paper proved to be a bit much; knowing what was ahead of me. I'm assuming I must have dosed off from fatigue. The light tapping on my car window aroused me. I was a little disoriented until I saw Mr. Nelson's face. Then everything came rushing back. I quickly opened my door.

"Mr. Nelson, thank you for meeting with me."

He had aged tremendously in the past four years. The salt and pepper hair was now completely silver. He walked a little slower and appeared to be tired.

"Good to see you young lady. My you are all grown up now."

He extended his hand to me and for a moment I hesitated. I hated being touched. He must have sensed my apprehension.

"I don't bite you know. These false teeth do not like people, just a good steak."

I gave him a half smile and extended my hand.

"Now that's more like it. The world needs that beautiful smile young lady. Now, what can I do for you?"

"Mr. Nelson you said if I ever needed anything… I have a brother. I need to find him. Can you please help me do that; find my brother?"

He looked a bit surprised although he camouflaged it rather well.

"Why don't we have a seat over there on that bench?"

As we walked to the little garden I tried to pull in the words I had rehearsed a million times before.

"Now, tell me about this brother."

I cleared my throat and began. "I don't know very much. I know he is about five years older than I am. His mother is Caucasian. He has our father's last name; Hunt. His mother's name is not Omelia like I thought, but Grace. I believe he was born in Shirlene, Illinois like I was, but I think he was raised by his grandparents." I waited for some sort of response. He appeared lost for a moment.

"I'll see what I can do."

That was it, no questions, and no comments. I gave him all of my contact information and that was that.

"Thank you Mr. Nelson."

"You are welcome young lady. Your mother would have been so proud of you. I will see you at graduation Miss Magna Cum Laude."

I didn't know what to say. So I just said "I will wait to hear from you" and waved. His reply shocked the devil out of me, if there was any left from Ms. Ann's beatings. The shock, which soon replaced fear in my eyes, must have been evident.

"Don't worry, she won't be coming. She doesn't have a clue to your whereabouts."

As I breathed out the slow breath it was only then I realized I had actually stopped breathing.

"Thanks again," I said and went on my way.

I'd wondered why he was so far away from Florida. Now I knew. I don't know how he knew but I had too much on my plate to worry myself with it.

When I parked my car at the Arena I sat there for a moment. I thought about the last 9 years of my life. Out of everything that I'd gone through and all of the conversation or should I say shouting matches Ms. Ann had with me, one stood out in particular. I took my journal from my purse and turned to my June 6, 2009 entry. It was worn from usage. I had to read it one last time.

When my mother left me I was angry at her for leaving me with Ms. Ann. Then I was angry at her for not taking me with her. The only thing that kept me sane and from becoming a murderer was knowing of my family, my real family. I used to hear my mom talk when she thought I was asleep. "Yes, she has a half brother she doesn't know about. Lord knows I would be the last to tell her." I always wanted to ask her how you could be a half of anything. Either he was my brother or he wasn't, but then she would know I was eavesdropping and spank my behind. So I did the smart thing and went to sleep. Just thinking that perhaps there was someone out there that loved me and wouldn't mind having me around gave me hope. Even if it was just a little bit of hope, it was still hope. I swore to myself that as soon as I turned 18, when I became nobody's child, I would find my brother. I did not want to look for my father. I think he should have looked for me. He knew I existed, and he should have cared enough to at least see if I was doing o.k. but he didn't. Besides, I was content with looking for my brother. I felt like we both came into this world without asking and neither of us had any control over the decisions our mothers and father decided to make. The only information I could remember was that when I was five, he was ten, so that made him somewhere between four and five years older than I am. I remember hearing my mother say his mother was white and lived across town with her parents until she met someone and left him with his grandparents. I knew his mother's name was Omelia. Who could forget a name like that? He got the "privilege, as my mother put it, of getting my father's last name, Hunt. Now it was time for me to return to Eaddy, Illinois. God knows I had had enough of Kristina, Florida and Ms. Ann. I had a good feeling about this. Somehow I knew it would work out and I had Ms. Ann to thank. If she had not told me every day I was nobody's child, I would never have been strong enough to start this journey. I may not be anybody's child, but I am somebody's sister and there was nothing she could do about it.

I closed my journal and brushed a tear from my eye. I may not have been ready four years earlier to search for my brother. Fear got the best of me, but now, now I was ready. Ready to look for the brother I never knew. It was time. I believe my mother had somehow made this decision for me.

Chapter 5

"Ladies and Gentleman, Distinguished guests and Class of 2014, Magna Cum Laude! Hannah Renee Corel-Waiters!"

The room erupts with roars, cheers, whistles, and chants, but somehow I didn't think any of it was really for me. In a trancelike fashion I made my way to the podium. For a moment I just stood there searching the room, scanning for a relative, some blood, even my mother as crazy as that sounds; somehow I had believed her when she said she would always be there.

"Good Day UASA, Faculty, Alumni, Distinguished guests and Class of 2014, we made it! I dare not say; today we begin the rest of our lives because everything we have done already is what has brought us to this point. Every triumph, all of the hard work, the long hours, burning the midnight oil and the self-discipline it took to obtain our degree. You should be proud. Now, a new journey begins. One that encompasses a wiser person, more accomplished, better prepared, and equipped to pursue what was once merely a dream. Some of you will go on to pursue an even higher education. Some will follow other passions and dreams; other will start that dream job. Whatever your path, the world awaits you. One thing we can all attest to, if you can beat the Texas heat, you can beat anything.

It is Gandhi that said, "You must be the change you wish to see in the world." Now, we must go back to our families, our homes, our new careers, for some new locations; and create the change necessary to make not only ourselves better, but our surroundings better. Better in the actuality that you had a goal, you pursued that goal and made it a reality; and this process

12

can be duplicated no matter where you are and what you do for the rest of your lives. That is change, the true formula for success.

So as you celebrate with your families, your friends and loved ones, be sure to celebrate yourself because you made this happen. Yes, with the love and support of many people, but the ultimate choice was yours and you made that choice. The commitment to become a higher learner, a higher thinker, and now you stand out above the crowd; celebrate yourself. Success to you! Go Roadrunners!"

After the ceremony was over I tried to make as quick an exit as possible. I knew Jane and her family had invited me to be a part of her graduation celebration, but I just wasn't in the mood. I was trying my best to make a break for it when Mr. Nelson caught up with me.

"Outstanding young lady. You were brilliant. You make an old man want to go back to school."

"Thank you Mr. Nelson."

"Oh, the pleasure was indeed mine. I have a little something for you."

With that he handed me a medium sized gift box with a yellow ribbon on top. "Thank you Mr. Nelson, you didn't have to do that."

"You deserve it Hannah, more than anyone I know. I will be in touch as soon as I find the information you need. Until then, don't party too hard young lady."

"Thanks again Mr. Nelson, for everything."

Although he was only the court appointed Attorney in my case to become a legal adult, free from the system and Ms. Ann, I was glad he was there for me. I don't know why, but it made me feel a little lighter.

"Hannah, Hannah!"

"Oh God why now?" I did not have to turn around to know that it was Brice Chandler calling my name at the top of his lungs in a crowded room. Ol' country self. Probably didn't want a darn thing either. That boy had annoyed me through four years of College. How he got through Engineering School I will never know. Somebody should be getting a check for him. I mean, how many ways can you tell a man no? Heck no, nix, absolutely not, by no means, negative, never, no way, not at all, not by any means. How many ways can you say, you are not my type? He might have been one of the smartest men in the class, but he was still rather stupid. I turned around and there he was. Cap hanging to the side of his big head. Glasses falling off his nose, and that big goofy grin plastered across his face.

"Hey Hannah, I want you to meet my parents."

I was ready to tell him off one last time and there he was standing there with his parents, who just happened to look normal. He had to be adopted.

"Hi Hannah. It is a pleasure to make your acquaintance. I'm Jordon and this is my wife China. Toni has told us so much about you."

I wanted to say, who the devil is Toni, but instead I extended my hand and said, "Nice to meet you Sir, Madam."

He continued, "What are your plans now that you are an Engineer?"

Before I could answer Mr. "Get on my nerves" himself speaks on my behalf.

"Oh Father, Hannah has some great job offers. She still hasn't told me which one she's decided to take, but she can't go wrong whatever she decides."

"Is that right?" Mr. Chandler asks looking in my direction.

"Yes sir. I still haven't made a decision yet though."

"Well congratulations Hannah. Your parents should be very proud."

"Dad! Brice gives his Father the look. But before either of them have time to be embarrassed I said, "They are. Nice meeting you Mr. & Mrs. Chandler" and make my exit. I couldn't even be angry with Brice. I guess he wasn't so awful if I really thought about it. If you took away Brice Anthony Chandler's glasses, his big teeth, and his clothes; he might not be so bad. But then I would have a toothless, blind, naked nerd. Nope, couldn't use him.

When I got home I treated myself to a rare bottle of pop and placed a TV dinner in the oven. I wasn't sure about opening Mr. Nelson's gift. It was still rather strange for him to be in Texas and stranger even, for him to come to my college graduation. After about an hour of not watching the blaring television I decided to see what was in the box. I guess I really had to prepare myself mentally. I just didn't know what to expect anymore. Everything I did was with caution nowadays.

I don't know what I expected but I was not prepared for what I saw. There was a card from the Mr. Nelson congratulating me on my graduation with a U.S. Savings bond inside. But under the card was what disturbed me. It was a Bible. Not just any Bible but one I recognized. I had seen it on numerous occasions. It belonged to my mother. Her brown, worn leather, King James Version with her inscription on the outside. Inside was a letter addressed to me. I don't know how long I sat there in a state of shock. Question after question raced through my mind. Where had it been all this time? How did Mr. Nelson of all people have it? Who or where did he get it from? I wanted to open the letter but I just sat there staring at my mother's hand writing. The way she always wrote my name, curving certain letters. I didn't want to disturb the envelope by ripping it open, yet I knew I must know what was inside. It was something just for me, and from my mother. Everything I had gotten from the day she died I had to get it on my own. When I left for college I didn't know what to do. I had nothing. Sure I had a scholarship, but it did not cover room and board for the summer months nor did it cover my meal card during that time. Some days I ate noodles, cereal, and other days I ate nothing. I wore clothes from the Salvation Army or other second hand stores and I only purchased generic brands of everything. I did not have money for the doctor so I knew I could not get sick. If it wasn't for Jane's uncle selling me the old car I knew I would not have made it. I realize they were being kind when they sold me the car for $200.00. Maybe it was pity. I didn't care I didn't have to wait two hours for the last bus trying to get home from work each night.

Taking in a long deep breath, then exhaling very slowly I carefully opened the letter. My hands trembled so much it became a difficult task.

"My Sweet Baby Hannah,

I guess one day I will have to stop calling you baby, but I sincerely don't believe I ever could. I love you so much. Out of everything that has ever happened to me, you are the most wonderful. You are beautiful and I consider it an honor to be called your mother. Did I tell you I love you? Oh sweetheart I really do love you. If you are reading this letter, it means that I am no longer in the earth. Although I may be in heaven I am in your heart, in your smile, I am in your blood so that means we can never be separated. I need you to know two things my darling; you were sent to not only me, but to the world because you are special, please don't ever forget that no matter who says or does what. The other thing is you are strong and that strength will get you

15

through anything. You are the very reason I never gave up. You are the reason I went back to school and graduated with my High School diploma. You are the reason I put one foot in front of the other each day God gave me. The first time I saw you I knew I did not need anything else, my life was complete. By now you should be with Ann. This was one of the hardest things I ever had to do. Decide who would raise my little girl if I could not. The fact of the matter is this Hannah, those that were willing just did not have the means. I knew you would have needs and wants. The others just weren't a choice at all. I could not put you in an environment of drugs or an atmosphere where you could possibly be abused physically or sexually. The thought of that just made me sick. Ann promised me she would be there for you if the time ever came and I could not; I pray she kept her word, God help her if she did not. Just know I only wanted the best for my little girl, or should I say my beautiful, brilliant young lady. I am so proud of you. No matter what you do in life you will be great at it I just know it.

Now for plan B. By now you should have seen a very important envelope. Since you were three years old I begin to save money for you. Oh, it wasn't much, but it was what I had. In addition to this money I took out a $250,000.00 insurance policy on myself with you as the sole beneficiary. This policy was not to be paid to any guardian or court appointed attorney, but deposited directly into your special bank account. The bank account could not be touched by anyone but you, but not until you turned 25 years of age or graduated from College, whichever came first. Either way, I am so proud of you. You always made my heart glad. I know you will spend the money wisely; you were always wiser than your years. If I believed in reincarnation I would say without a doubt you have been here before.

Your Mother,
Kimberlee Jonae Corel

PS

I know you may have some questions for and about Jonathan (Mr. Nelson) he is a long time friend and you can trust him."

I couldn't cry. I could only lay in a fetal position on the floor of my apartment and moan. I needed to see her one last time. I longed to hear her voice again. I wanted to say I was sorry for being angry with her for so long. To tell her how scared I was about everything. What if I got life wrong? I don't remember what she was wearing that morning when she dropped me off to school that day. I could no longer remember if she had on the necklace I made her in the third grade or not. "They" thought it best that I not see her in the casket. That it was best I remember her as she was, but I just wanted to kiss her good-bye.

I spent the rest of the evening alone. That is just how I wanted it to be. I finally had to turn off my cell phone because Jane would not leave me alone. She didn't understand and there was nothing I could do to make her. To be honest I was sick of trying to. Jane's family were a party people. They found a reason to throw a party and dance until dawn. They were some two-stepping, any kind of sliding, drinking and eating people. I usually got a good laugh each time I went for a visit home with her, but tonight I just wanted to be alone; with my mother.

Chapter 6

For the next week I don't remember doing much of anything. I don't know what I had to eat or when I slept. I know I did not talk to anyone and I did not cry. I put my letter and my Mother's Bible under my pillow and got in my bed. I didn't think much about the favor I asked of Mr. Nelson. I had far too many other things on my mind. For the first time ever I did not have to worry about where my next meal was coming from. I could actually breathe a little not thinking I might end up on the streets or living in my car; or wondering if I got sick who would take care of me? I didn't know what to think when I finally looked through the rest of the paperwork and found out that the $5,000 my mother managed to save for me plus the $250,000 insurance policy had accrued with nine years of interest was now $578,203.32. I could not comprehend that kind of money at 21. I felt much older but I still was only 21and this was much too overwhelming to even think about.

When the package arrived Wednesday afternoon, ten days after my talk with Mr. Nelson, addressed to me I didn't know how to process it. A lot had happened since my talk with him and my emotions were more mixed up than ever. I opened it with immeasurable anticipation. Inside was a bundle of papers tied with a little pink ribbon. There was a little note card included in the package as well. I opened the note with trembling fingers.

"Dear Hannah,

I believe you will find this information helpful.

I do wish this journey is successful for you, but regardless of what it may entail, look to God."

Mr. Nelson.

PS

"I am here if you need me."

There in the bundle of papers were newspaper clippings, old photographs, birth records, and guardianship papers.

The next day I packed my bags and headed to Virginia. I'd decided to take the job in Washington but before reporting to work I needed to do something. I had fourteen days before I had to start my new position at Terrofare International, where the dictum is "Using today to build a better tomorrow." Whatever that meant. I don't know why I chose Washington. I had received other job offers, one right here in San Antonio. Maybe it was the weather. It seemed to always rain in Tacoma. Sounded much like my life. Maybe it was the mountains, if I had nothing else; I could always look up to them. Maybe the fact that the container ships leaving and entering the port continuously would help the emptiness I always felt inside. It could be that the city meaning "Mother of the Waters" might be able to mother me. Maybe my fate rested in the city known as "The City of Destiny." Was it possible that it held one for me? I don't know. I just knew I needed a change. I wanted to go where no one knew me and I could begin to find out who I was besides orphaned, abandoned, abused, and rejected.

I was still processing the news of my big brother. He had just gotten his residency at a nearby Hospital and was practicing medicine. That made me proud. He obviously had been an early graduate like yours truly and went on to medical school. He had graduated at the top of his class. Married a year later and his wife had just given birth to a baby girl three months earlier. What was so amazing is that he had never been far away from me at all. Until High School the only thing that separated us was a single street. I wondered how it was that I never met him, ran into him on the playground or in the grocery store or riding our bicycles. The answer to that was all in a county line. He lived on Gayle Avenue and I lived on

Calhoun Street, a world of difference. Gayle Avenue was in Bridgeworth County and considered to be a "white" county and Calhoun Street was in Creek County, and considered to be a "black" county. The difference, they got the books, better teachers, and busses with air conditioners in them, more scholarships, better stadiums, and more funding. I got to attend the local school right down the street while he had to wake up an hour earlier and be bussed forty-five minutes away to the new school where there were bigger houses, gated communities, and more politics. When he went to school I was still asleep. When he got home from his football, tennis, and glee club activities I was already in bed. By the time I entered Middle School his mother was gone and he was living in another city and attending High School. I must have looked through my treasures at least a 100 times. My brother was a doctor, an endocrine specialist. I had a niece. I was somebody's Aunt. I wasn't alone. I had somebody in this world. A connection. It was time for me to meet my brother.

Chapter 7

"Excuse me, Dr. Hunt… Dr. Tobias Hunt."

Without even looking up at me he says, "You need to see my secretary Miss."

"She wasn't at her desk." Before I could get my next sentence out he informs me, he is sure she will return soon and that I should just wait in the reception area until she did so. He did all this without ever giving me his full attention.

"It is more of a personal matter. Is it possible that I buy you a cup of coffee after your shift?"

"I don't drink coffee and I just want to get home to my family. Now, as I stated before Vicky will be back soon and she can take care of whatever it is you need."

"What I need is to talk to you, Tobias Lincoln Hunt." At that he stops and looks up for the first time. Probably something to do with the middle name he had dropped since junior high school. His middle name, Lincoln just happened to be our father's first name. I guess no one was supposed to know that. I suspect that is why I now had his undivided attention finally.

"Miss what did you say your name was?"

"I didn't. I'd just like to talk to you whenever you get a minute. I will call your office tomorrow to see if you could possibly pencil me in," was my reply with as much sarcasm as I could muster up. With that I turned on my five inch black pumps and headed for the elevator. I wanted to call him a few choice words but the only ones I could think of society would say I fit the same description.

When I got back to my hotel it took me a while to bring my adrenaline under control. I contemplated going home but I knew I couldn't without seeing this thing through. Eating was out of the question so I decided to lie across the bed and try to calm my mind a bit. For some reason my mother's letter kept entering my mind. Each time I tried to dump the thought it just bombarded its way right back into my thought patterns. After realizing this battle was only causing me more unrest I got up and took out the only book I ever really saw my mother read on a regular basis, her Bible. Since the day Mr. Nelson gave it to me, it and my letter had become permanent party. I didn't know exactly what I was searching for so I just opened it up and let the pages fall where they may, which happened to be on Psalm 68; I began to read. I was still having a hard time focusing. My thoughts seemed to be out of control so I decided to read aloud. Maybe this would help. I went back to the first verse and started to read again.

Psalm 68

1. *Let God arise, let his enemies be scattered: let them also that hate him flee before him.*
2. *As smoke is driven away, so drive them away: as wax melteth before the fire, so let the wicked perish at the presence of God.*
3. *But let the righteous be glad; let them rejoice before God: yea, let them exceedingly rejoice.*
4. *Sing unto God, sing praises to his name: extol him that rideth upon the heavens by his name JAH, and rejoice before him.*
5. *A father of the fatherless, and a judge of the widows, is God in his holy habitation.*
6. *God setteth the solitary in families: he bringeth out those which are bound with chains: but the rebellious dwell in a dry land.*

I stopped. I just couldn't read anymore. Did God really mean what He said? I read it over again.

1. *A father of the fatherless, and a judge of the widows, is God in his holy habitation.*

2. *God setteth the solitary in families: he bringeth out those which are bound with chains: but the rebellious dwell in a dry land.*

It had been a long time since I prayed. I was sure God did not have an interest in anything I had to say. Plus, there were a lot of things about Him I just did not understand. My life had too many whys. I placed the Bible on my chest and placed my head on the pillow. I needed a minute to figure some things out.

I opened my eyes but I can't really tell you why. Something had jarred me but I didn't know if it was a dream or reality. Maybe I was just hearing things. I closed my eyes again wanting to be engrossed in the solitude of sleep.

"Housekeeping!"

My eyes popped opened again. I could not figure out why housekeeping would be at my room in the middle of the night. I was in a strange city. No one knew where I was and I seriously considered not answering, but her persistent knocking roused me from my dozing. Cautiously, I rose from my bed. While walking to the door I looked over at the clock on the microwave, 9:12 am. That hit me like a ton of bricks. It was after 9 in the morning. How could it possibly be the next day? All I did was put my head on the pillow a few minutes.

Chapter 8

I wanted to arrive early for our lunch meeting. I needed to be at the advantage. I chose a table in the center of the room, I really couldn't say why. I watched him approach the maître d'. Looking at him you could not tell his father was an African American at all. Unlike my 5'3, he was at least 6'2 or 6'3. There was no doubt about it, he was handsome. He carried himself in a way that let people know he was in charge, no questions asked. In his grade school pictures his hair was curled tight around his face. Today there were no curls.

True to his superior attitude, he arrived 30 minutes late. Maybe he was hoping I would go away, but despite our rough start the day before I really wanted, no I needed for this to work out. Sitting in the middle of the room made him a bit uncomfortable. I could tell by the way he scanned the room before taking a seat opposite the table.

"Miss, state your business please. I have a busy schedule and I need to make this quick."

"Hannah, my name is Hannah Corel-Waiters and I promise this won't take long. Would you like to order first? Something to drink maybe?"

"I assure you drinking is the last thing on my mind right now. What I would like to know is what made you invade my office and demand that I meet with you today?"

I knew I was stalling for time, plus I was trying really hard not to let his attitude get to me. This was just too important. I tried to put myself in his place and wondered how I would feel if the roles were reversed. That gave me the courage I needed to go on.

"Alright then, I'll get right down to business. Please accept my apologies for yesterday. The last thing I wanted to do was offend you in any way. Maybe after you hear what I have to say you will understand a little better."

"Miss Waiters, I have appointments lined up for the entire afternoon. Will you just tell me what you want so we can both get on with our lives please," he interrupts.

"Mr. Hunt…Dr. Hunt I have reason to believe that you are my half-brother…"

Before I could go on he laughed hysterically and stood up to leave. I was mortified.

"Please, Dr. Hunt, just hear me out. There is nothing I tell you that I cannot prove with documents."

"Lady I don't know who you are or what you want but please don't waste my time. Have you looked in the mirror lately? Just in case you haven't you and I have nothing in common, God forbid a blood-line. Just to let you know, all my relatives are accounted for. We are a hardworking, decent people that don't expect handouts but go to school, get jobs and make a contribution to society."

"Did you grow up in Eaddy, Illinois? Did you graduate at top of your class from Connelly High School? Where you were reared by your grandmother Omelia?"

He leans over to get right in my face and spews out, "All common knowledge! At least now I know you can read."

"Lincoln Hunt ring any bells? It should because he is OUR father. Your mother Grace and my mother Kimberlee both have him in common."

"I know of no such person Miss and if you ever come near me or my family again I will have you arrested. Why don't you try using the time and energy you used to come up with this ludicrous story and do something with your own life."

"You may be able to deny it with your skin pigmentation, moving to a different place, choosing only white friends, and straightening your hair, but DNA does not lie does it Doctor! I came here because I thought there might be a chance for us to get to know one another as family; brother to sister, sister-in-law, and aunt."

"Go find some other family to victimize. My family is off limits to crazy people. Understand this lady, I'd better never see you around my job or my family or you will regret the day you were born."

With controlled anger and calculating venom, I responded, "You will need me before I ever need you."

"What on earth could I ever need you for? My life is perfect. You probably don't have a job. Did you even finish high school? Look, I don't have any money if that is what this is all about."

By now I am standing toe to toe with him. He did not intimidate me in the least bit. I looked him directly in the eyes and said, "You may be on top now, but no doubt about it, you will have a long fall down. I just hope you break your neck in the process" and walked out of the room with my head held high and my heart full of hatred.

Chapter 9

I drove all night. I could not wait to leave. Being there was just too much for me. The way he treated me was worse than anything Ms. Ann had ever done to me or not done for me. He denied my very existence, my right to an existence and my ethnicity. He was ashamed of who he was, where he had come from, and I was a threat to his lily white life. It wasn't just the hateful things he said, but the hatred in which he said them. The way he looked at me and talked down to me as though I was subservient to him. He had treated me like some crack head off the street trying to get money for the next hit. Yet I had asked him for not one thing. I went there not wanting anything from him, except the possibility of a relationship. It took everything in me not to say, "No baby, it was your Mother that was the drug addict. That thing that had you was the one with a pimp. She left you with your grandmother to rear and never came back. She was the one who lay down with your daddy and made you a part of my life." But I knew he had no control over what his mother did.

As I drove I looked out over the horizon, not really sure what I was looking for. Mr. Nelson's words rang through my ears repeatedly, "Look to God." "Look to God." I wasn't sure if there was a God. My mother always talked about Him and up until I went to live with Ms. Ann I thought maybe there was a chance He may have existed. Only I had too many questions that did not fit into the whole God factor. Would God allow one person to be in so much pain? Would God allow such rejection and loneliness? Why would I be sent to live with someone who was incapable of loving me? Ms. Ann claimed to know God and that alone assured me that He could not be real. Her evil was all too real. I don't know if I could ever be a whole person again. I couldn't help remembering the crucifix in certain places of my brother's office. It was apparent someone believed in something. Yet the hatred in his eyes towards me was far more real. He didn't know me, yet he hated me. He denied my very right to be. The last thing in the world he wanted to be was black. I guess I was a reminder that no matter how much he ironed the curls from his hair or how far in the suburbs he moved, his blood line had my DNA. One thing I did know was that Tobias Hunt could drop dead tomorrow and I would not shed one tear. He wanted to pretend I didn't exist. Fine by me, to me he was dead. I ran to the only person that would welcome me without reservation.

When I rang the door bell I did not have anything rehearsed to say. I was dirty. Probably smelly as well from taking on the summer heat, but other than getting here I had no other plan.

When the door opened all I had in me was a "Hi".

He looked surprised, then worried, but I could offer him no explanation. I knew he could tell I had been crying by the puffiness of my eyes, but he did not ask questions and I gave no answers. My hair was a mess; uncombed for two days. I felt weak. I don't know if it was from not eating or what was eating at me. All I knew is that I needed a friend.

"May I come in?"

Trying to lighten the atmosphere he jokingly remarks, "You know my arms are always open." When he said that I don't know why, but I literally ran into them. I know he must have been taken back. I almost knocked the man down, but he quickly recovered. I let him hold me. I needed to be held, I wanted to be held. I needed love. I actually found some comfort in his arms and I wanted to stay there until I felt better. I never realized he could be strong. I did not see that one coming. After a while he asked if I wanted to sit. I didn't answer I was too exhausted to open my mouth. When I didn't answer he took my hand and led me into the living room and we both sat on the couch. He looked at me. Searching for some answers, but I had none. So we sat in silence. His arms wrapped tightly around me. I put my head on his shoulder and listen to him breathe. I closed my eyes to rest just for a moment. I wanted to forget it all if only for a little while.

When I woke up I had no idea where I was for a couple of minutes. I did not recognize any of my surroundings. Nor did I have any idea about the time of day. There was an afghan thrown over my legs. It looked as though someone's grandmother had made it.

"Hi sleeping beauty. I was beginning to wonder if you would ever wake up."

All too quickly, the past few days came rushing back like rising flood waters. I still did not feel like talking. He must have sensed it.

"I made you a sandwich Hannah."

"I'm not hungry."

"You should eat it."

I did not want to prolong any conversation especially about my appetite so I grabbed the turkey and cheese and did what he suggested. Before long the sandwich, the apple, and the pop were gone.

"What time is it?"

"10 o'clock."

"Are you serious? I slept that long?"

"That's called exhaustion Han."

"I should get going."

"No, you should get some rest."

"Do you mind if I shower."

"Oh, I recommend that you shower" he answers playfully.

"Ha ha. I need to get my suitcase."

"It's late. I can give you a shirt to sleep in. My sisters take my things all the time."

As I showered I replayed the last few days in my mind. I wish it was as easy to wash away the residue of life as it was to remove the dust from my travels. When I finished all my hygiene I emerged wearing the long black tee shirt. The house was almost completely dark by now. I took an extended shower and then even longer with my other personal care. I guess I was stalling.

"Hey, don't you look ready for the senior prom."

"Don't play. You know I could pull it off if I wanted to."

"Now that I have to agree with; if anyone could do it, Hannah Corel could. Are you ready to talk now or do you want to sleep on it?"

"I think I will sleep on it."

He beckoned to me to follow him down the hall to a bedroom I could tell was obviously a guest room.

"If you need anything, anything at all I am right across the hall. Sleep well Hannah."

"Thanks" was my only reply. There was a full size bed along with some other contemporary furnishings in the bedroom. There was one picture on the wall of a lion and some books on the nightstand. I turned on the television to occupy my time. I must have napped for several hours. For me that was all the rest I got in one night. Lately, that was all the sleep I got in days. After flipping through the 999 channels, I realized absolutely nothing was on television worth watching. I got up and grabbed one of the magazines from the shelf. I must have thumbed through every last one without really looking at any of them. I paced the floor. I looked out of the window and stared up at the stars. I listened to the neighbor's dog bark at only God knows what. Around 2:30a.m. I heard a distant train pass by, then another at 3:00a.m. Finally I just had to get out of the room. I opened the door and went out into the hallway. I stood at his door for a very long time before deciding what was best for me.

When I slipped under the covers behind him as he slept it took him a second to register what was going on. He was doing better than me because I didn't know myself. I was living moment by moment at this point in my life. He rolled over and I moved in closer and laid my head on his chest. It had been the rhythm of his breathing, the beat of his heart that had allowed me to sleep before. I wished this time would be no different. I soon realized that I needed more and apparently he did too. I could see his face courtesy of the moonlight. He had beautiful eyes; big, brown, sweet, caring eyes. Right now they were questioning. I kissed him. At first soft, gentle but he pushed me away.

"Hannah, I know you are hurting. I wish I could make it stop, God do I wish I could make it stop. All I can do is be here for you as long as you allow me to be. As much as I want this I cannot take advantage of you when I know you are so vulnerable. Do you know how long I have dreamed of this night? I can't. It won't be right and deep down inside you know it's true. You deserve better than that."

I never answered him. I kissed him again; firmer this time.

"I'm not that strong Han." He barely got the words out, but I still wasn't listening. I needed him that's all I knew. I moved my hands down his smooth chocolate skin until I got to the buttons of his pajama top. One by one I unbuttoned them.

"Hannah…Han…look at me. We need to talk."

He jumped up, turned on the lamp beside the bed struggling with his composure and demanded I talk to him. It wasn't what I had in mind.

"I haven't heard from you since graduation Hannah. I have been worried sick. You don't answer your phone, you don't answer your door and then you just disappear without saying a word. Jane didn't know anything. The Center had no information, nor your neighbors and any of the study group. You don't treat your friends like that. You just don't. Now you just show up out of the blue…Hannah please, please let me in."

"You are NOT my psychiatrist Brice! And you are certainly not my daddy! Stop trying to get in my head!" With that I stormed out of the room and into the spare bedroom slamming the door behind me. After flinging myself on the bed I just rocked back and forward for I don't know how long. I ignored the knocking on the door. I wasn't able to respond anyway. When I felt the weight on the bed I continued to rock back and forth.

"Oh Hannah. Sweet sweet Hannah."

This time it was he who did the kissing; just a feather like kiss on my forehead as he caressed my hair and then my arm. I felt myself breaking and I didn't know how to stop it. Like dropping a glass from the kitchen counter. You know it is going to fall and break, but there is nothing you can do about it except watch it go down in slow motion and shield yourself from the renegade pieces.

"I can't keep it together anymore Brice, I just can't."

"You don't have too Han. Let me help."

"Do you think I'm crazy?"

"No. You're not crazy. Beautiful. Wonderful. Smart. Caring. Fun. Strong. Never crazy. You know you don't have to carry all this by yourself. Leaning on someone else doesn't make you weak, it makes you last."

"I saw him Brice. I met him. I met my Brother."

I am sure I never told him or anyone else I had a brother, but when you are having a meltdown you seem to forget little facts like that. He never responded either way. Just kept holding me and caressing me and listening to me intensely. I was glad he did not interrupt.

"He treated me like trash. He belittled me, demeaned me and denied my very existence. He is a doctor. Practices medicine everyday and doesn't know who or what he is. He goes to great lengths to hide his ethnicity. God forbid anyone knows he is biracial. I always thought finding him would be good for me, for us, like I'd have a real family. He denied not only me but my race. The possibility of finding him one day is the only reason I survived living with Ms. Ann all those years. She always said I was nothing and nobody's child, but I knew in my heart that was not true, I was somebody's sister. Now, that is not true any longer. Maybe she was right."

I must have talked for hours. He listened to every word I spoke. Every now and then he gave a brief interjection, but I think that was just to let me know he was still with me. I can't tell you what time I fell asleep but for the first time since before my mother died, I rested.

I was awakened by him entering the room with a prepared breakfast. For the next few days this became our routine. Us talking into the wee hours of the morning and him serving me breakfast in bed. I usually attempted to make something for us to eat for dinner while we argued over who was cheating at whatever game we were playing. He was competitive and I was competitive and that equaled a problem. He never pressured me about information, sex or leaving. He just listened and gave me a safe place to stay. Just when I thought things were perfect, his mother showed up one day and I just happened to answer the door in my night shirt, or his rather, and he was in the shower. That lady looked at me and demanded I tell her where her precious son could be found. After that she stormed past me like Hurricane Katrina.

Why do people go in the other room to talk about others like they can't be heard anyway? I was definitely fooled the first time I met Mrs. Chandler. I don't remember her ever saying one word. Oh but she was making up for it now. China Chandler was without a doubt showing her behind and she was making sure I saw every bit of it.

"Toni bear are you shacking up? Why is she staying here? How long has she been here? Is she one of those loose girls? You know we taught you better than this. Is she pregnant? Does she want money because we don't have any? We used it to put you through school so you could have a better life, remember, a life with choices?"

"Mother, please stop. Hannah is my friend and she is welcomed to stay here as long as she likes. That's what friends do. You know you are being downright rude and that is totally unnecessary."

"Well you need to tell me what's going on here."

"Me and a friend were about to go out for dinner mother so we are going to have to talk about this a little later. Hannah are you ready?"

I had no clue we were going anywhere, but I was more than happy to play along with this charade if it meant getting away from Mother Superior. "Just let me grab my purse," was my only part in the dramatic scene. I was dressed and ready to go in record time.

"Well, I will just have to see what your father has to say about all of this."

All I heard was the door close really hard when I went into the bedroom. When I emerged Brice was looking out the living room window watching his mother drive away.

"You ok?"

"Never been better. You ready to grab that bite to eat because I am starving."

"You are always starving and it all goes right to that big head."

"That means I'm smart. Don't hate."

"I have another name for it."

We rode in silence for a few minutes then I just had to ask him, "You sure it's ok, me being at your place and all?"

"Han I pay the bills at that house. I respect my parents and I love them very much but I have to do what I feel is right for my life. As long as you want to be there, as long as you need to be there, is fine with me."

With that he looked at me and smiled then continued, "Besides, I could use a cook and a maid." Before I knew it I had hit him upside the head with my purse. I had a few choice words for him, but my upbringing would not let me say them. My Mother might just slap me upside my head. Hearing him grimace in pain was reward enough for me though. I don't know why he thought he was funny.

"I think it's about time I got going anyway. I still need to find a place in Tacoma and so many other things that come with relocating."

His demeanor changed from playful to serious mode as soon as the words left my mouth. I felt the change. It made me a little nervous so I continued to talk. "We both have exciting new careers and we are about to start a whole new chapter of our lives. Yours here and mine in Washington. I guess it is time to join the real work force as legal adults."

"I guess" was all he had to say.

The rest of the night was downright chilly. He just didn't have much to say so we mostly ate in silence. Having talked night after night it had now come to this, silence. I tried to make small talk but he would only give one word answers and that gets under my skin. He knew it too. The truth is, what little I had was already in storage and I wasn't sure I even wanted to take the job in Washington anymore. I should have been there already, but instead I drove right back to San Antonio. I still don't know why. When we got back to his place he tossed his keys on the table sitting in the small foyer and proceeded to walk to his bedroom, but I grabbed his hand. For a minute he looked at me and I stared back but neither of us said anything. Then he casually said, "It's late and I'm tired, I'm going to bed." When I said, "Not without me" he did no protesting, just took my other hand and led me into his bedroom.

It is funny how some people can fool you. I spent the entire college experience trying to avoid what I ended up with when it was all said and done. I never imagined Brice to be anything but a nerd. He was loyal, smart, goofy, energetic, dependable, and boring. Nothing I was remotely interested in. I guess I was only fooling myself. He made a good study partner, a great friend, but anything beyond that I had no use for in my life. I dated here and there throughout my college life, but it never seemed to work out. There were those boys that wanted sex and only sex and I was not giving it up or out. Then there were those who wanted to find the perfect girl to please momma while they ran around with those girls who were putting it out. Neither interested me. Maybe something was wrong with me. What did I know anyway and especially about men? My mother didn't have a man. Ms. Ann didn't have one. Most of the people in their circles didn't have one either.

For a long time afterwards we just laid there. I had just had the most wonderful experience and I didn't see it coming. I expected him to be a klutz. To not know what to do, but it was I who was left speechless. What next? Where did we go from here? I thought Brice would be a safe choice. No strings. Now I didn't know what to think. Initially it had not been the love making I sought, but what happened afterwards; the holding and cuddling, the talking. That's what I needed and wanted, but he gave me all that first and reeled me right in.

"You sleep Han?"

"No."

"I don't want you to leave. I mean you don't have to leave."

"I have a new job to start. Someone is depending on me."

"I figure if you really wanted to be in Washington you would be there by now."

"I have to work Brice. Isn't that what you go to school for, to get a good job and work?"

"I will take care of you. You don't have to work. It's not like your degree is going anywhere. I think we should give us a try. It might just be worth it. Besides, what good is all that work if you don't have someone to share your life with? Six months. That's all I'm asking is six months. If it doesn't work out then that's ok we gave it a shot."

"I am all mixed up Brice. I still have to work through so many things."

"We can work through them together."

"You deserve better than that. You know it and so do I. It wouldn't be fair to you."

"Promise me you will at least think about it Han."

"I promise."

"That's all I'm asking."

With that he pulled me closer into his arms and we both went to sleep.

Chapter 10

I was all packed and ready to go. At least that's what I told myself repeatedly. One voice told me to stay and do what you want to do for the first time in your life; while the other said it will never work so get out while you can. I felt bad leaving without saying good-bye, but I didn't have the strength to do it any other way. There was just too much going on in my head and my heart and I knew that I had to get away. I needed time. I knew the 2,204 miles of nothing but highway would certainly give me that. I had not even processed Tacoma yet. In those few days with Brice I had actually pushed everything to the back of my mind. My only concerns had been sleeping, eating, and being with him. It felt good, too good. It scared me. Wasn't life supposed to be a struggle? That's all I had ever known was struggle. I was still trying to wrap my head around the letter from Mommy, the Bible and Mr. Nelson; I felt overwhelmed. I rented a car when I knew I could have bought a brand new one. What did I know about cars? Who could I trust to help me or tell me what to do? My mind just kept going and going and going until the sun was setting again. I had gotten through the tumble weeds and the dust and I guess El Paso was as good a place as any to spend the night. I didn't know much of anything about the city, but I knew it would stay that way. I was just too tired to care. I half expected Brice to call after finding out that I had skipped out on him. He never did. Jane was different all together. She rang my phone off the hook until I told her I needed to save my battery and promised to call her and tell her exactly where I was staying for the night; address and room number included. After grabbing a salad and gassing up the car I found a hotel for the night and that was all she wrote.

For some reason when I eased out onto the interstate on day two of my trip I had an overwhelming longing to hear Brice's voice. It took everything in me to keep going. I wanted to turn around and go back. I wanted to call him and say I was sorry and yes, I wanted to give us a try. My mind replayed our last few moments together. Maybe it was not waking up to breakfast in bed this morning. Amazing how when you have never had something just how easy it is to become accustomed to it. It wasn't about the food. It was about for once in my life having someone that cared about me. As much as I wanted to stay I could not handle a pity relationship. Brice had seen me at my absolute worse and I know as much of a nerd as he was, he didn't deserve me. He had a good heart and someday he would make someone a good husband. I was just not that someone. For the last nine years I had been at my worse. Through puberty, tweens, teens and in betweens right up until I could actually drink legally I'd had a pain inside that no medication, alcohol, work or sleep could help. Ms. Ann never knew about the times I went into her medicine drawer and counted out enough pills to end it all. No one knew about the many times I just wanted to walk in front of a bus or slit my wrist and the other hundred things I knew would help me leave this world a little faster. He did not know that part of me. He only knew the witty, fiery, smart aleck, I don't need anybody Hannah. He did not know the bitter, resentful, full of anger, scared, lonely Hannah that I went to bed with each night. The only thing that gave me hope was the possibility of finding my brother and perhaps getting to know him. Now, I had a new pain that held hands with the old ones and I was sure they were becoming good friends.

Each day as I drove I couldn't help thinking Brice never called to even check on me. I knew he was hurt, but still I longed to talk to him. As I drove from Texas to New Mexico, from Utah to Colorado, and finally Idaho, Oregon and at last Washington I longed to hear his voice. When I saw the sign that read, Welcome to Tacoma, I realized it wasn't going to happen.

When I got off on the exit to the hotel my new employer had provided something happened. I don't know what took place inside my head when I realized I was half way across the United States and truly all alone. I had a job, a very good job, but nothing or no one else. Not my best friend, not Brice, not anyone. I was petrified.

When Jane answered the phone I was almost hyperventilating. I managed to get out a whisper, "Jane." That was all it took. She went into panic mode. I think she broke her record for asking questions. I lost count at nine.

"What's wrong, are you ok, where are you, are you alone, is someone hurting you, are you lost, are you sick, can you call 911, do I need to get my uncles, answer me!?" All in one breath. If I wasn't trying to have a nervous breakdown it would have been comical.

"Jane, I don't know what is wrong. I just can't shake this feeling of fear. I am scared and I don't know what to do or where to go. I don't know if I'm supposed to be here. I just don't know anymore. I just feel overwhelmed."

"Take a deep breath Hannah and just let it go. Let it all go. Where are you?"

"About a mile from my hotel."

"Ok just keep driving and breathing. Think about all you have come through. Everything you have survived. This is your time Sister. Now you can finally live your life for you and not for anyone else. Make the most of it. Cut the rope to your past and allow yourself a new beginning."

I listened to Jane as I drove into the hotel parking lot. I just wanted to sit for a minute. Maybe it was road lag, if there was such a thing. I felt like I had been running for my very life since the day my mother died. Now that it was time to stop I realized I didn't have any brakes. It is one thing to jog. It is another to sprint, but it is a whole different story to run like a lion is chasing you and it is only a matter of time before he catches you and makes you his dinner. Everything from the past several weeks was boiling inside of me and I just had to have a time of confession.

"I saw my mother's lawyer Jane. I have her Bible. I slept with Brice. Maybe I should turn around and come back to San Antonio. I went to see my brother. He is a real butt head. I don't hate Miss Ann anymore; she's just not worth it."

"You slept with Brice!!"

All I could hear was her banging her phone against something, yelling, "You slept with Brice!" Bang, bang, bang, "Is this thing on? You slept with who? I know I had to hear you wrong." Bang, bang, bang…"Peanut butter and jelly! Cheese and crackers! What in the Sam Hill!"

It was apparent she had selective hearing and that she was trying her best not to curse me out. I was spilling my guts to her and she was livid about my sex life. I had to tell somebody I had lost my virginity. I mean the man at the gas station just didn't do. The old lady in the grocery store was out of the question and a billboard just cost too much. Why not my best friend Jennifer, but oh no, she was acting like my mother and it was stressing me out.

"Jane! I don't need judgment, just an ear. I feel like my life is falling apart and I don't know how to save myself anymore. I don't have to fight but I can't turn off flight mode. I am stuck in high gear. I never have to hear Ms. Ann's voice again, yet the tape recorder still plays. I have enough food but I can't eat it. I have money but won't spend it. I have the brother I have always longed for and I hate his guts. I have always had a plan. How to get out of Ms. Ann's house, how to survive high school; how to make it through college, get good grades, and take care of myself. I knew just what to do to get to this place, but what do you do when you finally get there? Where do you go from that place and how do you do it?"

"I'm sorry Hannah. I can't say I know how you feel, but I can listen and be here for you. Do you want me to fly out for a few days?"

"What about your new job?"

"I don't start for two weeks. That is just enough time for me to help you find an apartment and find out what Tacoma, Washington has to offer someone as fine as I am…what! Besides I have to look in your face when you tell me about this Brice thing."

"Jane!"

"Sorry, darling. I love you boo, really I do" she said chuckling.

"You have a funny way of showing it. Anyway, Brice is a best kept secret for your information."

"Hail Mary! What you say! I could be there TO MAR ROW with popcorn and a slushie to hear this drama. Just say the word!"

"As much as I want to say yes I know I have to grow up sometime. Besides, the popcorn and slushie thing does not work for me. You know I hate popcorn."

"Party pooper. Anyway, on a side note, don't worry about your brother. I can guarantee he will need you before you need him. At least that is what my granny always says. Along with a few other words I am not grown enough to use."

"Granny knows."

"Now that is the truth and what she doesn't know her 38 makes up for it."

I couldn't help laughing at Jane. It was a sound I still had to get used to. Hearing myself be amused and maybe one day be happy is something I only dreamt of.

"You know Hannah. I think that sometimes just when we think there is no hope everything we have longed for comes rushing in like flood waters. Just to make us remember that there is still a God up there."

"I don't know Jane."

"I do. That is how we know there is a God. Again, that is what my granny says. At least I think it's my granny or maybe Bud light but it's still the truth. Just involuntary that's all."

Through my laughter I manage to say, "You need to stop."

"No my sister she needs to stop. As soon as they gave the benediction Sunday she pops a can of beer. I had to pretend she was catching the spirit when the usher asked what that foam was around her mouth. I grabbed her and made a mad dash for the door before she took another sip."

"Nooo! Did she believe you?"

"Girl I think I convinced her, but I know God didn't buy one word of it. Got me lying in the church. All I could hear in my head was burn baby burn. I went to confession bright and early the next morning."

By now I am literally crying. Strange, for years I had been crying tears of sorrow, but not today.

"I swear she is two people; one a saint and the other a rank sinner. The delivery man is just as confused as he can be. One day she invites him in and another day she shoots at him swearing up and down he the voodoo man."

By now my stomach is hurting and my eyes are red and no matter how I try I can't stop laughing.

"But I love my granny now. Yes I do. I love my granny. Well, I guess it is time for you to check into that nice luxury hotel before they think you are casing it for a robbery."

"I guess you are right."

"You ready?"
"As ready as I will ever be."
"Talk to you soon friend."
"Thanks Jane."

Chapter 11

Much of the next month was a blur. Terrofare International welcomed me and my fresh brain and put us both right to work. Between orientations, training, and more training I did not have time for anything else. When I got home I was elated about my air mattress and Chinese food. On the weekends I read and studied just to stay abreast of what the next week entailed. The only thing I had managed to do was find an apartment not far from my job. It really came highly recommended by one of my team workers who had lived in the area for a number of years and that was good enough for me. I had no furniture, no curtains; the blinds were good enough for the time being, and no pots or pans. My job should have been a stressful place, but oddly enough it was calming. There was always something going on. Something to prevent from happening, something to fix, or something to discover and this left me no time to think about the past. It felt good to be needed, considered, and validated. I woke up at six in the morning and went to bed around midnight and I was beginning to love my life. When you have been told so many times that you are nothing, you will never be anything, and the only luck you will ever have will be bad, you have to work extra hard not to believe it. I was meeting new people, learning new things, and doing things I never imagined I could.

From the first time I walked into my office, my office on the 19th floor, I decided not to carry the burdens of my past anymore. Tacoma was a long way from anywhere I'd ever been; so I made the decision to start over; completely over, starting with my name. I dropped my first name and began to use only Renee. It suited me better anyway. I made up in my mind that I would no longer wait for Brice or any other man to rescue me; I would sink or swim on my own. Jane was my only connection with Hannah. I'd changed my phone number and gotten a local unlisted number and a post office box so that not even the mail man could find me.

I guess it was about six months after I settled into my new life that Jane called me to say someone was looking for me. I must admit for about a millisecond I hoped it was Brice, but then I remembered I had placed him in the category of a weak man and I had no use for a weak man.

"Do you know someone named Jonathan Nelson?"

"What did you say his name was?"

"He said his name was Mr. Nelson and it was imperative that he contact you."

"Mr. Nelson, he is the lawyer I told you about. What could he want with me? How in the world did he find you?"

"Girl I don't know but it sounds serious. He left his number. Do you want it?"

I wanted to scream "No," but I knew Mr. Nelson had never been anything but kind to me; although I couldn't help but wonder why he never rescued me. My thoughts were racing through a world I'd left behind and never had any intention of returning to when Jane interrupted me.

"Han, you ok?"

"I'm fine, what makes you think otherwise."

"Well, mainly because I have been calling your name for the last five minutes and you have said not one thing for starters."

"I guess I was lost in thought for a minute. I really can't think of any reason he would contact me."

"Maybe he just wants to see how you are or something?"

"You may be on to something. It's probably nothing. If he contacts you again just let him know I am doing well. Nothing more, nothing less."

"You don't think you should at least give him a call. I mean if he took the time to track me down to find you it might be more than a social call now that I think about it."

"You worry too much Jane. Just forget it."

"You sure?"

"Positive," I said and thought that was the end of that. I was quite annoyed when she called again two days later to say that Mr. Nelson had returned yet again only this time with a package that he said was of the utmost urgency to be delivered to me.

I was a bit perturbed at this point with the whole situation. What did he want? What could he have to give me and why? Somehow I did not feel in my heart it had anything to do with my mother and nothing else or no one else concerned me. I was finally living. For the very first time in my life I was actually starting to believe that everything might be ok for me. Maybe I did have a future and a hope like Jane always told me.

"Han I know you may be angry with me but I am sending this overnight to you. I won't send it to your apartment, but I am sending it. I just don't believe it is something you should ignore. I can handle you being angry with me for a while. What I can't handle is you living with regret for the rest of your life."

"Why would you say that Jane? Things are finally better for me."

"I don't know Han, I just have this gut feeling is all."

"There you go with your feelings. You can't trust feelings. They tell lies everyday all day."

"Oh Han don't get upset."

"I'm not upset."

"Yes you are. You just sucked your teeth."

"Excuse me," I said rather annoyed.

"You sucked your teeth. You only do that when you are upset."

"What are you talking about?"

"I know you girl. It's what you do. All through college you did it and you still do it now. Listen, sometimes you have to face the past if only to bid it good-bye."

"Jane, please not today ok, just not today. Just put it in the mail please."

"I will. Just try to keep an open mind. Believe me when I tell you there is no one in the world who wants the best for you more than I do. You are strong Hannah. I know with certainty that I could never have made it through all the things you have. Every time I think I have a problem and want to complain I think of you and realize I don't have a right to complain."

"Don't get mushy on me now."

"It is the truth. There are so many things I want to do, but don't have the guts or the will power, but not you, you do just what you set your mind to."

"Jane when you have nothing you don't really have a choice."

"That is where you are wrong. I see people every day in the streets selling drugs, homeless, doing things that the devil himself would be ashamed of but they still choose to keep right on doing what they want to."

"I thought about all of that Jane if you want to know the truth. Pain seeks relief anywhere it can find it."

"But you didn't though."

"Only because I knew that stuff did not take pain away. It only camouflaged it."

"See that is it. How could you know that being so young? I have a lot of people in my family so much older and they do such crazy things. They are surrounded by family and refuse to listen to anyone because they think they know better. Yet you are an orphan and you know what to do."

"Don't do that Jane. Please don't. I am no saint. There is a lot that I haven't told you. I think if I did you would leave just like everybody else."

"That would never happen."

"That's what you say, but I know how it works. You may keep talking to me but our relationship would change. You wouldn't look at me the same or trust me as much, but I know it would change."

"That is not fair Han. Try me first before you sentence me. You judge me for what you think I would do. That's just not fair."

"I had an abortion Jane."

The silence on the phone felt like an eternity.

"I did too."

I don't know what happened but both of us cried. The kind of cry that says I wish I could do it over. How could I have done such a thing? I am just happy to be able to talk about it. It was the type of cry that gave me a freedom to talk so I could breathe again.

"I didn't know what to do Jane. I was so scared. I'd just gotten here. I never heard from Brice. He didn't use protection and I wasn't on anything. I was just learning how to take care of myself. I'd just started my new job and I panicked. I panicked. I confided in someone at work and it was their recommendation. She was an older woman about the age my mother should have been. She said I had my whole life ahead of me and that was plenty of time to have babies later. I murdered a man's child and never let him know it existed. I can't look at little babies now. It was my chance to have someone to love and I aborted it."

"Alone is how I went. I didn't tell anyone. Not one soul. All of my family looks to me to be the one. The one to make it. The one to bring honor to the family name. The one everybody sees as being different. The one who can't make a mistake. The expectation was so high I knew I could never live up to it. It was a boy. I heard them say it. I cried all the way home and for the next two weeks. I couldn't eat or sleep. Then one day my granny came in the room and said, "Child if you don't tell me what's eating you we gonna have to bury you and I know you don't want to break my heart like that." I told her if she knew what I'd done her heart would break anyway. Then she told me, "Let me be the keeper of my own heart. That is not your job." When I told her everything she pulled me close and said, "I forgive you, now you must forgive yourself." I asked her how and she said I had to say hello and goodbye properly. When I asked her how this is what she said, "Write a letter to him. Tell him whatever comes to your heart. Before you start the letter though you have to close your eyes and see him, hold him, and be happy for him. Then you write. When you are finished with that letter put it aside and begin your goodbye letter. This letter you must also say whatever you would want him to know. It doesn't matter what it is. Write as though it is the only time you will ever get to talk to him."

"Did you do it?"

"Yes, I sure did. When I finished the letters she took me to the store and we purchased two balloons; one blue and one white. She made me put the hello letter in the blue balloon and the goodbye letter in the white balloon. We drove to the country and released them. That's when I made peace with baby Joseph."

"Who?"

"Baby Joseph. That's what I named him. The people at the clinic lied to me. He was a real person so granny said I had to give him a name."

"Do you still think about him?"

"Every day. I just don't cry over it anymore. Me, granny, and God made peace about it."

"I don't know how to do that. I knew it was wrong but I chose my life for his."

"Han if you could change it what would you do?"

"Have my baby."

"That's all that matters."

With that we both went to bed. I felt a little relieved to talk about the ordeal, but I still carried my baby in my broken heart. Somehow I didn't want to release it. It was the only thing I'd ever had since being orphaned that no one could take away from me. I'd done that all by myself.

Chapter 12

When I received the certified letter forwarded to me from Jane I didn't open it for a couple of days. Something about the hand writing, the thickness of it, and the seemingly urgency of it made me uneasy. I specifically waited until Friday night when I knew I had no other plans than to stay at home and watch old movies and to read it. I most assuredly picked it up a hundred times, but had a hundred and one reasons not to open it. I needed to work out. Then I had to clean my house. Next it was grocery shopping for food I never cooked because I did not like to cook for just me, plus I still had a lot to learn about cooking certain foods. About 10 pm Sunday night is when I became tired of being held captive by a piece of mail.

"Dearest Hannah,

I do hope that all is well with you. I think of you often and whisper a little prayer every time I do. Life is not always easy but it is still a gift worth opening each day.

It is with regret that I inform you that your custodial guardian has fallen ill. There is nothing more the doctors can do for her besides make her comfortable. They have given her very little time. Initially, I was hesitant to write this letter to you, but after much soul searching I realized I had no other choice.

Angela has requested to see you and has asked my help in locating your whereabouts. As promised before, I would never violate your trust in me, but I do recommend you make peace with whatever you are running from. I am enclosing my phone number as well as Angela's number.

Remember, look to God,

Jonathan"

That was it. She was sick. She wanted to see me. He thought I needed to go. News flash, I was grown and as far as I was concerned Ms. Ann could rot in hell. That is all.

I felt a volcano of anger and resentment towards the both of them. How dare they invade my privacy, my peace? I had paid my dues to Ms. Ann and Jonathan Nelson had been paid for his services. Hell would have to freeze over before I ever set foot in her presence again, dead or alive. I took that letter, set it on fire and lit my cigarette with it. I had had enough of people pushing me around and telling me what to do. Let her suffer like she made me suffer. Let her be sad day in and day out like I was. Let her wonder how life was going to turn out for her. Let her lay terrified and paralyzed by fear. Just like Jane's granny always said, "You'll get yours, just keep living." When Jane asked me about the letter I lied. I told her it was some business with my mother that had been mishandled and needed to be rectified. Some things even friends don't need to know.

I don't know why but when I went to bed that night I felt like the weight of the world had been lifted off my shoulders. Maybe it was the feeling of knowing that Ms. Ann wasn't immortal. It could be the fact that I could now travel anywhere I wanted and never have to worry about bumping into her. For the first time since the age of twelve I had a complete night's sleep. There was one thing Mr. Nelson said that I agreed on, life is not easy. I was living proof of that, but more than ever I was determined to enjoy it.

Chapter 13

Just when I decided to live Terrofare International decided I needed to work more. I really had no time for much else. I was beginning to wonder if the sun really existed. I never saw. I went to work in the dark and I came home in the dark. I ate breakfast, lunch and dinner in that 34 story building. Some weekends I slept, too worn out to do anything else. Other weekends I had to bring the projects home with me. This meant my partners came along to put our heads together so we could close one deal only to start another. Making the most of a hectic situation we decided to create our own play. Somebody brought steaks, another drinks, and someone else desserts. There was Ms. Jean who was somewhere on the flip side of middle age, heavy set, size double D, 5'2 fire cracker that was most certainly African American, not black. She went to church every Sunday and played with the devil Monday through Saturday. Michael was the military brat who decided not to move on with his family when they were shipped to yet another location. Like me he had no family in the area. He was closest to my age and as carefree as they came. I wasn't sure what his ethnicity was and did not care. He spoke one culture and acted another, but if you needed help with anything at all, Michael Louis James was your man. Then there was Shirley, the people pleaser who was the most beautiful woman I had ever seen; blonde hair, green eyes, not a hair or cellulite out of place, who was defiantly a melancholy mess, but she knew her job. We had Connor, oh la la la gorgeous Connor Fitzgerald Lee; 6'2 flawless body, bone structure, teeth, captivating blue eyes and perfect red hair. A few years wiser, confident, and well educated Connor. There was Donavon who reminded me way too much of Brice. Yep he was the nerd that everybody loved. He had charm, wasn't bad looking, average height, had a very strong family background, and all the women loved him. I'd known him for almost a year and I don't think he brought lunch not one of those days. If his mother didn't bring it, some other silly woman did. Last but not left out was Johanna; big, baking, biracial, Johanna Hemsley, not to be mistaken for the filthy rich, deceased dog Helmsley's. She was morbidly obese, had a PhD in Engineering and bathroom psychology. If you had a problem she had an answer and the food to make sure you didn't starve while you were talking to her. She took you to her hand clapping, foot stomping, hat wearing, oil slinging, everything will be alright church where she was better known as Sis Jo in charge of hospitality. Of course I was the baby in the group but in numbers only. I felt so old and oddly enough I fit right in.

We always had to wait until Jo left before we got loose and sometimes that took a while. She was always trying to get you saved, take you to church or hug you. I had made the mistake of promising her that one day I would go to church with her. I knew there was nothing I could do to get out of it short of dying. Knowing her though, she would still probably have the funeral home to do a drive by on the way to the burial.

Life was settling in very nicely for me. Besides the feeling of needing to take the 50 plus club vitamin, things were good. For the first time in my life I was surrounded by people that liked me for who I was. No apologies needed. Ms. Jean and Jo helped me pick out furniture. Connor put me on a budget; I never bothered to tell anyone about my inheritance. Jane still thought my car was on credit. Before work Donavon, Connor and I hit the gym most days. It felt good doing something I knew was beneficial for me. Yes, Washington was working out just fine.

I never imagined in a million years that something good could come out of anything that happened in Ms. Ann's house. Amazingly, those times she locked me in my room were paying off. To make sure I didn't lose my mind I read any and everything I could find while I was being held captive. It didn't take me long to figure out her routine. When she wanted to entertain or go out and not pay a sitter it was all too easy for her to think of a reason to punish me. I was punished for looking at her wrong, sucking my teeth, not saying hello, speaking in the wrong tone, not combing my hair correctly, making a 98 and not a 100, waiting too long to respond to her, sleeping in, going to bed too late, or just being in her house. I knew when something was up. It was usually around the third of the month, fourth Sundays, and most holidays. I didn't care much because it did not mean I was alone, it meant I didn't have to be around her and that to me was like Christmas. Some days it was hot because she turned off the air conditioner to allegedly save on the electric bill; but my books took me to a cool place where I could live an entirely different life. Many times she forgot to cook so I was hungry until I learned to stash food in my room in places she would not snoop through. I put food in my sanitary napkins container, in my old jackets in the back of my closet, and inside my pillow cases. But it all paid off though, all that reading. Every time my co-workers said, "Now how would you know that" or "You are too young to remember that," I always had the same reply, "I read it somewhere."

That is what first drew me to Connor, his mind. He had been educated at the most elite schools, and knowledge always fascinated me. It seemed like each time we all got together he lingered a little longer than the others. The ten year age difference was dissipated in our conversations. We had nothing in common except our minds. His family was well to do, close knit, and lived in a gated community. My family, well I had none. If anyone ever brought it up I'd say I was an only child reared by my single mother who had recently passed away. That was all I needed to say. Nothing changed the subject quicker or made people uncomfortable more than grief. They just did not know what to say or how to sympathize so it was always awkward enough to move on quickly. That was the exact way I wanted it.

Whether Connor and I had a relationship as much as we had an extended friendship I wasn't sure. We had an understanding. He talked as much as he wanted to and I listened. I talked when I felt like it. He did not push or pry because he'd found out that if he pushed, I pushed back; real hard. For him and a select few of my co-workers my apartment was the hang out, the getaway, or the hide out. There were no spouses or mates, no children, and no drama. We went to festivals together, hiked mountains, went to the theater, or anything else we wanted to do. Mostly we just hung out talking a lot about nothing. That's what I liked about them; I was Renee and Hannah never came up.

I tried to ignore the haunting feeling that I was leaving Jane in my moving forward. She was the sister I always wanted and literally the lifeline that was thrown when I was going down for the last time. I remembered the first time we met; I was distraught to say the very least. That day I'd decided after having one more thing go wrong maybe it was not meant for me to ever have anything. I was hungry and did not have any food. I had an eviction notice for my apartment and I had nowhere to go. I'd gone to every agency in town but no one could or would help me. That day I just gave up. I figured if God wanted me to have those things He would give them to me. Then I thought maybe I was just not supposed to be born. Maybe my life was so bad because I was a mistake and nothing and no one could make it better. I kept thinking and thinking and thinking and thinking until I was standing over a bridge convinced the best decision I could make for myself was to jump. It all sounded rational to me. I didn't see the young girl sitting on the bench behind me, but she made sure I heard her.

"Look if you are going to jump I need for you to do it another day. I have a weak stomach, I don't do blood, and my make-up is too perfect to be crying over strangers."

I stared at her for a minute, but was speechless at her flipped remarks about such a serious matter.

"Anyway, the way I see it, there is nothing that a bowl of gumbo and a good heart to heart with Jesus can't fix. At least that is what my granny says" she continued. "Well, I'm not Jesus and I don't have any gumbo but I can tell you how to get both."

I was becoming annoyed with her. I am sure it was evident but she just kept right on talking with a twang in her voice and an accent I wasn't familiar with.

"Funny you don't look like a loser to me. I consider myself to be an expert on picking losers. First there was Bobby who thought he couldn't live without me, or Joslyn, or Janice, or Jamie. I thought I was his one and only but as it turned out, I was just another "J". Then there was Sean; the perfect gentleman. Good head on his shoulders, well dressed, educated and knew where he was going. I just hope I would have known where he was going before he headed to my closet so I could have been spared the sight of him standing there in my bra, panties, and makeup. Yeah, didn't see that one coming. And last but not least loser number three, the roommate from

Hades. The one who never pays rent, always in a crisis, doesn't know how to cook or clean, and sleeps with your man. I have a doctorate in Loserology. Just would have never in a billion years picked you as one. I mean look at you, you're beautiful. If I worked out until Jesus came or until we find out what really happened to little Caylee, I still would not have a body like that. My hair can be your hair though as soon as I go down to MiMi's and buy the wet and wavy b4 for $39.99. I'd have to put it on layaway of course, but in six short weeks it would be mine."

"Enough already, are you trying to cheer me up?!" I screamed annoyed and amused.

"Is it working?"

"Whatever you do, never study psychology!"

"Hi, I'm Jennifer, but my friends call me Jane. Student, broke, Bayou breed, Bayou dead. Please to meet you."

From that point on we became inseparable. I became a part of her family. Her aunt worked for social services and I was able to get some help. Her uncles made sure I had reliable transportation, and her father called me his daughter, something I'd never heard before. They were always celebrating something or someone and that meant lots of food and dancing. I was always being sent home with plates of food. One of her aunts always knew someone that just happened to have some clothing or a pair of shoes and in my size. Imagine that. The bond between them was as tight as any I'd ever seen. Jane's family originated from Louisiana, but some looking for a better life migrated to Texas. When it was time for Jane to go to college there was no question as to where she was going because she had to be near family. Their way of life and commitment to one another was a fairy tale to me.

I don't know why I was closing the door on her. The pain was indescribable but something in me needed closure and my mind said this included her. Only my heart was protesting. Still, when the feelings became overwhelming I just snuggled up a little closer to Connor and well that was that. It was only at night that she came to mind. It was at night when I should have been sleeping that my mother danced through my heart. Something about when it is quiet, too quiet that forces you to think.

I was ashamed to tell Jane I was spending a little too much time with

Connor, that sexy white boy from work. She would be mortified if she knew I was drinking a little too much, partying way too hard and had taken up smoking. The last she'd heard I had found Jesus. Only she had no idea it had taken me less than a week to lose him; just one late night call because the sex was too good and I couldn't tell him no. She would on the other hand be happy to hear I ate birth control like breath mints. The truth is I did not want to see Jane, her new husband or her big round pregnant belly. We were both different people now and maybe that is just the way it was intended to be.

There was no doubt about it, if Jane knew how I was living she would be ashamed. Her aunts and uncles would be at my door with a belt then have me baptized in holy water. Hannah Renee had taken up lying. I'd lied about Ms. Ann and the letter. To me Ms. Ann had been dead for years; her funeral was just a formality. I lied about my mother, mainly because I did not want to share her with anyone. I lied about my father saying he was killed in the war. No questions about it, it was the lies that made me pull away. Fooling the people around me was easy, but I could never fool Jane. This made her a threat to my new life. For once I wanted to be someone else besides that little orphaned girl.

Chapter 14

It was a typical Saturday when the delivery man showed up at my door. Johanna was in the kitchen. Donovan, Michael, and Connor were watching sports and I was having yet another conversation with Ms. Jean about nothing. I was sure it was another one of Ms. Ann's tactics to hunt me down. I felt violated. No one had my physical address except Jane. My assumption was that she had forwarded something to me. That had to be what she'd been trying to tell me with all her phone calls I was so conveniently ignoring. It had been several months since the last one arrived. I didn't even look at the envelope; just signed for it and tossed it aside.

"Don't you think you should open that," Shirley asks.

"And you're in my business why..." I said it before I knew it.

By this time Johanna emerges from the kitchen. "Who was at the door?"

"Delivery man" Donavon announces not looking up from the game for even a second.

With zeal Johanna assumes that the new curtains for the guest bedroom have arrived. Ms. Jean is all too happy to inform her, "It is not draperies but some mysterious letter that Renee won't open."

That was all it took for Johanna, spoon in hand, to waltz over to the mantle where I'd thrown the letter to stick her nose into my affairs, like always.

"Renee, who do you know from Richmond, Virginia?" She blurts out.

If it were possible for the color to drain from my almond skin this

56

would have definitely been the moment for it to happen. The blood rushed from my head just momentarily and I reached out for the coffee table next to me.

Connor asks, "Baby what's wrong?"

There was good reason for me to give Connor the look for calling me baby in front of all those people, especially when no one knew we were lovers. Every eye in the living room instantly focused on him, missing my fall from grace. The chair just wasn't close enough for me to make it. I slid to the floor and by some miracle missed hitting my head on the glass table.

"Renee, Renee, talk to me Renee please talk to me," Johanna was demanding.

"Should we dial 911," Shirley nervously asks.

"No she has a strong pulse. I just think she passed out. I told you she wasn't eating enough. Don't have enough iron in her blood," Ms. Jean diagnoses.

"Give me my purse I have some smelling salt in it," Johanna says.

"Smelling salt! What is wrong with you! You will not be putting that under her nose. Is that even legal?" Connor spews out sounding a lot on edge.

When I regained consciousness the room was buzzing with chatter. I did not want to talk or move. I just wanted them to leave me alone.

"Baby are you ok? What's wrong, do I need to take you to the emergency room?"

Connor was getting on my nerves and causing me to feel sicker by the minute. Now there would be even more questions asked that I would not be answering.

"I'm fine. I just haven't been feeling well." More lies. They were the only answer I was willing to give. How could I say I was just shocked to momentary unconsciousness? The only person I knew that lived in Richmond was Tobias Hunt. Judging from our last encounter, I knew if he was contacting me, it was bad; very bad. My mind raced so much until I thought it better to close my eyes to find a little peace.

Shirley thinks I should be forced to go to the hospital. Johanna is having a prayer meeting rather loudly. Donavon is content to allow everyone else to handle the situation. Michael is just plain nervous. Ms. Jean had a cool cloth on my head by now and Connor is playing the dotting lover. They were all getting on my nerves, especially Connor. Somehow I knew from that moment on my life would never be the same again.

It had been well over a year since I'd walked out on my brother at that restaurant. I never expected to hear from him and I swore on my mother's grave I would never contact him again.

Chapter 15

It took some convincing before the crew would leave, but eventually everyone did, Connor being the only exception. Getting a politician to tell the truth would have been an easier task. By now they all knew about our relationship. I couldn't help thinking, when it rains it pours. He never wanted us to be a secret. At least not among friends anyway, but I knew better. There was no doubt in my mind it would only complicate things, especially when we were finished having fun.

After everyone had gone home he came and sat next to me on the couch. Neither one of us spoke for a long time. Finally, I broke the silence. I was sure he would never go home if I didn't give him some answers. That was his personality. He wanted to fix everything. Only I knew some things could never be repaired.

"I'm alright Connor, promise. Just a little tired that's all." More lies. I really did not know how to stop. Every time I told one lie I had to tell ten more to cover up the previous lie. It was becoming exhausting.

"If I believed that I wouldn't be here darling. Something tells me this goes much deeper than that package and I just want you to know I am here and I don't plan on going anywhere."

With that he took my hand and kissed it. Cringing inside I said, "You know as well as I do we've been working long hours. It's catching up with me is all."

"You may be tired, but I know something is wrong. I have never pried into your past life. It didn't take me long to figure out that it was off limits. When I look at you, even though you are smiling, I can see that you are guarding a piece of your heart I can only one day hope to be a part of. Just like I can see that, I also saw something on your face tonight that made me want to shield you from whatever terrified you so much. You may not be honest about it, but you and I both still know it is true."

When he finished speaking he stood up. I surprised myself when I asked, "Are you leaving?" Maybe it surprised him too. He looked at me for a long time. Feeling like I was prostrate on an x-ray table I fidgeted a bit.

"Talk to me Renee Corel-Waiters. For once may we talk about you? The real you that not one person at Terrofare International has ever had the privilege of meeting, including myself. What are you hiding? Why are you so afraid? When I hold you at night I can feel your pain. When you don't know I'm watching you I see such sadness in your eyes at times and it breaks my heart. Relationships are more than physical. I know that sounds ludicrous coming from a man, but when a man knows she may just be the one, he wants all of her."

Maybe it was the gut feeling that whatever I was about to find out couldn't be handled alone. There was a great possibility that it was true that I was worn from running, lying, and hiding. Then it may have just been the way his voice quivered when he poured out his heart to me. No telling, but I allowed a part of me to step forward.

"Hannah."

"Excuse me. Does Hannah live in Richmond?"

"No Connor. My name is Hannah."

His face became a little flushed, but he didn't leave. The breath I'd been holding rushed out like someone had slapped me on the back. When he joined me on the couch again I took that as a nonverbal to continue.

"After I moved to Washington I began to use my middle name, Renee. My mother died when I was twelve and I am grateful that I've never had the misfortune of meeting my sperm donor." Waiting for him to leave I paused to give him time. He didn't move nor did he say anything. Both made me nervous. Looking dumbfounded, he sat staring into my face. Fighting back tears I got up and headed for the bedroom in desperate need of air. I felt like I was choking and just needed to breathe but struggled with taking one breathe at a time. Before I reached the bedroom door he grabbed me from behind.

"I'm here. I'm not going anywhere Renee…, Hannah; I love you."

"How could you love me? You don't know me. You don't know that the person in which the courts made my custodial guardian was dying and wanted to see me and I loathed her so much I refused to go. I was happy she was getting what she deserved after all the evil things she did to me. You don't know when I relocated here I was pregnant and had an abortion. You don't know that I have a half-brother whom I hate; the doctor who lives in Virginia. You don't know that I've been avoiding my best friend in the world; the only person who has always been there for me. The only one who has stayed and loved me through it all and I'm not talking to her because of jealousy. She has the husband, the baby, the family, the love I know I will never have. You don't know me at all. I don't know who I am yet, how could you? How could you love such a stranger, because that is who you have been sleeping with?" Feeling certain I'd given him enough to no longer need an excuse to leave I attempted to walk out of his hold. He wouldn't let go. Demanding that he loose his hold on me I commence to yell and scream at him. "Why should you be any different than anyone else Connor? Just leave me alone. You make me sick. You don't love me and you know it. You've never taken the little black girl home to your precious family have you?" Even though I pushed, pulled, and shoved he just repositioned himself and held me even tighter until I'd literally wore myself out. When he was sure I had no more strength he pulled me to him close enough to whisper in my ear, "I'm not going to walk out on us." With that I broke into tiny little pieces I was certain could never be put back together again.

"I'm tired Connor, so tired. I just can't do it anymore."

"You don't have to do this alone anymore Renee."

"Sometimes I feel like I was some type of experiment that failed and the inventors have not figured out what they wanted to do with me yet. Why are people born to have pain and suffer? My whole life had to be some big mistake because as much as I try I can't see any reason for it. No one knows or cares that I even exist. Why can't I just go to sleep and never wake up?"

"Sweetheart please don't say that. I need you just as much as I know you need me. God Renee I can't imagine the world without you in it. You have an inner strength that forces others to take notice. Why do you think everyone wants to be around you? We make social calls to your office, your apartment, or the gym not because we don't have anywhere else to go, but because we draw strength from you. That smile of yours illuminates any atmosphere. It is beyond me why you've had so much pain. It is beyond me to construe, but I do know you were meant to be here. I'm certain of it. Whatever it is you have to face Sweetheart I'll be there, I promise."

The uncertainty of his words toyed with my heart. The rational reasoning part of me argued he was just caught in the middle of a bad situation; but every time he called me Baby, Sweetheart, or Darling and caressed me so lovingly my defenses were weakened. Overwhelmed is how I felt and going to bed was all I could manage at that point.

"I need to lie down Connor."

He almost carried me to the bedroom and from there I just rocked back and forth until I fell asleep fully dressed and in my make-up, leaving the letter from Richmond sitting on the mantle.

Chapter 16

The low muffled sound of voices lured me into consciousness. Getting out of bed was not on my to-do list. Climbing mount McKinley would have been easier than facing the crew after the previous evening unfolded. Mentally and physically I was drained and I knew it. It was difficult for me to recognize this new feeling. I'd never been here before. Connor obviously was moving about in the kitchen. By the sound of things he was not alone. Donavon and Michael I was sure were at the gym. Johanna and Ms. Jean would be in church just as sure as the sun rose in the morning. The only person I could think of that would come by early Sunday morning was Shirley. It didn't matter much anyway. I was not engaging in any activity this Sunday morning. Thinking was low on my list of priorities; nevertheless, my mind returned to the good doctor repeatedly. The day we parted ways I knew from his stand point and mine that it was for forever. A matter of life and death is the only reason I could imagine ever hearing from him and even that shocked me. Judging from what I knew about the both of us we did have something in common after all, pride.

There was no way to get around reading the letter, but I knew just from the extreme fatigue I was feeling I wanted Connor with me. Before I could talk myself out of it, I picked up my cell from the nightstand and texted him, "Good morning :)." Less than sixty seconds later the man who claimed to love me stood over my bed.

"Good morning Sweetheart. I was beginning to worry. I've never known the great Renee Corel-Waiters to sleep past seven a.m. on any given day of the week."

"What time is it?"

"Almost noon."

"Excuse me. Why didn't you wake me up?" Already I was becoming overexcited. Me sleeping the morning away was another clue that my body was not feeling right.

"Honestly, I thought about it, but then I thought better of it. You didn't miss anything, believe me."

"Who's in the kitchen?"

"Johanna."

"Johanna!" I sat up in the bed in disbelief and almost shock. I couldn't believe what I was hearing. Johanna did not miss church for anyone or anything. Heaven forbid she was late. She took her God and her church duties very seriously. Serious, like you have three days to live serious. Serious, like Jesus will be back this afternoon, not tomorrow. My stomach immediately begins to do flips and the smell of the food in the kitchen made it worse. Johanna must have sensed something. Most times she got on my nerves with her feelings, but I still knew they always checked out, even if I never told her she was right.

"Stop it Sweetheart," he says, easing onto the bed beside me.

"Stop what," I asked feeling myself getting irritated already. With his arms around my waist he sits for a minute in silence.

"You are thinking too much my dear."

He was right and I knew it. I was tired of running and I was tired of hiding. Whatever else I had to face in life I just had to go ahead and do it. With that I asked if he would bring me the package from the mantle so I could deal with it and move on with my life.

When he returned Johanna was right behind him being a mother hen. A part of me did not want her there, yet another part of me did. There was still so much she did not know about me. Connor and I still had much to talk about after my confessions the night before. Trying to figure out a way to tell her I preferred some privacy and not hurt her feelings or be disrespectful after she'd missed her church service for me was difficult at best. After vacillating back and forth for a few seconds I proceeded to serve her walking papers. When I made eye contact with her the tenderness in her eyes turned my heart to mush. She extended her hand to me and I gladly took it. With Connor on one side of the bed and Johanna on the other I opened the package from Richmond, Virginia addressed to Miss Hannah Corel-Waiters.

To the person of Hannah Renee Corel-Waiters of Eaddy, Illinois, descendent of Kimberlee Jonae Corel and Lincoln Hunt.

This is a personal matter in regards to your half-brother Tobias Hunt, also of Eaddy, Illinois, born to Grace Shepard and Lincoln Hunt, but reared by his grandmother Omelia Shepard.

With great sorrow I inform you that your brother is gravely ill and is not expected to live. He has a rare form of cancer of which there is no cure. His only chance of survival is a bone marrow transplant. His family members, close friends, and co-workers have all participated in a bone marrow drive in his honor, but to date the National Registry has been unsuccessful in finding a donor match.

Words cannot express the great sorrow I feel as I watch my grandson as he slowly dies each day and the pain in the face of his beautiful wife Kelly. Knowing that he will never see his daughter, Ally, grow up is just heartbreaking. I understand that the two of you are strangers, but one thing does unite the two of you, and that is blood. No matter how it may have been denied it does make you a possibility for a donor match. I know I am asking a lot and maybe I have no right to ask such a thing, but my grandson is all I have in the world.

Enclosed is the hospital information and my contact information. Should you decide to visit or if you find it in your heart to consider the possibility of exploring further into the simple test to see if you could be a match you have the information. Your name has been added to the family visitors' list at the hospital so you will be able to visit without difficulty.

Please forgive me for invading your privacy, but I know that if for no other reason you deserved the opportunity to say a proper good-bye.

Sincerely,

Omelia Shepard

The three of us sat on the bed without uttering a word. There were no words in me. No tears. Nothing. I felt completely and utterly barren. My soul was desolate. Leaning back against my pillow I felt the urgency to close my eyes. Maybe it would help. It did not.

My feelings towards Tobias Hunt were exactly the same. If he was going to die let him die. I said I would never do anything for him and that was concrete. He was still a butt hole, now he was just a dying one. His superior attitude was unforgettable and unforgiveable. Why do people live differently when they know they are dying? Why wouldn't you live each day like it was your last on earth anyway? Why should an emergency, a catastrophe, or an illness make you suddenly realize what and who matters in the world? One thing was certain for me and I had no doubt in my mind about it, my half-brother was not interested in a relationship just my DNA. Clearer than anything was the fact that it was his grandmother who found me and wrote the letter and that told me all I needed to know.

The portrait of his wife and daughter flashed through my mind. There had been a beautiful family picture sitting on the desk in his office. The image was not hard to recall although it had been many months since I'd seen it. Taken in the middle of a field, the three of them sat bare foot in jeans and white shirts on a blanket looking like no one or nothing else could ever matter. My mind and my heart went to the little girl, my niece, as odd as that was to think about her that way. When I left Richmond that day I took everything to do with that experience and buried it. It was the only way I could go on with my own life after so many years of holding on to the fairy tale of happily ever after. Now, I'd been forced to reopen that box once again and Ally was the only reason. It wasn't for her grandmother, her mother, and certainly not her father. I without a doubt had to at least consider some things concerning her. Like someone should have considered me. Children aren't normally depressed. They don't wear long sleeves in the summer and they should have appetites sometimes. Even if you say they are with the babysitter and you never see the sitter come and go it should be a sign to someone. The child was my only concern.

The day passed slowly and quietly. Comical is how I would have to describe Connor and Johanna. Protective and nerve racking is what it all amounted to in the end. He was the affectionate lover and she was the woman of God on a rescue mission. I really did not have much to say about it all for the time being. How far was someone expected to go when being asked to change their life for someone that did not give a rat's behind about yours? How likely was it that Dr. Tobias Hunt would even send a flower to my funeral if he knew I'd finally met my maker? My mother always taught me to love, to forgive, and to lend a helping hand. Funny how it took this time in my life to discover just how much I wasn't like her anymore. It was a struggle to remember how she looked; her voice, her smell, and her beliefs all seemed to be slipping away from me subtly. That was my greatest sorrow; I was losing my mother all over again just when I needed her most.

Jane came to mind many times during the course of the day. My heart's desire was to talk to her. I must tell her the truth about everything. Coming clean was not an option. Not when it came to Jane and not for myself either. I had to admit that I was in love with Connor and that I needed people in my life. Love was a necessity of life. It was vital that I embraced love and stop running from those around me that were so willing to give it to me. Amazingly my fears were becoming less of a problem even in the midst of all of the turmoil. Why I felt a strange sense of peace washing over me is a mystery to me. Perhaps it was the calm before the storm. Peradventure it was Johanna constantly praying when she thought I was sleeping. There was a great possibility it was having someone at my side through my crisis. Only time would be able to tell the story. It felt good and for me that was like winning the lotto. I'd forgotten what good felt like.

Johanna finally went home, but not before she'd cooked, cleaned, done laundry, and made me promise to call her even if it was during the night if I needed to talk. Assuring her I would be just fine she reluctantly left. There was no such happening with Connor. Truth is I wanted him to stay. I needed him to stay and I am sure he knew it. It had taken me several months to realize why I opened my heart to him. Sex was not it, nor was it position or money, but the fact that we could say so much without having to say much at all. Just one hand squeeze, look across the room, smile, text at the right time, card for no apparent reason, or call was who he was for me. As much as I didn't want to believe it, it was true; someone really loved me and had been patient enough to wait until I wasn't afraid to love him back. That night I did not sleep much at all as with so many other nights during the past few years. Not because I was afraid, nightmares, or sickness, but I was talking. Talking about things I'd kept bottled up for so long. Things that had held me hostage for so long. Things that I could not take a chance on being judged for feeling, doing, or thinking. When I went to sleep during the middle of the night for the first time in my adult life I was confident enough to trust whatever decision was right for me. No pressure from anyone, in particular, Omelia Shepard or Tobias Hunt.

Before I drifted off to sleep I already knew I would not be reporting for duty at Terrofare International the next day. There were some tough adult decisions to make and that took time and my undivided attention. I called out for the very first time, wrong decision. My phone went crazy. Little Renee never got sick or called out. My team thought it was something to look into, some for no other reason than being down right nosey, others had genuine concern. My only recourse was to turn off my phone and my computer. "You've got mail" was not vital information in this moment of my life.

Chapter 17

The only audible sounds in the room were that of the machines. A beep followed by a swish and a few clicks, then the sound of pumping, another swish and it started all over again. It happened every 30 seconds, 2,880 times each day since he had arrived; eleven days before. The elderly woman in the corner was barely noticeable. She held on to her beads caressing them gently. Her eyes were fixed on the figure lying in the bed; motionless, pale, and almost comatose. Nurses left small meals for her each day. The doctors insisted the bed on the other side of the curtain remain empty so that she could rest, but she still did not. She left his bedside only to use the restroom when nature could no longer be ignored. She took catnaps in the recliner when her body demanded it. The other hours of the day she brushed his hair, hummed his favorite childhood song, and held his hand. Each night she tucked him in promising to be right there when he woke up. True to her word she remained at his side with each sunrise, only he never heard a word of her promises, at least that is what the doctors told her. Only she had her own beliefs. Standing no taller than 4'10 her round frame appeared frail at best. Her thinning bluish gray hair curled in soft tresses around her sad oval face.

Standing in the doorway, I was reluctant to make my presence known. Closure was why I knew I had to come and see Tobias, but now seeing him I was certain it would not be that simple. My stomach churned and my heart beat faster. I hadn't known what to expect but this was not it. Remorsefully I hated that I did not allow someone to accompany me. Seeing him so sick put all my personal feelings in utter confusion. When I was very small I used to dream of meeting him. Us becoming friends and being there for each other was what my heart desired. As far as I was concerned we had both been victims and that made my heart compassionate for him; until my first encounter with him. Seeing him crumbled in his hospital bed took me right back to those feelings again.

"Hannah...?"

"Yes, yes Ma'am I'm Hannah. Sorry I did not mean to disturb your visit."

"You could never do that. I have prayed for this moment a million times. I'm Omelia by the way."

"It's a pleasure meeting you Ms. Shepard."

"Come over and say hi. I am sure he will be pleased to see you."

Frozen I stood staring at her. Why was I even here? What could I do? What should I say? The overwhelming feeling to run seized me and that is exactly what I did. Feeling faint, nauseous, and guilty I left that room with every intention of never going back. Hardly knowing where I was running to I escaped through the first exit I could find. Breathing hard and feeling like the chief of sinners I got onto the elevator. Only God knows what happened next.

"Miss, are you ok?"

As I stared up at the people in the elevator I finally recognized one thing Johanna always said was true, no man is an island.

"Her pulse is a little fast but strong. I think she fainted."

Unknown to me the man standing over me was not the only person concerned for my welfare. Quickly I begin to realize I was surrounded by white coats and scrubs. Somehow I'd managed to get on the wrong elevator to have my moment of weakness, not to mention shame. I knew I had to make a quick recovery.

"Thank you, but I'm fine. Just a little lost," I said getting up with more helping hands than I could ever need.

"Where are you trying to go?" This from a middle aged Caucasian doctor resembling anybody's uncle.

"Out, I was trying to leave. I guess I got a little turned around." Why was I talking so much?

"Oh..." From another who didn't look to be much older than myself, which just happened to be quite the Hispanic hunk.

"You have family here?" The other two asked almost simultaneously. My guess is they were trying to keep me talking while they assessed me.

Still a little shaken I said, "My brother, Tobias, Tobias Hunt."

Now why I said that I will never know? Maybe it was the lack of oxygen to the brain. Could be I was surround by testosterone or maybe it was white coat syndrome. Only God knows and He certainly was not telling me, but from that public announcement on, it was on.

The entire room fell silent in a holy hush. Even the elevator paused it seemed.

"You mean Dr. Hunt?"

It was not hard to miss the looks. Apparently I'd stumbled onto some of his colleagues. Realizing I'd said too much. I tried to make an escape when the elevator doors opened. It wouldn't be that easy. One of them pursued after me.

"Wait a minute Miss. Are you talking about Dr. Tobias Hunt? I could show you to his room."

Great, by now I have an audience. Every doctor on that elevator stood staring waiting for my reply. Just what I've always wanted, but somehow this had not been my fantasy when I played the naughty nurse.

"No thank you I'm just trying to find my way out."

Persistently and intrusively Dr. Emmanuel, according to his name badge, takes me by the arm and decides it would be easier to show me rather than tell me the way out. He received no argument from me. Ready to leave the hospital was an understatement. Clueless and still feeling a bit overwhelmed I eagerly followed his lead. I already knew the first thing I planned to do was hail a taxi and go to my hotel room and sort through this whole muddle. Bewildered, my next thought was to just go right back to the airport and fly home. I never saw my mother after I left for school that day so confronting death had not been an option. In this situation it confronted me and I most assuredly did not have an answer for it. Seeing someone else that was a part of me lying lifeless was something I did not prepare for. He was still the closest relative I had in the whole world. He may not have liked me, wanted me, or accepted me, but it was still true.

It wasn't until we bumped into Tobias' grandmother in the hall just outside the family waiting room that I realized Dr. Emmanuel had deceived me. The look I gave the doctor was nothing short of murderous.

He looked half apologetically and partly sympathetic for his behavior but I was still upset with him.

"Oh Gabe, thank goodness you found her. She was so upset and I didn't know where she went," Ms. Shepard says almost at the point of tears. All the while she was putting a death grip on my arm. Maybe she thought I was going to run away again or maybe she was trying to comfort me, I couldn't tell.

"Hannah… I am elated you could come."

No doubt I knew the lady entering the room was Kelly, Tobias' wife. Their family picture was forever etched in my memory. This was turning into a circus and I felt like a monkey in a cage. Apparently, everyone knew who I was. For some reason this annoyed me. How was it everyone knew who I was and how I looked? How was it that they were expecting me; or so it appeared? There was obviously no element of surprise on their part. When Kelly embraced me without warning, well, I just did not know what to do or say. Not hugging back was rude, but I did not know these people. So I just stood there staring from face to face wishing I could get a bus out of this horror movie. Not sure if it was my body language or my facial expression, but something made the schemer, Dr. Emmanuel come to my rescue.

"Maybe you should sit. You've had an adventurous morning to say the least."

Again, I gave him a dirty look as he helped me to a chair in the waiting room. As I found myself sitting in the chair he offered I thought to myself, "It is official, my life has officially fallen apart." Moments like those were when I missed my mother the most.

Kelly spoke first, "Just take your time. I know this is a lot to absorb at once."

Nodding I still did not know what to say.

Dr. Emmanuel spoke next. "You know he spoke of you often. Every time we played golf or tennis he somehow mentioned a younger sibling."

Positive shock registered on my face when the young doctor who could not be more than thirty, with the tall finely sculptured body, and the brilliant smile, and the dreamy eyes said such preposterous words. Cursing is what came to mind, then throwing a chair or two, but this was not the time or the place. Maybe I was living in the twilight zone. It was still a mystery why he was still sitting next to me. Really, didn't he have a patient to see? All I wanted to do now was go home. Back to the first normal I have ever had and that was in Washington.

Again Kelly spoke, "I am sure you must be exhausted Hannah. Let's get you unpacked and settled and then you can have your visit a little later today."

"Wonderful idea" his grandmother interjected.

Nothing short of relief is what flooded my soul. I was getting a way out. My mother had to be smiling on me.

"That would be great," is all I could answer. I didn't really have any bags. Packing light with only a couple of blouses to interchange with the two bottoms I'd stuffed into my small bag. I'd come straight from the airport to the hospital because this was not to be an extended trip. I relished the idea of finally getting into a cab and going somewhere to think.

"Then it's settled. We only live a few minutes from here. We could stop and get a bite to eat on the way if you are hungry."

Was my mind playing tricks on me? Why was she acting as though I was going to their home?

Standing with the intention to leave I turned and said, "I will call a Taxi and be on my way," just so there would be no confusion.

"You'll do no such thing! Tobias and I would have it no other way. You are family and family should be together, especially in times like these."

There was a sadness in her eyes that she had managed to conceal up until this moment. That sadness is what made me agree to her terms, for the moment anyway.

Chapter 18

When we drove up to the two-story home located somewhere in the suburbs I still had not found my emotions. After Kelly gave me the address to their home I texted Connor and Johanna my whereabouts promising to fill them in on the details later. That was not an acceptable answer for either one of them. They were bombarding me with questions I just did not have answers to. On the drive over we made small talk about my flight, the weather, and food. At that present time I didn't believe I could stomach any food if Jesus offered to share a meal with me. Not wanting to be impolite I did agree to a hot cup of tea once we were inside.

Slowly and graciously I entered the home of the half-brother who just over a year ago treated me with such venom. Scanning the room there was nothing about their home that screamed extravagance. Comfort yes, family yes, but nothing said high society. The atmosphere and the decorum were quite warm. Seeing the fireplace in the sitting room made me relax a little. Momentarily a middle aged woman enters the room.

"Hi Mom." The two greet each other with a peck on the cheek.

"Hannah I would like you to meet my mother, Charlotte. Mom this is Hannah, my sister-in-law."

All I could hope for was that the "What the heck" that went through my mind had been just a thought. From the looks on Kelly and her mother's face it had not been.

"Pleased to meet you Miss," I said through my embarrassment.

"Likewise Hannah" was all she said before making an excuse to go and check on the baby that was having her morning nap.

I felt bad. Rude is something I never wanted to be. If at all possible I wanted to find the good in any situation. Lately that was difficult.

"Pardon my rudeness Kelly, I…" before I could finish my thoughts I was interrupted.

"Hannah, there is no need for an apology. This is overwhelming I am certain. Why don't I show you to your room and we can talk later over a cup of tea."

Smiling I said, "That would be nice." I liked Kelly, can't say why but I did.

Sitting on the bed in the guest room a little later I felt the urgency to get down on my knees and pray. Can't explain it, don't know why, but the feeling was so strong I could not refuse it. My mother had been addicted to prayer. I'd seen her on her knees a million times it seemed. I had not followed her path. What would I have to say? What could He have to say to me? Between Mr. Nelson and Johanna I was seeing a different part of God and it confused and intrigued me. All I know is that if what they said was remotely true, He was the only one that could help Tobias, or me for that matter. Kneeling down beside the bed I became tongue tied. My thoughts were sporadic and my voice unwilling to cooperate. My heart was flooded with conversations that were never scripted.

When I got up it was with the feeling of defeat and stupidity. At that moment my phone rang.

"Hello."

"Hi Darling. I was just thinking about how much I love you. I miss you."

Slamming into his conversation my response was curt, "Then why aren't you here"

"Renee?"

"What Connor!" I snapped.

"What's going on?"

"Oh I'm just having the time of my life Connor" I said sarcastically. "Life's just great. Things couldn't be better. Oh how privileged I am," I continued. Why stop when I was on a roll.

"Talk to me Renee." I became silent on the phone. It was something about the emotions I heard in his voice. His voice, calm, soothing, and filled with concern made me want to see him, be with him if just for a little while. Somehow he never responded to my emotional dramatics, just to the pain inside. He knew the whys of it all. It was what I did to keep from crying. Crying wasn't something I indulged in at this point in my life; if I started I would surely drown in sorrow.

"I will be there tomorrow Darling, ok?"

"Alright."

"I love you Hannah Renee Corel-Waiters. I can't promise everything will be fine, but I do promise to be there with you every step of the way. You want to talk about it?"

"Not enough time in the world. Besides, your break should be ending soon anyway."

"You know me all too well Baby. I will see you tomorrow."

"Promise…?"

"Promise Baby. I will be there."

Relieved, I decided it was time I got some answers to this mysterious family reunion. The house was still so very quiet. No Kelly, no Charlotte, and no baby Ally. I so wanted to see Ally. Even if I never had the privilege of being a wife I was certain I wanted children. I wanted a family and if I must adopt I knew I would as soon as I was stable enough.

Intrusive was not where I was headed, but it sure felt that way. Walking through the house I thought it might give me a better idea of who these long lost relatives were. Each room had a color scheme of some sort. I loved color, although my apartment walls were bare. My contract stated eggshell and antique white was as far as I could go. When I stumbled into the library it instantly brought joy to my heart. Shelves and shelves of book lured me into the room. This room had a fireplace as well with two winged back chairs adjacent to it. The focal point of the room was a beautiful oak desk. Before I knew it I was sitting on the plush carpet in front of the fireplace with one of my favorite books in hand; Leaves of Gold.

"There you are."

Kelly startled me. Lost somewhere between shock and reason my senses had become dulled and I had not heard her approaching.

"Oh I'm so sorry; I didn't mean to wander through your house."

"Hannah…you are to make yourself at home. I see you found Tobias' favorite room and his favorite book as you can tell from the worn pages.

His grandmother gave him that book when he was just beginning to read. This looks like a perfect time for tea don't you think?"

"I couldn't think of a better time."

"I tell you what, I will put on the tea kettle and you keep reading, deal?"

"Deal." Amazingly I felt so comfortable around Tobias' wife. She just had that type of personality. It had to be awful for her. Seeing him that way was a struggle for me and I hardly knew him. Yet, she held it all together. That was another mystery to me since this whole saga began to unfold. My moment of peace had passed. Getting up from my position on the floor I headed out the room. I attempted to follow Kelly to see if I could offer some assistance, but stopped short. Why was there a picture of me on the end table? My high school graduation picture sat among the other family pictures. This just did not make sense to me. A tear streamed down my face as I searched for answers.

When Kelly reentered the room I was still staring at the picture. She never said a word. Putting the tray down she gently took my hand and lead me to one of the chairs near the fireplace. After giving me a box of tissue she served me a cup a tea.

"No matter what is going on in my life I always feel better when I come to this room and have a cup of tea. Especially since Tobias has been so ill. This is his room. I guess since it is his room, it has become our room because we come in here to spend time with him when work won't allow him to get away from that desk."

"I can't imagine how hard this must be for you."

"I have hope, good family support, and faith that no matter what happens I know he would never give up without fighting with everything in him. So if he can stay strong I have to remain strong as well."

Nodding, I didn't know what else to say so I took a sip of my tea.

She continues, "You must have a thousand questions. I know I would."

"I'm certain he told you about our first meeting."

"He did. Something he regrets until this day. He's written you a hundred letters, but ashamed, he's never mailed any of them. It took him six months to find you. He wanted to make things right, but at the same time frame the private detective located you he begin to have symptoms.

He thought he was just taking longer to recover from a lingering cold he'd been challenged with. Then other symptoms became evident. He tried to ignore them, but one of his close friends, you met him today, Dr. Emmanuel, convinced him to have some labs run." She looks into the distance trying to manage her emotions.

"What can I do? I mean is it too late."

"Hannah that's not why Nan and I felt it was important for you to come here. We knew it was important to Tobias."

Getting up from her position she took a small wooden box from the shelf hidden among the books.

"I believe this is as good a time as any for you to have these."

When I opened the box there were about twenty letters all addressed to me.

"That's where Nan and I obtained your address. When I asked Tobias why he never mailed them he said he still had not found a proper way to say he was sorry. He was positive the only real way to ask your forgiveness was in person. He put that as a priority once he started to feel better, only he…"

Tearing up for the first time she looks away again for a moment. Disturbed about everything I wished I knew the right words to say or the correct thing to do. Sadness had been a normal part of my life for a very long time now. Still, I never had a proper answer for it when it constantly knocked on my door. This time was no different. Once I opened the little box of letters the revelation that I never needed to read them was so real. Just the truth that he'd written them, the truth that he searched for me until he found me was consolation enough. Now the picture on the table made sense. He had indeed accepted me as his family.

"Whenever you're ready I'd like to see him."

"I think that is a great idea. There is someone you must meet first though. I'll be right back Hannah."

With that she left the room. My heart was so overjoyed for the first time since my mother died. Only the joy was constantly being chased away by the grief of finding something you'd lost only to have to lose it again. There was a family for me, but how long before I would lose it to death? How long before I would have to say goodbye?

"Hannah this is Ally. Ally say hello to Aunt Hannah."

My heart melted when little Ally extended her arms to me. She was beautiful; perfect in every way.

"May I hold her?"

"Of course. She knows your picture. We go through the family tree and she repeats after us when we say each name. Ally, say Han nah."

"Nah nah."

"I know it sounds like Nana but she is saying your name."

I really did not care what it sounded like; it was music to my soul. As I held baby Hannah tears of joy welled up inside of me. Wanting to take in every moment I dropped to the floor and sat her in front of me so I could soak up every detail. Only she would not stay, she'd get up and come right back to me and sit on my lap. We must have played for about an hour.

Chapter 19

M s. Omelia Shepard was sitting at her grandson's bedside when we returned. This time it wasn't as hard to walk into Tobias' room. For once, I wasn't alone. Kelly was with me. Something about knowing I actually had a family that wanted and loved me, as best they knew so far, gave me strength. The same strength that helped me get through school, out of Ms. Ann's house, and become a college graduate. I had something to fight for. I had a reason to go on because I hoped for better. The better being finding my brother and getting to know him and it put a fight in me when I felt like giving up and dying. Walking up to his hospital bed I felt that feeling again, the fight.

As before the beeps, swishes, and clicks serenaded the room, but this time I wasn't petrified by the sound, smell, or look of it all. Kelly went straight to her husband's bedside and gave him a kiss. She then begins speaking to him as to include him in every detail of the conversation.

"Honey, look who's here, Hannah! Isn't it great! Now the entire family is here."

Grabbing my hand she gently pulls me over to where she is standing next to the bed. Me feeling as awkward as a person could possibly feel just stood there staring. For a minute I was lost in Tobias' features. We had the same dimple in our left cheek; amazing. I assume I was too angry to notice it before. His hair had more of the curls that were in his pictures from days gone by. Today he appeared more awake.

"Go ahead Hannah, say something," Kelly urged. "He can hear you."

"Hello Tobias" was all I managed. When he opened his eyes and extended his hand to me I swear I almost wet myself. No, time did not stand still, no, I did not hear music playing, and no, I did not see a light from heaven; although I did get a little light headed for a moment. Especially when I noticed I was holding his hand. He squeezed my hand lightly and then drifted back into sleep. In just that simply touch, that light squeeze I knew him. Can't explain it, but I felt his childhood, his pain, his struggles, and his disappointments. Suddenly I knew without a shadow of a doubt life had not been so easy for him.

On the drive to the hospital Kelly informed me that the registry had notified the hospital of a possible donor. With all my heart I prayed it was true. I wanted him to be better. Maybe there were many lives he still had to save, one of them being mine.

The afternoon passed quickly into evening as we sat in the family waiting room. We visited as often as we were allowed and made idle conversation other times. It was interesting to see the flow of traffic that entered and exited my brother's room. He was loved and it was evident. There was a steady flow of colleagues, co-workers, neighbors, patients, and friends visiting Tobias Hunt and his family throughout the day. With enough food to feed an army from people that just had to do something, it was shared with other families waiting to get some good news about their loved ones.

My mind constantly went to Jane. I missed her so much. Since the day we met I'd never survived a crisis without her to talk me through it. The truth is, I was afraid to call her. So much had taken place I just wasn't sure how to begin. Most of all I didn't know if she wanted to talk to me. Our last conversation had not gone so well and I was always too busy to answer the phone or text back when she wanted to talk. Her grandmother always use to say, "Never burn the bridges you cross over on, you may need them again." Now I knew exactly what she was talking about without any second guessing. Not only had I burned my bridge, but I had laced it with dynamite and destroyed any hopes of ever crossing again. I wondered how old the baby was now and how they were doing? How she'd transitioned into her new job and how married life was treating her. One thing I knew for sure is that it was time for me to grow up. I knew I could no longer make excuses about anything. She was right about my hatred for Ms. Ann and so many other things. Just like I had to find closure with my brother I still had a long list of other matters I had to attend to.

When it was time to leave the hospital I wanted to visit with Tobias one last time before leaving, but this time alone. It was me that grabbed his hand this time and squeezed it. The old folks in my neighborhood growing up had a saying when you looked like you had something to say but was too scared to open your mouth, "Spit it out child." That is what I did with my brother.

"I forgive you Tobias. Although I don't know you, I still love you because we are family. God decided that and I guess it is something we just have to deal with. Is that alright with you?" I wasn't quite sure what to expect but I was so tired of being held captive by fear. I stood for a moment looking down into his face. He appeared more peaceful than when I first saw him earlier in the day. My thought pattern was interrupted when I felt him squeeze my hand, this time it was a much firmer grip than before. I knew what it meant. He didn't need to say a word. "I'll be back tomorrow Tobias."

Chapter 20

It almost took an act of congress to convince Kelly and Ms. Omelia that I would be fine spending the night at my hotel. She seemed a bit upset when I insisted on calling a cab once we returned to their home. It's not that I didn't want to be there, I just needed a little space to process the last twenty-four hours of my life. How could I explain that to her? Before the night was over there were two things I had to do; talk to Jane and figure out a plan about this whole Ms. Ann thing. Then there was that Connor thing.

After promising I would spend a night or two before leaving she gave in, but not before arranging for me to have a ride to the hotel, "Certainly NOT a taxi," she was adamant. I wasn't all that surprised when none other than Dr. Gabriel Emmanuel arrived to escort me to my hotel. I let him know with my eyes and body language I did not appreciate his deceiving me that morning. Being polite but still giving him the cold shoulder I'm sure he got the message.

When the dashing doctor opened the passenger door to his 1998 Volvo a few choice words floated around in my head. Thank God I was learning not to say everything I thought. To each his own, but the cracked windshield and missing back seat took my mind to a far different place. We mostly made small talk on the way to the hotel, which was a thirty minute drive. I couldn't be rude forever. His heart had been for his friend and I couldn't knock that. The conversation just seemed so natural. He was not the ordinary doctor. He was down to earth, playful manner, and from the looks of things, frugal. Frugal like we share a happy meal on a date kind of thing.

By the time we reached the hotel it was after eleven. Feeling a little bit exhausted I thanked Gabe, as he insisted on being called, and threw myself on the bed. It had been an extremely long day. Although there was a three hour time difference my body still felt like it was after midnight. Connor's flight arrived late the next afternoon and he'd arranged for a rental car so I didn't have to do anything but wait for him.

Jane was still on my mind. Not contacting her wasn't an option anymore. My only reluctance was being indecisive about the time difference. We'd both burned the midnight oil all through college, but things were so different now. It was now much greater than year since we began our own lives, but it seemed like an eternity. We were only an hour's time difference apart but that was still late, especially with the uncertainties of the new baby schedules and demands. I decided texting would be my only option. "I'm sorry" was all that came to mind. After waiting for a few minutes I decided to prepare for bed.

After showering and checking my phone about a hundred times I switched on the television, mainly for the company. I wasn't much of a television watcher, but it was always on since being on my own. At first it was a night light, then a noise maker, and eventually a habit. When the phone rang it startled me something terrible. My thoughts were so far away.

"Hello."

"Hi Sweetie, how are you holding up?"

"Oh Hi." I tried my best to conceal my disappointment that it wasn't Jane calling. "I'm fine Johanna. Just a little tired, but doing alright."

"Are you sure?"

"Promise. Just trying to figure out how to store everything is all."

"Sweetie that is a whole lot of storing. One of the things I have learned about you and am still seeing the more I get to know you is that you are one tough cookie. God made you super strong. My church has some people you could teach a few survival lessons to."

"Not sure about that." Feeling my emotions take a nose dive I almost wished I'd stayed with Kelly and Ally for the night. Weirdest thing, one minute I felt happy and excited, the next I was frightened and sad. Sometimes I wondered how many people there were in the world like me.

How they got by, who they received counsel from and if they ever really got to the point in life where they could truly, honestly, become happy.

"Hello, hello…hello" I could hear Johanna on the other end of the phone saying, "I must have a bad connection," when my mind jumped back into life.

"Johanna, I'm here."

"Oh, I thought I'd lost you."

If she only knew. When my phone beeped I was relieved to see Connor's picture show up on my screen. "Johanna, I need to get to bed. I'm a bit fatigued I'll call you tomorrow."

"Wait, I wanted to pray before we end our call."

It was already common knowledge that I was a heathen so admitting prayer was not on my mind, but Connor Fitzgerald and being in his arms in less than 24 hours would not be a confession. Besides, Johanna prayed far too long. A moment of prayer with her meant telling Jesus how the world looked and what to do to fix it. She told God all your business and then some. It was the difference in cold food and going from hungry to starving.

"OK Johanna, thank you for the prayers," I said pretending I misunderstood her and hung up the phone. Then I prayed she didn't call me back to correct my mistake.

"Hello."

"How's the sexiest woman in the world doing?"

"She is doing just great now that she is talking to you."

"Now that's what I like to hear."

Strangely, I was wide awake now, blushing and a lot too hot and bothered.

"Wow, is that all it takes for you Mr. Lee?"

"Well I must say I am intoxicated by that walk of yours. Then there's your irresistible fragrance, and let's not forget that thing you do?"

"What thing might that be Sir?"

"You know that thing that makes me want to hurt anyone that stares at you a little too long."

"Oh, that thing…"

"I love you Renee. I never want to imagine my life without you in it. You are like no other woman I've ever met. I love that dimple of yours, those big beautiful eyes, those sexy legs, and that look you get on your face when something is bothering you. You are an amazing woman and…"

"Hey I'm not dying!"

"Guess I miss you more than I thought I would."

"Gee thanks."

"You know what I mean baby."

We talked on the phone into the early morning hours. He was full of questions and I was willing to give him answers, finally. Including him made him happy, that was evident. For some reason he needed to feel like he could solve my problems for me, slay my giants, and then turn around and comfort me as a lover. He needed to be a hero and I wanted prince charming so I imagined we fit. When I began to drift off to sleep he told me to get some rest and before I knew it, we would be together. I did not protest one iota.

Chapter 21

It was the tapping on the door that caused me to reluctantly rouse from sleep. Certain they must have the wrong room, I opened the door with attitude ready to inform the intruder of their grave mistake. My appearance did not matter and neither was my morning breath a concern. That bed felt great and I wanted in. It was with a vengeance I swung that door open ready to grill whomever this unwanted visitor could be. Lo and behold there standing in front of me was Connor.

"Surprise!"

Indeed it was a surprise. He was not supposed to be here yet, but before I could respond he grabbed me and kissed me. My questions and scolding him for fibbing were all forgotten. I did not know how much I'd missed him until I saw him. I guess we both didn't realize how much we missed one another. He took a step back with the intent to say something, but I did not allow him to speak. I wasn't interested in conversation. I needed him to make me forget that I had some important decisions to make. In the balance were some serious decisions that affected so many lives in a major way; to include my own. "Connor I missed you so much…" That was all he needed to hear and I knew it. He closed the door, picked me up, and took me to the bed where I'd spent a portion of the night alone and made up for our lost time together.

Much later, I felt his gentle kisses luring me into consciousness, but I wanted to stay where I was cuddled close to him. "What time are we going to the hospital Darling?"

"Ummm, what time is it?" I said without opening my eyes. I felt safe with him, not to mention loved. He was so protective and I'd decided to stop fighting it. He wanted me to be alright and did everything to try and make sure I was ok and I was happy too. That felt good. If I asked him to get me ice cream in the middle of the night he went. He rubbed my back, my feet and any other place I needed him to massage. Sometimes I did things just to see how far I could go, but he never went far away. Many times I was mean on purpose to see what it would take to make him leave, but he always said, "I know what you are doing and I'm not going anywhere. I love you Hannah Renee Corel-Waiters, so you may as well get used to it." In many respects he'd become my teacher. There were so many things I did not know but he was so patient and gentle. He never made me feel ignorant, just loved. No doubt about it I was book smart. I knew a little too much about surviving in this life. Could write a book about pain too, but I understood I still had much to learn. He loved being my teacher it was evident.

"It is 11oclock baby."

"They're not expecting me until late this evening. Kelly knows my friend was scheduled to arrive this afternoon." I put emphasis on the afternoon part. "If we don't make the five o'clock visit then we will have to wait until the 8 pm visit."

"Your friend, is that all I am to you?" he said playfully pushing me away.

"Your pretense at being coy is horrid at best." On a serious note I laid back on the pillow for a moment. "Connor I really don't know what to do. He is sick, really sick and I know I just met him and spent a lot of time trying to hate him, but he is still my big brother and the only relative I really have. What do I do Fits?"

When I said that he looked at me. He knew I called him that when I was scared or upset. It didn't take a rocket science to decipher which one I was feeling at the moment.

"You should follow your heart sweetheart."

"Should I be afraid? I mean I'm not sure how things are going to turn out, but I want a chance at least to see it through. Kelly was nothing short of perfect. Ally, well I wanted to just sit right there on that floor and hold her forever."

"When will they find out about the donor?"

"Not sure about that one. I really don't understand all that, but I know just in case it doesn't work out I want to see if I am a match."

"Well if you can see if you are a possible donor match, I can too."

For a second or two I looked at him not really sure I heard him say what I thought he said. My face obviously said it for me.

"Yes Renee, I'd like to see if I am a possible match. I want you to be happy and as much as you pretend and try to hide your feelings, I know you love your brother. If you didn't you wouldn't be here."

Unsure what came over me, could have been exhaustion, the shock of seeing my brother being reduced to such a frail shell, or realizing I was hopelessly in love with Connor, but I started to cry. It scared Connor half to death. Had it not been for my temporary break down I would have laughed myself silly at the look on his face. One minute he was saying, "Oh darling don't cry, I'll fix it, I'm going to make it all better," and the next he was saying something in another language, I'm sure it was French and I'm sure he was cursing. Laying my head on his chest I said, "You amaze me." He took it from there.

By the time we finished playing, talking, and playing some more we were both exhausted. Sleep was in order. He told me we would go to the hospital at eight o'clock and I nodded and closed my eyes and snuggled closer to him. Just before I drifted off to sleep I said it for the first time, "I love you Connor." Feeling his heartbeat increase I smiled and drifted off to sleep, but not before he tightened his hold on me and kissed me on the cheek.

Chapter 22

We arrived at the hospital around 7:30 that evening. I wasn't sure if Kelly would be there, but I was certain Ms. Omelia would be. Connor was attentive to my every whim. If I coughed he had tissue, sanitizer, and a concerned look. He wanted to feed me, pat my back, and hold my hand sometimes all in the same moment it seemed. Having him with me was reassuring. My hope for Tobias' recovery was increasing. Not sure why I was beginning to think he would get better, but I did actually think he would. I was feeling tired and trying to come down with a cold or something. Odd, I was never sick in the past. Maybe because I knew I couldn't afford to be ill. My heart may not have been able to handle being sick and alone. Or just that my mother's prayers were still watching over me. The climate change did not help the matter and neither did the cold air in the hospital. I'd slept most of the day and yet I was still exhausted.

Conversing with Ms. Omelia I'd learned the doctors were trying some experimental treatments with the hopes that it would buy them some time in finding a donor. Connor and I were having ourselves tested for a possible match early the next morning and that made me feel so good inside. Even if it didn't work out I knew it was something I must do. Being honest with myself the only real reason I'd traveled was to see what I could do. My heart still held on to the truth that neither of us was responsible for the choices that our parents made, but as adults we could not point fingers. Johanna taught me this, "You could spend a lifetime hating and blaming, but the only person missing out is yourself." I wanted a life, not the shadow of what could or should have been. I never wanted to wonder about the "what ifs" of me not coming to see my brother and reaching out to help him if I could. Hatred and unforgiveness were probably the heaviest things a person could carry. Weight without relief or release and I needed both to have a chance at a decent life.

The waiting room was filled to standing room only. How alarming to see the number of people who were so seriously ill. Families waited together, some holding hands, others quietly sitting, some pretending to watch television, while still others were clearly distraught. Obviously sickness had no age limit. The old waited for the critically ill young and the young waited for the middle aged dying. There wasn't much conversing on this particular evening. Without a doubt someone was going home minus a loved one and the sorrow was worn on the faces of their families. My mind went to my mother and then my brother. That's when Connor squeezed my hand and pulled me a little closer to him. My face had its own story.

When I'd introduced Connor to Ms. Omelia there was curiosity in her eyes, but she only said, "Please to make your acquaintance" and went back to her cross word puzzle. The same puzzle she was doing the day before. Something was obviously on her mind as well. Studying her face when she wasn't looking I could only imagine her pain. She looked tired. More than a grandmother should. No one ever mentioned his mother and I dared not ask. Ms. Omelia was his mother in every way. She reared him, provided for him, and loved him; that was clear. Now she grieved for him hoping and praying for answers.

Finally it was my turn to visit with my brother. A little apprehensive just like the day before I walked down the corridor. My mind kept saying that previous day was a dream, or it was the medication, or a joke. He would feel differently today about seeing his half-sister who was just as illegitimate as he was and as golden brown as almonds. Connor wasn't allowed to visit despite his protesting. I longed to be able to have him walk beside me down the endless hall. There was a need in me to have something to hold on to but there wasn't anything. Sometimes faith came but fear chased it away.

When I stepped into the hospital room my brother was wearing headphones of some sort and he did not see me. Laying there with his eyes closed he looked peaceful. He had more color and that was a little reassuring. Today he didn't seem as tensed with pain as the first time I visited. The room even had a different feel, didn't know how that was possible but something was different. Looking at Tobias in that hospital bed made me remember just how vulnerable we all were. My mind went to my own life. Where was I headed and would I get there or would I wonder aimlessly like I'd done for so long? Tobias was a dream for so long in my life and now maybe it was a reality, but even so there was still a hole in my heart. This helped, but it had not healed like I imagined all those lonely nights at Ms. Ann's. Maybe nothing could completely heal pain, just lessen the sting. Paying no attention to Tobias at this point I let out a little yelp when he reached out his hand to me. Taking his hand without saying a word I stood there; suspended in that moment. He smiled just a little and closed his eyes again. Feeling peace about us I was now certain we were reconciled, as brother and sister, as people. That was all I had ever wanted.

The next three days proved to be extremely taxing. Connor and I did our swabs and some other tests as planned. The doctors continued with the experimental treatments for Tobias. They warned it was far too early to tell how things would go but all of us could clearly see for ourselves. Tobias was getting stronger. In his grip, in his posture, and it was evident. Spending as much time with him at the hospital, Kelly and Ally at their home in the evenings, and with Connor at night was more than I imagined could happen for me. Kelly was understanding when I apologized for breaking my promise about staying overnight in their home, but I wanted Connor with me and I would not violate their home by bringing a stranger into it. The truth is, I did not want to share them with Connor and I did not want to share Connor with them. We were becoming a real couple and I wanted nothing more.

We'd decided to fly back together so that meant changing our flights and staying an extra day. He was insistent upon paying for the change and obtaining first class accommodations as well. When we needed a break from the walls of the hospital but weren't yet ready to return to the hotel we walked downtown. Window shopping, holding hands, and talking and laughing like the world was a perfect place. Each time I saw something that made my eyes twinkle he felt it was his solemn duty to purchase it for me. When I protested he ignored me and bought it anyway. Materialistic was not who or what I'd ever been. One thing I knew without vacillation was that money could not buy the things that really mattered. It could not bring my mother or my baby back. It could not save my brother either; all of that was in God's hands. Despite Ms. Ann's efforts it did not make her happy regardless of her pretense. The cars and houses still weren't enough. There is no way a happy person could ever be so mean, shallow, and downright evil. No, I did not miss the college days when I thought I would starve to death, freeze to death or just plain die from fear of being alone and unloved for the rest of my life. After a while you learn how to cope, compromise, and count the cost. Cope with certain things to ensure you have relevant needs. Compromise the lesser of the evils and make sure you were able to pay whatever your decisions cost you in the end. Survival had taught me to love who loved me, embrace those who embraced me and want what wanted me. You could train your heart to believe whatever you told it long enough. When Connor called I answered, when he touched me I responded, and it made us both happy. What was so wrong with that? He had secrets I'm sure of it, but so did I.

Coming back to the rain, the traffic and the corporate world was welcoming. I was in a new phase in life and I loved it. New people to get to know, but more important I was searching for the real Hannah Renee Corel-Waiters. The only thing I knew about myself was what I had been told, it wasn't enough. What you are not told is what eats away at you. I'd learned to fill in the blanks for myself when communication broke down with the ones that were supposed to nurture and guide me because the silence was too much. Only my answers to the questions had come from misconstrued information, pain, and disappointment. Either way I failed the test of trust and love time and time again. This time I hoped it was right, but I knew time would be my only judge.

Chapter 23

After a while I ceased asking Connor about certain issues. The consequences of my inquisitive nature were not how I wanted us to spend our time together. My life was as good as I knew it could be for someone like me. Things had changed so drastically in such a short time and weighing the scales I knew the balance was in my favor. College graduate, corporate position, friends, and now family, plus being with someone that wanted me just for who and what I was is more than my mind ever had the capacity to dream for my life. Connor didn't like me smoking so I stopped, it was not ladylike and that was not the image I wanted to convey. He liked helping me pick out my clothes to ensure I looked professional. For that I was grateful to him because he knew more about such things than I did. It was a small price to pay for someone who didn't hesitate to give me anything I asked. He made sure I went to the salon weekly and the spa bi-weekly. If we weren't spending the weekend in a cabin somewhere, sailing in another place we were just hanging out being with each other. His sexual appetite was something serious, but I was fine with that too. When he had a rough day we made love, when he was worried, frustrated, or bored, same thing; sex. Why should I complain or protest? Giving him what he wanted and how he wanted it was the way I displayed my gratitude to him, it was my way of pleasing him.

Life was good. Connor and I were spending more time together and growing as a couple outside of work and my apartment. We were becoming more of an item minus the group we had always spent time with. We didn't go to clubs as much but we went to festivals, to vineyards, parks, museums, and art galleries. His apartment had become a second home to me, I think I was infatuated with his library most. We both had a thing for books and that was always a conversation for us, among other things. Having someone to talk to on such an intimate level was an answered prayer for me. Work was still work, but I had something to look forward to afterwards. Cooking wasn't something I was thrilled to do. Johanna was the master chef and I gladly allowed her to have the platform when we were all together. Now, especially since we didn't do the group thing as much anymore, we did a lot of dining out. Connor loved introducing me to new things. Two things he knew I hated were sushi and escargot. I learned that he actually loved sweet potato pie and I preferred pumpkin, go figure. He was thinking of going back to school again and I was in hot pursuit of happiness. Some days I was so close I could touch it, feel it, and hear it. Other days my analyzing chased it far far away. Most days I was able to chase away the bad thoughts, but on others they lingered much too long.

We were making our own group of friends as a couple and that was exciting; people who were not associated with our place of employment. Colleen and Jeff were friends we met at a restaurant, when Connor just did not want to wait for service so he took the liberty of asking if we could share a table with them. Colleen was a valley girl if you ever saw one. She had the walk, the talk, the attire, and the hair to prove that life had always been kind to her. In all of her, "whatever's" and "shut-ups" she had substance and that is what I found appealing about her. She volunteered at the local soup kitchen, went on mission trips, and held premature babies of mothers who were substance abusers. This program was a special part of a program to help heal through touch in the local area newborn intensive care units. Jeff was unique in that he was the brightest thug I ever met. Recued, as he called it from going down the wrong path by a teacher, he'd gone in the military as an alternative to going to jail. It was "The best thing that could have happened to me," he said. He worked with troubled youth at a middle school and the way he looked when speaking of his job made me envious. They were a sweet couple. Interracial in their relationship they appeared to know what they wanted out of life. The only fault I found with them is that they were too touchy feely for me. Having no qualms about public affection they went at it anywhere. Holding hands and an occasional peck on the cheek was as far as Connor and I went. All of your kissing and heavy panting was not for public viewing. Still, they were fun and we got along well and that was great for us.

Sometimes we hung out with Daisy and Ralph. The two were hilarious. They argued about everything, agreed on nothing, and never had any money. Yet miraculously they went anywhere and everywhere together. They had been married for ten years. Having been high school sweethearts she was the cheerleader and he was the all-around sports man. They'd been married right out of high school. He went to work on his father's local farm and she owned a salon. Having children was out of the question. Both of them came from large families and according to them they had already done enough babysitting and child rearing. If we wanted adventure they were our couple. Bungee jumping, skydiving, and white water rafting are what they lived for. Truly, I could say none of those things were on my bucket list, but Connor was so persistent when he wanted something. Right up to the panic attack I had when he was forcing me to jump out of a plane. He made me so mad I am positive I embarrassed him when I screamed, "The black people I know don't jump out of planes!" The entire room grew silent and his face turned beet red and that was just what he deserved. Not to mention that night I wore a chastity belt to bed.

He had this way of pushing me sometimes that I resented because he was my weakness. All he had to do was start talking about our future. Looking for a house when he finished his degree or hinting at settling down. If those failed he just kissed me in the right places and begged. Just like the walls of Jericho I fell every time. Connor believed you only live once so you should live it up. My belief was you only live once so you should get it right, but I was still struggling with right. Between his adventures on the weekends and the hectic place work had become, my body was going through some things. Although I missed our friends I was glad to be free of Terrofare International whenever it was possible. Lord knows I could do without the reminders of work. The atmosphere had changed drastically in the past several weeks and for many of us it was almost unbearable. The strategy team I originally worked with was no more. We were all sent to different departments to work. Some pending management decisions as to further employment.

Chapter 24

It was strange to me that I still had not met any of Connor's family. There were pictures of them plastered all over his apartment, but yet to me they were only a figment of my imagination. When I brought up the subject he either became evasive or had some excuse. They traveled a lot or they were always busy. Each time I pried I could tell it irritated him and he became a little distant. Distance I didn't like so I was learning to do what I must to close the gap. Sometimes he went for a run or any other place he thought of to get away. When he returned he always had a gift for me, some trinket he just had to pick up. After his outings I also waited for him to return ready to do whatever I deemed necessary to reassure him I wasn't going anywhere. Touching him where he needed to be touched, stroking him like he wanted to be stroked, and saying what he longed to hear. With confused signals being sent I just wanted proof that he loved me the way he swore he did. Funny, it was easy to ignore the blaring alarms that were constantly sounding in our relationship. Connor's insecurities of other men, especially black men were burdensome at best. When I walked past and got a second look from an unsuspected admirer he punished me in subtle ways. Pretty was something I never felt described me and so those men with hormone problems did not bother me. He was a different story. He was withdrawn and sometimes more aggressive in bed. Later he always apologized and was again the devoting lover and protector. I always forgave him. My fight was dwindling. I could never remember being so tired, not at my worse had I ever felt so fatigued. My answer was to just let it go and keep moving.

Kelly and I spoke several times a week, which included talking on the phone to little Ally. Tobias was getting stronger and stronger with each new day. His recovery from where he had been to where he was now was nothing short of a miracle and we all knew it. The experimental treatments were going well and there was hope that he may be able to have a bone marrow transplant in a few weeks. He promised as soon as he was well enough that they would come to visit me. Imagine that, relatives coming to see me. Sometimes I had to pinch myself to make sure I wasn't hallucinating. The only thing I could honestly say was irritating the heck out of me was a nagging cough I could not get rid of.

Out of all the people in the world Shirley and I had become close friends. Michael had a girlfriend and I mostly saw him at work, although he unfailingly checked on me daily. He was indeed the brother I was supposed to have. Johanna was still determined to be a mother to me. At times I embraced it and other times I resented it. She was sure to let me know she did not approve of Connor and I spending so much time together. By that she meant having sex and shacking up. I wanted to tell her so many times, "Sex is good Johanna you should try it," but I knew my own mother would reach down from heaven and slap me across my face. She meant well. According to her she just wanted us saved, but the jury was still out on that one.

Work was grueling. Our company was going through a merger and although it had not been put in writing, they wanted our very souls. Panic gripped department after department as little pink slips were being given out like birthday cards. People that had been with the company for decades now had no hope of retirement, sending children to college, or paying off mortgages. One employer was doing the work of three people to compensate for the people being fired or that were caught in the downsizing, as they called it.

Oblivious to the constant challenges I was having with doing ordinary things I hid my recurring health issues from Connor. I wanted nothing to interfere with my life the way it was. I couldn't talk to Kelly or Tobias because finally a donor match had been found and they had enough to worry and pray about at the moment. For several weeks now I had been living with Connor. Going by my apartment only to check on things, pick up mail, and water plants. He was content to have me with him more than any place else. We carpooled to work in the mornings and even then we took his car. Twice a week he went to school. Education was a requirement to getting ahead in life and getting ahead was all a part of his plans for us. He told me I would be going back to school the following spring to pursue my master's degree so I needed to prepare myself. Joking I said, "Yes sir." He didn't laugh. So when he completed an application for me to enroll in online classes I didn't know what to think. Not wanting to start an argument I said nothing.

When he came home at night I had dinner waiting and we ate together. Eating alone was not on my to-do list so I waited for him. Surprising him was one of my specialties. I made sure food was not the first thing he got when he came home. I made it my business to find the naughtiest things to wear to greet him in when he got home. He loved naughty and I loved to make him feel good. We had places at work and home we'd initiated as ours. I knew just what to do to drive him crazy and I found great pleasure in making him my puppet when it came to making love. It did not take me long to figure out when I sexed him up I got what I wanted. He was happy and that meant he wasn't prying into my head trying to make sure I still wasn't the sick little girl he'd first met two years ago.

He paid all my bills; purchased everything I ever needed, and gave me an allowance each week. He insisted I save my wages each pay period. Sometimes I felt awful about not telling him I had money from my inheritance, but I really didn't think it would have mattered. Honestly, I think it was more of a control thing for him more than anything else. My role was to be helpless and I knew I would get many awards had I been in Hollywood. He was my hero, every girl wanted one, at least this one did anyway. Yes, we were playing house very well. Whether or not he would marry me I had no way of telling, but what we had was fine with me. He liked my hair straight, not curly and I could not cut it. He preferred me in dresses, just above my knee and not too much cleavage. No big hoop earrings, no long nails, just the usual French manicure and pedicure he paid for twice a month. Was that a bad deal when I did not want or need for anything? A mature man was just want I needed. He helped me invest money. Made sure I had the proper health insurance, and proper life insurance and anything else that mattered in life. I'd never had anyone to teach me what he did.

Church had become a thing of the past. Johanna eventually stopped asking me to go with her. I wished she hadn't. Connor and I didn't go to church at all. Instead we made love on Sunday mornings and then went to the gym. He was Lutheran and I had no idea what that meant. My mother had raised me Baptist and to me choosing equated an argument and so I steered clear of the subject of religion. He didn't know it but I still slept with my mother's Bible under my pillow and after he went to sleep I always read it. The scriptures from my first trip to Richmond to meet my brother were always with me. Could God really put the solitary in families? Could He really take away the pain I'd stopped speaking of and tucked away so deep within sometimes I forgot about it. Sometimes I wished I could have a conference call with God Almighty. Maybe even get Him on a video call. Questions still plagued me at times in my life. Was I on the right path? Was Connor the one? Did he love me or was he just substituting me for something else? Was it cheating if I sometimes pretended he was Brice when we made love? Were the things I'd learned in Sunday school true? So many questions but never any answers.

All things being considered, I had no reason to complain. My life did not include starvation, Ms. Ann, or the panic attacks I used to have. My trepidations about not having a nest egg were subsiding just a little. I knew one wrong thing could wipe out my money so I had to keep working and saving and being frivolous wasn't something I could participate in. My sleep patterns were definitely better. Even when I felt myself becoming restless I read some of the scriptures my Mother had highlighted in her Bible and I was always able to rest. My feelings of guilt sometimes got the best of me. How would she feel about me sleeping with a man and the Holy Bible? What would she think of what I'd become? Missing her was always a part of my life. Her voice, her smell and the way she saw life. I was losing that. She always saw good in the worse situations. She recognized something nice to glean from regardless of how bleak the situation may have been. Brice was that way. I think that was the reason I so hated him and loved him at the same time. He gave me both sorrow and joy and there were days I secretly wished I could hear his voice. My mother had been my number one cheerleader. She believed I was the prettiest, the smartest, and the greatest at anything I did. Our home had a hall of fame just for Hannah Renee. All of my achievements, awards, ribbons, badges, and scribbled art were displayed for anyone who came to our home to see. I was her gift and she never allowed one day to past without telling me so. My life was busy now. Becoming crowded, and for some reason I just knew that was all I ever needed to heal me. It hadn't. Deep down inside the little orphan girl was still alive and well. She was just covered with more stuff now.

Chapter 25

Johanna surprised me one Saturday night when she called and invited me to church. It had been such a long time. They were having a special guest speaker and she wanted me to please, please, please be her guest. She had to remind me of the promise I made so long ago to attend a service with her again. Then she solidified her case by saying how I had been on her mind. How God had been putting me on her heart and she was certain she was supposed to be a part of my life. I needed a mother figure and she was sure God had brought us together for that very reason. The "Yes" that came out of my mouth shocked me. Lately I was feeling so dreadful physically I knew something had to change. Connor wasn't thrilled at the idea but I did not care. I was careful not to display my feelings. Instead I kissed him and one thing lead to another and just when he wanted me most I stopped and I whispered in his ear, "Please baby May I go? I promise I will still be a bad girl when I get back. Then we can go to your favorite toy store…" before I could finish my sentence he rolled me over and slid home, but not before giving me permission.

When Johanna picked me up the next morning I was so relieved. Connor wasn't happy, but he had given his word and I knew he would not change his mind. That is how I'd learned to play his game on his own terms. Before leaving he had to critique my clothing. Passing the fashion inspection it was time for him to lecture me about having my own mind. He said I should not give others permission to tell me what and how to think. To myself I was thinking, "Isn't that what you are doing" but I was too excited about leaving his grip for a while to chance saying anything.

I fought back tears when Johanna hugged me and held me just a little longer than normal.

"My I've missed you baby girl."

Responding to her was out of the question because it would induce tears. She had no idea that was one of my mother's favorite pet names. It always let me know I belonged to someone. After driving for a few minutes I regained my composure.

"Good to see you too Johanna. Time flies when you're working overtime all the time."

"We have to make time for the ones that matter though. That is why I am here today. You look as gorgeous as ever."

"Thanks and you as well. Do I have to call the Reverend to tell them that Sister Jo has been shopping in the junior section and not the church mother's section? I know the mother board doesn't know about that skirt or those shoes. Humph! What's his name and does Jesus approve?" Laughing she scolds me for making her blush. We made small talk the remainder of the drive. Catching up felt good and seeing an old friend was even better.

The first and only time I'd visited Johanna's church it was loud, today was no different. My head started throbbing as soon as we walked through the door. Church hadn't even started yet and the organ was blaring and people were dancing all over the place. Apparently prayer had started a riot.

"Ooh, church is going to be good today! Do you feel that?"

Hannah Renee did not feel a thing, except a little scared someone's shoe was going to come flying through the air and hit me in the head. Or that the lady pounding on that tambourine was going to catch the Spirit and throw it in my direction and I wouldn't be able to duck in time. That was about all I felt. My radar had long since been broken. When "Sister Jo" wasn't looking, I texted Connor a love note. Feeling pretty good about not getting caught I texted him back when he responded. That's when Mr. Black and White appeared out of nowhere to inform me that, "The Lord's House was a no texting zone!" He was not quiet about it either. For just a second I wished I could have crawled under the seat I was so embarrassed, but there were already several others there already. I'm sure there was no room left for me.

When the real service started I totally forgot about Connor or my phone. That choir started singing one of my mother's favorite songs and it was all over for me. The enforcer appears yet again but this time to give me tissues for my waterfall. Johanna was too busy shouting down the aisle to notice and I was glad. I did not want people fanning me and making a scene because the heathen was crying. The other choir or praise team as they called it got on the stage and began to sing and the lady behind me begin to scream. Seriously, I was at a loss for what to do. By this time Johanna was back from her trip to the Holy Land and whispered to me, "She is ok, she's just happy that's all." Now I wondered about that. Happy made you laugh, chuckle, or smile. What part of happy made you scream like that? Of course I dared not ask. My mother taught me you are supposed to be silent when the Lord was moving. These people had not received that memo.

About two hours into the service, after the hairdos were done, the make-up had run, and the hats had flung; the Reverend finally got up to teach his sermon. By then my bottom hurt, I was hungry and beginning to despise ushers. Really, I felt like I had been one of the people from the missing persons bulletins and someone had figured it out.

"No mister penguin I do not want to move up front. No sir I would rather sit on the end and not the middle. Sir I have enough tissues could you please just leave me alone; you have earned your star for today" were all on the tip of my tongue!

Listening to the man speak was not the easiest thing I'd ever done. I really was giving it my best to pay attention and everything but distractions were all around me. Each time he gave a good point and I tried to store it for later someone yelled, "Preach preacher!" and I forgot what I was trying to remember. So I would start all over again the next time I knew I was hearing something vital, and yet again, distraction. Someone being chased by something or someone only they could see got up from their seat and ran around the church. Then it would happen again and someone would jump from their seat and high-five the person across the aisle. But then he said something that made my surroundings succumb.

"God does not have any orphans; only heirs."

My heart was racing. He continued, "You see God puts the solitary in families. You may be saying what family is that preacher? Well I'm glad you asked. When you become a member of the body of Christ you join all the other children of God. That's why we are called brothers and sisters you see. We all have the same Father, Abba, or Daddy. None of us are illegitimate once we come to Him. You see God makes us heirs to His Kingdom. Turn with me if you will to Psalm 68. That's Psalm 68 and verse 6. I will be reading from the New King James Version. It reads as follows:

God sets the solitary in families;
He brings out those who are bound into prosperity;
But the rebellious dwell in a dry land.

Turn to your neighbor and say, I got family, I,I, I…I have a family. Look at your other neighbor and say; I have people that love me! I am not alone. God made sure of that!

Listen to what the New Living Translation has to say about it.

God places the lonely in families; he sets the prisoners free and gives them joy. But he makes the rebellious live in a sun-scorched land.

Have you ever been lonely? Surrounded by others but still all by yourself? Got a man, but still feel by yourself. Have you ever felt out of place? Felt you just didn't belong? I have the answer for you. You just haven't met your family yet. You just need to make it to God's house and come on in. You don't need a key. All you need to do is come down here and say, Lord I'm home and He'll welcome you in.

Would there be one. The altar is now open…"

No doubt my eyes were red from crying and I was now make-up less. That was the same scripture from my mother's Bible. The one I had read hundreds of times hoping that one day I would have someone to love me and someone who would love me for who I was. When the usher decided to give me the box of tissues I wasn't at all concerned. For the last few minutes no one else had been in that room but me. I'm not sure what it feels like when God is talking to you but maybe my heart did.

Johanna being Johanna took it upon herself to grab my hand when the speaker announced that the altar was open. Fight her is what I wanted to do. It was bad enough she made me stand up when they called for visitors and later told me I was not allowed to be served communion. She sent up flares to the ushers that I did not have a Bible. Now I was being drug to Jesus! I was so finished with her! If I wasn't afraid God would have struck me down I would have started running in the opposite direction. She may have delivered me to the preacher, but my mind was still sitting back on that pew. After all that is where I had been when my heart first felt Him. At least I think it was God, but how can a person be sure of such things?

The speaker was still giving the message. "Many of you down here have searched in all types of places to fill that loneliness. You've trying to belong, to fit in and to find some relief from your pain. Today I've come to tell you that you've come to the right place."

Shaking now I yearned to go back to my seat. People were all around me and my mind was so distraught I didn't even remember where I had been seated in the huge building. People on all sides of me wept and cried out to a God you could not see but feel. Some knelt and others lay on the altar. Getting out was all I wanted. If Connor had been with me he would have helped me and taken me home. Maybe God didn't give everyone a family. Maybe that was only for certain people, good people. My mother was gone. My father had not loved me. Why would someone else? After all, I was a murderer, a liar and a deceiver. Needing some air I turned left and then right trying to find an escape route but to no avail. I was feeling the exact way I did at my mother's funeral. Like I was suffocating and there was nothing I could do about it. Where was Johanna? I couldn't find her in the crowd. I felt like I was going to die right there in that church. Frantically looking around I finally spotted her just ahead of me assisting someone who had a fainting spell or something. Pushing my way through anyone or anything that got in my way I literally ran to her grabbing her like she was my last hope. She saw the panic and fear in my eyes and grabbed me just as my knees buckled under me. She went down with me and I slumped over in her arms crying.

"Oh baby girl, it's ok…it's ok" she kept saying rocking me back and forth. I didn't know if I believed her or not I just knew something was happening I couldn't stop or explain. Crying was all I could do and hold on to Johanna for dear life.

"Young lady I have a message for you," the speaker said. "Sister Jo I need for her to hear me and hear me good." That is when I knew he was addressing me. Me, I had been singled out by either him or God. Either way I was horrified. What if He hated me too?

"Sister…what's her name Sister Jo?"

"Hannah, but we call her Renee."

He continues, "Hannah…my goodness, a woman that took her broken heart to God in the Bible when no one else could give her what she wanted. After she had been picked on and mocked year after year. Even the priest accused her of being drunk in the temple when all she was doing was pouring out her heart to God. My God!"

The people in the church started clapping and now Johanna was crying too and ushers were standing at parade rest to the left and to the right.

"I have a message for you Hannah. Just like Hannah in the Bible, God has granted your request. This time next year your life will be so different, so beautiful, it is literally going to scare you. I want you to remember this moment. Because you see Hannah, God has a plan for your life; He has a family for you. He has seen your tears, your broken heart and your loneliness. Such loneliness you can't explain it. God is going to teach you how to trust Him and to love Him. You and your family are going to serve Him because your story young lady must be told.

Sister Jo, hold on to her. That is your baby. Do you hear me? Do not let her go. Pray for her, love on her, be there for her. The Lord put the two of you together. This, my sister is a Kingdom connection. Let me pray for you both." Whatever he said I suppose was only God's business because I do not remember it. Closing my eyes I wanted to relish in the peace I felt. Unlike anything I had ever experienced.

When the service ended I was still weeping. Johanna never left my side though. Not when her friends greeted her after church and not when we walked to the car. Before we exited the building someone came running up to me and gave me a couple of CDs. All visitors, I was informed, received a copy of the message for that day. The other CD I was told contained the prophecy. I had no clue what prophecy was but I said "Thank you" through my tears.

Once in the car I asked Johanna, "What's prophecy Johanna?"

"Prophecy is when someone tells you something that is going to happen in the future, foretelling. Basically they are speaking on God's behalf. God also uses it to comfort and encourage a person that really needs it."

"I don't understand."

"That's what happened today when Pastor David James spoke to you remember? The things he said were going to take place in your life. Didn't you feel better after he spoke to you? That was to encourage you and allow you to know that God has not forgotten about you. The CD has the words he spoke. It is a good reminder for you especially if things get hard. You can just put the CD on and listen to it. God cannot lie. Always remember that Hannah Renee, God cannot and will not ever lie."

"Johanna."

"Yes baby girl."

"May I spend the day with you?"

"There is nothing in this world I would rather do then spend the day with you."

Peace is what I felt. I knew that's what it was called although my life had been void of it for so many years. I didn't want to let it go. What I felt today and what was said I so desperately needed to hold on to it just a little while. Connor was blowing up my phone. It didn't matter; I couldn't go home right now. I wanted to breathe freely for just a little longer. At the altar I felt like someone had placed an oxygen mask on my face and finally breathing wasn't a struggle any longer.

As usual Johanna cooked a feast and I was not ashamed to relish in the labors of her hard work. I enjoyed her food the way I did my mother's cooking. We talked a lot. I found out things I'd never known about her and I told her things I was never at liberty to voice to anyone. She had been adopted and never laid eyes on her biological parents. She said she had a wonderful childhood and felt God knew what He was doing and she dared not interfere with it. She'd married her husband William right after college and spent twenty wonderful years with him until he died of prostate cancer. They never had any children. She didn't know if it was him or her that was sterile but to them it didn't matter. He had been the only man for her and so she had dedicated her life to serving God and her work after his passing. After playing several board games and eating two desserts I lay on the plush carpet in the living floor and took a long nap. When I woke up it was dark outside and Johanna was watching game shows on television. Johanna's home was so tranquil I did not want to go home, but I knew I must.

"I guess I had better get going."

"You are probably right, but before I drive you home I want to talk to you first."

Uh oh, what on earth could this be about I thought to myself.

"Today was an answered prayer for me. You may not have understood it but I do believe that will come later. From the first moment I laid eyes on you I knew God had sent you to me. I knew from the first day you came to Terrofare International I must pray for you and be there for you. You are the daughter, the god-daughter if you will, that was promised to me years ago. No one can take your mother's place and that is the last thing I want to do, but I want to be there in whatever capacity you will allow me. So much healing has to take place in your life. Today that healing began and it will only get better from this day forward. I have something for you."

Removing the little emerald ring from her finger she took my left hand and placed it on the index finger.

"When my husband and I visited Italy years ago we purchased this for our first daughter. It was a faith thing. We both wanted children and so we decided to give our daughter something special when she was old enough to appreciate it. Today I understood this ring was meant for you all along. God doesn't just rattle off words so when He speaks I pay close attention. So I'm not going anywhere---no place at all. That means there is nothing you can tell me and it shock me out of your life. Nothing you can do that will make me leave and not return. No place you can go that is too far. I'm here baby girl."

By the time Johanna dropped me off it was eight o'clock at night. Judging from the last text I'd received from Connor I did not know what to expect. It did not take long for me to figure out he was livid.

"Where the (bleep bleep bleep) have you been!"

Keeping my voice low I answered, "You know I went to church Connor."

"Church is not all day and half the night Renee!!! Who are you sleeping with? Church was over hours ago. And don't lie about it because I drove by and there was not one car in the parking lot."

His voice escalated with every word he spoke. Seeing him get upset was nothing new, but not like this. He was never this angry.

"You were checking up on me Connor? How could you do such an irrational thing and why? What reason have I ever given you to spy on me?"

"You stop answering my text, you didn't take my calls, and you didn't come home. What did you expect me to do? Was I not supposed to be concerned Renee?"

"Trust me. That is what you are supposed to do. You know I went to church. When have I ever given you a reason to doubt my loyalty to you---when? You know my every move every moment of the day. All I wanted to do was go to church…church, that's it. I'm going to bed."

With the full intention of walking past him I headed for the bedroom. Shock registered when he grabbed my arm in an unfamiliar way. "No, we have to finish our discussion" he says.

"Connor this isn't a discussion. It is a full blown argument and you are touching me in a way that makes me uncomfortable."

Pulling me close enough to him so that I could not only see the pulse in the side of his neck going crazy, but feel him breathing on my face he says, "Who are you sleeping with?"

Maybe I should have been afraid. I wasn't. The feeling from the church was still with me. "No one Connor. I would never do that to you… promise."

Jerking my arm in an upward motion so that my hand is in his face he says, "Whose ring is this then?"

Now I understood a part of his dysfunctional behavior. Although I would think he could have given me more credit than to not know better than to wear another man's ring home. If I was going to cheat, I would definitely know just how to do it and get away with it. Many opportunities had presented themselves from high school teachers to college professors; even some loyal deacons at Ms. Ann's church, but that was wrong. Even though I was very young I still knew wrong when I saw it, heard it, and smelt it. Cheating was not for me. I was too selfish to share anyway. I wanted and needed to have my very own or I was out.

Wanting to lighten the moment I took my other hand and caressed his face. Looking into his eyes I said, "Baby this is a piece of old jewelry Johanna gave to me. I didn't want to be rude so I took it. You know how Johanna doesn't like to take no for an answer. I'm sorry about being so late. She invited me to eat at her place and I feel asleep on her living room floor. That's it baby, honest. Her church and her house were the only places I've gone today."

Although he was still holding my other arm rather firmly, I attempted to pull out of his grip. Staring me in the face for a few moments, searching for what I know not, he released me. When he did I took that hand and caressed the other side of his face and looked into his eyes again and said, "I would never cheat on you. I think you know that. You are the only person that I've been with besides my first and you know all about him." Moving close enough so he could now feel me breathe and my body against his I made my point clear. "You are it for me Connor."

With that he let out a deep breath and said a raspy, "I need you Renee."

"I know" I said kissing him.

"I love you so much Renee…"

Maybe he did love me in his own special way, but I now knew it would not be enough. When we made love that night I did not feel good---about a lot of things. Sick was the only appropriate way I could put it. Sick, both inside and outside and trapped just like the years of living with Ms. Ann. I was repeating my past. I fell asleep after laying in the dark for hours. That night I did not read my Bible.

Chapter 26

When I woke up the following morning I was not myself. I wish I could say it was a good thing but I knew in my heart it was very bad. Bad that filled the room and it enveloped me also. Literally I felt like it was the last day I would live upon the earth. As a matter of fact I was almost certain by the end of the day I would be joining my mother. Maybe that was what the speaker meant when he said I would have a family. Either way I needed to know some things about Connor Fitzgerald Lee.

Looking over at him in the bed next to me sleeping so peaceful after giving me such a hellacious time about going to church you would never guess he had a mean streak. I knew all about it though. Survival is what my life had always been about and so I learned quickly to do what I must. I reached over and ran my hand through his beautiful red hair. When that didn't wake him I took my finger and rubbed it across his sexy bottom lip. That did it.

Rolling over he said an annoyed, "Morning."

"Connor, if I died what would you say at my funeral? Or would you even go?"

"Stop talking like that Renee!" He sat up in the bed like a bolt of lightning.

"Do you believe in heaven and hell Connor?"

At that he moved close enough to me to put his hand on my forehead. "My God Renee you have a fever. Renee, baby, you need to go to the doctor. There is nothing wrong with seeing a physician you know. You have been coughing for weeks and now you are burning up with fever."

Ignoring him I continued, "Are you going to break my heart?"

"No, I will never hurt you. Why do you ask me such crazy questions all the time Renee?"

"I think you will. Yes, it's true; you will break my heart just like everybody else." Truth was, he had already hurt me by hiding me. He hurt me when he knew we needed to talk things out but instead he acted it out in our bedroom. He wanted me to be something I wasn't and we both knew it, yet I went along with it. He was dependent on the way I touched him, stroked him, and yielded to him and I was addicted to someone actually needing me in that way. We were both sick.

"Oh Baby, you're sick and I am taking you to the hospital whether you like it or not. I'm calling Johanna so she can meet us there. This is preposterous!"

"Connor…, you have to meet my mother. Let me introduce you to her."

Somewhere in time I lost three days. Well maybe not lost but I played tag with them now and again. All I knew now was that my mind was racing, then my temper decided to follow suit. I had never been surrounded by a lot of people, but those who knew me had been told enough I hated being cold. Why in the world was I so cold? The only thing I could think of was one of my apartment crashers had adjusted the setting on my thermostat. And what was that constant noise? Why was my chest hurting and better yet, why couldn't I open my eyes? I was so cold I wanted to scream. I tried, but nothing came out. Then I had a burning sensation in my arm and sleep took me captive.

Feeling like I'd taken a long disturbing nap I opened my eyes, not rested at all, but more tired than anything. For a second I focused on a picture I could not remember purchasing. Then a lamp not even a blind person would want. Starting to feel out of place my eyes shifted to the other parts of the room. Shock registered when I saw Connor sleeping in a hideous recliner. His face was as white as a sheet which only magnified that curly red hair I loved so much. Sitting right next to him, reading her Bible was Johanna. I knew then something had gone terribly wrong with me. Scared, tears began to roll down my face. When a couple of people I'd never seen walked into the room things became even more frightening.

"Well young lady, it is wonderful to finally meet you. My name is Jade Myers, and I'm your nurse. Are you in any pain Miss Corel-Waiters?"

Shaking my head I said no at first, but then I said yes.

"Where does it hurt, can you point to it?" The second woman somewhere around middle aged and not yet ready to be grandma asked through ruby red lipstick.

Thinking I would much rather tell her than point I opened my mouth but it felt as though I had swallowed a rock. That was where my pain was coming from. My tears became heavier and that is when Johanna pushed passed the two women and stepped up to my bed.

"Baby girl…it's ok you're in the hospital. You don't have to be afraid."

But I was afraid and she knew it. Reaching out to her she took my hand and held it. Connor was awake now, but he was staying in the background almost a bit stand offish looking weird. He was not my concern. My anxiety increased when two more people in white coats enter the room.

"Miss Corel-Waiters, good day to you. I'm doctor Woods. Do you know what year it is?"

My mind wasn't concerned about the year, but the pain in my chest and side aggravated the heck out of me. Almost unbearable to me I just wanted to scream but I couldn't.

The doctor continues, "Do you know who our president is Miss Corel-Waiters?"

He had given me a pad and pen. I had a mouth but for the life of me couldn't use it. Becoming frustrated I took the pad and pen and tossed them across the room. By now I was crying because the more irritated I became the more my pains intensified. Johanna standing guard still rubbing my hand asks, "Are you in any discomfort baby?"

Finally someone got it. Shaking my head vigorously I reached up to solve one of the problems myself but my hands were immediately restrained. Not before I figured out I had a tube of some kind down my throat and it felt like what I imagined a brief moment in hell would feel like. My eyes pleaded with Johanna to help me.

"What hurts baby girl? Show me."

On cue the nurse released my arms and I motioned to my side. Having communicated the problem the doctor examines the area and began giving orders of some kind. By now I was going in and out of the pain and the conversation.

Sometime later I woke up again. This time there was no one else in the room but Johanna. She was staring off into space at nothing in particular, but I knew that was what she did when she had something on her mind. By now I knew that something was me. There was no way for me to know how much time had elapsed since the first time I'd awaken. It was the same day I was certain because Johanna was still wearing the same clothes. The pain that antagonized me before was no longer present, but my mind was in jumbles.

"Hi there…" Johanna said in the sweetest voice. I hadn't realized she noticed I'd awaken. "You feeling better now baby girl?" she continued. She looked tired. Those big bright hazel eyes of hers had bags under them and she was moving a little slower than usual. Watching her walk over to the bed I felt sadness like I'd never experienced. Here I was in the hospital and there was no one waiting for me. No family. No person related to me by blood. No one to even call or notify that something had gone wrong in my life. Not one person on the earth to care. Just Johanna---a co-worker. Turning my head to the wall I began to cry and cry. A cry that elevated my heart rate, my blood pressure, and my anxiety. When the room again filled with staff enquiring of my pain levels I desperately wanted to lie just so I could have something to knock me out again. Maybe I was growing up, hopefully that was it, but this time I knew I had to face my demons. Dealing with me was first on my list. Johanna always told me if I couldn't appreciate anything else life should always be on the agenda. So I sucked it up, dismissed the feeling that I would love to go be with my mother and decided to live if God would just show me how. I hoped He was willing because besides desire, I had nothing.

The next few days things became clearer and clearer. Besides having had double pneumonia I somehow had a chronic kidney infection. All explained the severe fatigue I'd felt for several weeks. The continual coughing and night sweats had all been part of a real problem that would not be ignored any longer. According to my doctor I would have to be on antibiotics for several weeks.

Connor was everything I ever wanted him to be. He took time off work to take care of me. He did everything. The cooking (breakfast and lunch), the cleaning, the shopping, and he never asked anything of me besides what he could do to make me better. He was scared. Each day he brought me a fresh bouquet of flowers. The apartment was starting to look like a mortuary to me, eerie. Like in the days of old Johanna came over after work each day and made dinner. Then we sat and watched television. I was glad for the company. This new Connor was still a mystery to me. I needed time to figure us out again. He seemed to want the closeness I longed for but I wasn't sure what I wanted anymore. The feeling that he was closing me in and shutting me off from the rest of the world was still such a vivid image. We hadn't been intimate since I'd been released from the hospital, but he was surprisingly patient. The truth is we could make love. I just wasn't sure that was what I wanted anymore. Since that church service we, Connor and I just did not feel right. He didn't know I wasn't on any physical limitations after the first week of being released and I didn't volunteer the information.

The doctor recommended I take a couple of weeks from my job and I took his advice. Where I was headed from this point in my life was still a mystery but oddly after having such an experience I felt a renewed strength. When Connor went back to work after my first week being home I was overjoyed. There was a need for me to find me and figure things out and that was impossible to do when he was always there wanting to hold me, kiss me, rub my feet and please me. Johanna had given me a book about purpose and between reading it and my mother's Bible I was doing a lot of soul searching. The problem with searching is that you have to know what you are looking for so that you can identify it when you find it. I became lost in the search.

Shamefully, it wasn't long before Connor touched me in the right place and I was right back where I started. All it took was for him to be gone a little too long one day and I realized how much I missed him. Then I started rationalizing and concluded he wasn't that bad. He loved me and he never allowed me want or need for anything. Shouldn't I give him my all since he was dead set on giving me his? Of course I knew all the correct answers to my own questions, but he was so convincing and he felt so good after what seemed like so long. Then he turned around and shocked me even more when he made our love making all about me. It was what I wanted and how I felt and my mind was messed up to the point of total surrender. I could feel myself getting in deeper and deeper with no way out. My attachment and need for him to touch me grew stronger and stronger.

More and more I longed to hear him tell me how much he loved me and could hardly wait to be with me after our long days finally ended.

Since the pressure was off about going back to school we were more relaxed and that meant less arguments and more us time. During the day I found myself daydreaming about him and even doodling his name periodically. Somehow I'd stopped soul searching and dropped the little girl off that still had not decided who and what she wanted out of life and decided where I was would suffice. Becoming an expert at muting my mother's voice of reason and Johanna's voice of concern, my top priority became not being alone. Dying alone was motivation to make it work with Connor and allow the past to be just that, the past. My health had improved tremendously and so did our relationship. To me it was like a completely new relationship was forming and we could not keep our hands off one another. Deciding to trust him I ceased worrying about his late night texts and why his phone had a pass code on it that I didn't know. It was irrelevant. He came home to me each night and that was reason enough not to worry. To be honest I felt like I was on a honeymoon for the next few months and I told myself it had better be happy or else.

Chapter 27

Maybe it was the fear of losing me or the guilt of our relationship, whatever the reason Connor came home one evening and announced we were going to Sunday dinner at his parent's house. He almost had to administer the Heimlich because I choked on my food. No warning, just like that I was going to meet the family. My mind didn't know whether to rejoice or curse. By the time he finished pounding on my back I was two kinds of angry with him and resorted to name calling. "Fool if the person can still speak you just monitor them. Dang you learn that on public television."

"I was just trying to help Renee."

"No Connor that was pain!" My anger was displaced and I knew it. I could not understand why after all this time he suddenly wanted me to play the role of guess who's coming to dinner. I didn't feel right about it. It had been several months since we last spoke about it and I was actually becoming comfortable with the idea. Plus, Sunday was only two days away. Apprehensive did not begin to describe how I felt. Maybe it had been for a reason his family wasn't a part of our lives. Our relationship had taken a different turn and I liked where we were headed. Connor and I talked more, really talked. He listened to me when I spoke and tried his best to satisfy me in the ways I needed him too. He was trying and that had to count for something. Now with his announcement, he had to interfere with what was going fine. He had the nerve to appear excited. All I felt was extreme agitation.

The next two days were nothing short of a nightmare but meet the parents finally arrived. Nothing I put on was the best outfit. Constantly changing my clothes I grew more and more nervous with my indecisiveness about what to wear. Connor was growing frustrated and angry. The tapping of his foot in the living room and the wrinkles in his forehead when he checked on me every five minutes told me all I needed to know.

By the time we drove into Fairway Estates my nerves were on edge. Connor had been talkative the entire forty-five minute drive and I could not tell you one word he said. Nervous chatter is what I thought it was, but who knew. All I knew was that I had a very bad feeling in the pit of my stomach.

"Mother, Father I'd like for you to meet Renee."

Extending my hand to Mr. Lee first I said, "Please to meet you Sir." He nodded and didn't bother to accept my offer of a handshake. Curmudgeon and hubris are a couple of words that came to mind after Mr. Lee refused to shake my hand, but nodded his head instead. My heart told me this was going to be disastrous. The looks from the family when we walked in were also an indicator.

Mrs. Lee was more cordial with her rudeness. "How nice that color looks on you. It matches perfect with your type of hair."

Curse words were stirring up in my soul by now, but I only smiled and said, "Why thank you Ma'am" in my old Negro spiritual voice. She immediately turned red. Connor gave me a look, but he knew not to say anything to me at that moment because God knows I was too close to the edge. He had become a tongue tied ten year old since our arrival. I was beginning to wonder who in the world I slept with each night.

Dinner was served out on the veranda, by none other than Ms. Manners herself; all fifty courses of it. Fine china, silver, and crystal arrayed a magnificent table. It was exquisite, right down to the beautiful floral arrangement center piece; just among bad company. With each course every eye in the room rested on me to see if I knew which utensils to use and they had nothing to see. My mother had groomed me on table etiquette from the time I could talk. She always insisted I be ready to have dinner with the President at a moment's notice because—"You're going somewhere in life Baby Girl and I know God is going to use you so you have to know who you are and that no one else is any better than you are."

These people didn't know who they were messing with because I was a champion at ignoring and shutting out people. Let the games begin. I wasn't afraid and nor was I intimidated. They were just ignorant and fortunate for me I had been educated in this field of study. If I knew nothing else I was certain one of the reasons Connor was with me was because we had many of the same interests. He loved my mind and I was intrigued by his and so we fit.

When Connor's Father began to speak of his new set of golf clubs and insisted on showing them to him I knew something was up. Bracing myself I waited for one of his family members to insult me with him being gone from the room. It was a long wait. No one said one word. They completely ignored me and acted as though I was not in the room. The maid must have taken pity on me. She repeatedly asked if she could serve me anything else, but I politely declined. When Connor and his father left the room I ceased eating or drinking anything served. Contempt was very present and to me that spelled caution.

After about thirty minutes of ignore the black girl at the table I excused myself from the table. Pretending to need to use the restroom the family was relieved to have the help show me how to get there. Not sure how long I was in there I figured I had to return some time so I flushed the toilet just for the heck of it, washed my hands just for the sound of it, and dried my hands on the designer towel and preceded to return to hell. Not before I gave myself a once over in the HL designer collection beveled mirror. Hannah Renee looked stunning and yes I had to say so myself. My hair was flawless, my make-up was great, and my dress fit every curve of my body without being insulting. All of that did not matter because I never had a chance with these people anyway. Holding my head high and walking with confidence I headed to the table of disdain again. Not realizing I'd gone in the wrong direction. The house was in truth a mansion and I was as turned around as a schizophrenic off medication. Thinking my best bet was to text Connor and alert him so I didn't make a spectacle of myself I took out my phone but breathed a sigh of relief when I heard voices. Maybe I wasn't as lost and I believed. I continued to walk in the direction of the noise, but soon realized what I heard were male voices. Connor and his father to be exact; I stopped short.

"Why the devil did you bring her here? Were there no suitable woman in the state for you to choose from son? Some women you have a good time with and others you marry. It is acceptable to have a moment of insanity, but she is not the marrying kind."

"Father she is a good woman. She is intelligent, kind and loving."

He interjects, "She is good in bed. I know, I've had a few, but who is she? What is her ancestry? That kind just aren't adroit. My grandchildren must be unalloyed. Do you hear me Connor Fitzgerald Lee!"

"Yes Father I hear you."

"Don't you ever bring her into our home again, unless she is in uniform and then you'd better bring her through the back door. What am I supposed to tell my friends down at the club? My son has the burning desire for the wrong kind."

"But Father, she is better educated than I am in many ways…"

"I just bet she is. Make her your secretary or your nanny and do her whenever you feel like it. Just stop being a buffoon and think about your future. I will not allow you to bring embarrassment or shame on this family."

"No, you have it all wrong. Hannah is the strongest woman I know. She has been through so much I can't understand how she survived, but she did."

"So she is a charity case. Is that it? What about Senator Joplin's daughter Amanda. I thought things were going well with you two. Don't you still communicate with her? "

"Yes, from time to time but she is not my type."

"So what is your type, black and poor?"

"That's not fair Father."

Interrupting again he says, "Everyone has their place in this world. That's how God made it and you don't interfere with it. Do you hear me son? If you continue this charade you will no longer be an accepted member of this family. That means your inheritance will be forfeited as well. I will no longer entertain this matter. My dinner is waiting."

When the door opened my head was spinning. Somewhere between rage and felony is where I was positioned. Mr. Lee waltzed right past me without any acknowledgement. That was probably the best thing because at the moment I did not trust myself to do the right thing. Wondering why Connor was not behind him I peered into the study and there he was standing in front of a huge bay window. Shock engulfed the room when I demanded, "Take me home!" He did not argue. When his Father motioned for him to use the side door I looked him in the face, eye to eye, and said, "I walked in the front door and I will leave through the front door." My head was high and my walk confident as I descended those twenty-three stairs at the Fitzgerald's entrance. If I remembered nothing else from that day I went to church with Johanna, I knew I belonged in this world. When Connor proceeded to get off on the exit to his apartment I again said, "Take me home." He said nothing and that to me said everything. There was nothing between us now, not even words.

Chapter 28

It had been a little less than six months since my hospital emergency and now what I'd feared most was true. I was alone and obviously sick once again. My days were now filled with bitter tears and severe bouts of vomiting. If this was what people meant by being love sick I needed a return to sender box. My heart, my body and my soul longed for Connor. Then I remembered the words of his father now etched on my brain and I wanted to hate them both. Each day I put on a happy face and went to work, demanding my body and my mind follow suit. Fortunately our company was having an audit and there was not a minute of the day that could be considered free. Thinking about anything else but doing my job once I punched the clock wasn't even rational. Once I made it through the day I went home ate dinner alone just to barf it up again and then cry myself to sleep only to repeat it again the following day.

After about a week of vomiting, feeling weak and depressed I made a doctor's appointment. Although I had been having symptoms of fatigue, nausea, and aches and pains off and on for the past several weeks I just didn't want anything to ruin my happiness. Scared was what I felt most of all. What if there was something seriously wrong with my kidneys? Tobias came to mind. Lord knows I needed some medical advice, but I was still building a relationship with him. Kelly and I spoke several times a week. Ally and I spoke just as often, but sometimes I still wondered about where Tobias Hunt and I would end up. He was still healing and getting back to his new normal in this life and I still had not found what a normal life for me was. Crisis to crisis was my zip code and uncertainly was my address.

When I left the doctor's office my level of frustration was at an all-time high. Irritation and frustration are a toxic combination when you don't feel well. For several weeks now I had been asking my doctor about symptoms I was having but he repeatedly reassured me everything was fine and I should not worry so much. Listening was not his best characteristic and that was not only sad but could ultimately be deadly for some patients. I would not be one of those patients. Leaving that office there was one thing I knew without a doubt, I would never be returning to that office again. My body felt like it was shutting down some days I was so tired. If I did not have to work I would quit, I felt so bad most days. I am sure my emotions played a part in the situation but my heart told me something else was going on.

One night after one of my episodes I called Johanna. She wanted to run right over but I would not do that to her even though it was exactly what I wanted and probably needed. My weight loss had become noticeable and people at my place of employment weren't shy about their snide remarks. She was able to get a referral for a new physician and that alone was an anxiety eliminator. Overjoyed is what I felt when I was able to get an appointment the following Monday. Getting through the weekend was now my next hurdle.

Monday had not come soon enough. After working through the morning I grabbed a piece of fruit and drove across town to see Dr. K. H. Miller. I wasn't sure the last time I'd prayed. By now I just knew God was tired of me only coming to Him when I needed something or was in trouble. So I'd decided I better handle the mess I made alone, but today was an exception. Before entering the building I asked God if my prayer somehow made it past the roof of my car to please allow the doctor to find out why I was so sick again and help me to get well. Over the weekend I took Johanna's advice and made a list of all my symptoms and another of my medications. She wanted to accompany me and as much as I wanted her to be with me I still refused.

Having completed the new patient medical forms I needed a restroom in the worse way. Why was I making so many frequent trips? I wasn't positive but frequent urination had been one of my symptoms before and that made me believe it was my kidney again. When I exited the restroom the medical assistant was standing in the patient waiting room. Apparently it was time for me to see the doctor. The first thing I observed about Dr.

Miller was that she was patient. She listened to me or at least she appeared to anyway.

A battery of questions, a physical examination, and much lab work later Doctor Miller assured me I wasn't dying. She said she was almost a hundred percent she knew what my diagnosis was, but wanted to wait for my lab results and that would not be until the following morning. I thanked her and went on my way. To tell you the truth I felt a little better. Maybe it was a mind thing, but my heart felt a little lighter, at least about my health anyway. Connor was a different story.

The next morning the old feelings greeted me again and it was just too much to deal with so I took a sick day from work. That was the best thing I could have done. I was in no way prepared for what was to come just before noon. If my mother had come down from heaven and told me what the doctor called to tell me just twenty-four hours after my visit I still would not have believed it. What was I going to do? How could I be so stupid? Where did I go wrong? Why me? Valid questions but no answer would make any difference at this point.

The conversation re-played over and over in my head.

"Miss Corel-Waiters your kidneys are functioning just fine. So far all of your test results have returned negative and that is excellent news. Your iron is a little lower than I'd like to see, but I will prescribe some iron pills for you."

"Then what is wrong with me. Why do I feel so bad? I missed work today because I just didn't have the strength to go in. I vomit all the time, I feel weak all the time, I don't have an appetite, and I am losing weight?"

"I did administer one more test, based on the hunch I had when I saw you yesterday. That is the only lab that was positive?"

"Really, then what is wrong with me?"

"Miss Corel-Waiters you're expecting."

"Expecting what? I don't understand."

"You are going to have a baby Miss Corel-Waiters."

"A what! Oh no I'm not! There must have been a mix-up in the lab or something."

"I assure you there wasn't a mix-up Miss Corel-Waiters. I had two different types of labs run; a regular lab and a lab for beta quants. I suspect you are quite far along in your pregnancy."

Before she hung up she explained a few things to me, answered several questions and gave me a referral to an Obstetrician Gynecologist. I was good for nothing by this time. I thought I might need oxygen for a moment. My chest hurt, my head hurt, I was having difficulty breathing and for the rest of the week I completely disengaged with life. Shutting down was the only way I could survive. Still thinking there was a mistake made on someone's behalf I went to the local store and purchased three pregnancy tests. All of them were positive.

Chapter 29

As I sat in the hard blue chair next to the door that open and shut constantly I felt only pain. For once in my life I'd been without it and it felt so good, but it had returned with a vengeance. My appointment was at 2p.m. and it was now 3:30 and still I waited. Watching the patients come and go gave me no indications about their status' in life. Some appeared relieved upon leaving and others distraught. Most of the women had an escort or some significant other with them. The ages were across the board, but there was not a lot of diversity.

Two weeks had passed since I'd seen or spoken to Connor. The gossip at work reported he'd had a family emergency. I wondered what the baby growing inside me would be considered. There was much I could show him about an emergency. Try being pregnant for the second time knowing you did everything in your power not to be only to have the doctor say, "The antibiotics you were taking made your birth control ineffective." Then you come to the reality that your lover's family believes women of color were only good enough to be someone's mistress. Or better yet try giving everything to a man because you finally decide you're not going to be afraid anymore and take a chance on loving only to find it is not good enough. He can't live without his parent's approval so that's that.

Becoming frustrated at my delay I decided to complain about the long wait but before I could a young girl, about fifteen years of age reenters the waiting area. She was sobbing uncontrollably, "But I changed my mind. I want my baby, please I want my baby." Nurses are trying to quiet her but to no avail. Her sobs began to escalate to a scream, "I want my baby! I want my little girl! I didn't mean to kill her God. I'm sorry please forgive me!" Her escort, not much older than the distraught teenager, was visibly shaken and confused about what to do for her young friend. More nurses came with the intention of resolving the situation, clearly, they could not. When a doctor briskly walked from the back the girl becomes even more hysterical. "Don't touch me, don't touch me! You are a murderer! You said it wasn't a baby, you said it wasn't real!" By now, the escort, a few patients, and one of the nurses have been reduced to tears. I was one of them. Beginning to shake, my stomach becomes queasy and my palms sweaty. I felt like I couldn't breathe. Needing to find some air I stood up and ran to the first exit I could find. A second later and there would have been vomit all over the waiting room floor.

When at last I reached my car I was sweating for no good reason. My head hurt like I'd never felt before and I was dreadfully weak. Starting my car my intention was to drive home, but I felt so bad I really did not know what to do. The phone ringing in my purse did not make the situation any better. The last thing I wanted to do right now was talk to someone. Thinking better of ignoring the phone I picked it up with the intentions of taking the call until I saw the caller ID. It was Connor! "Oh God why now. Why now Connor?!" I threw the phone out of the window with everything in me. It was probably not the smartest thing to do in a strange city, at an abortion clinic, and feeling sick as a dog. That's when the tears came. How could I have gotten myself in such a position? What was I going to do? How could I tell my heart to stop loving him? My job was so demanding, how could I manage it and a baby? How could I face the people on my job when my baby bump appeared or even Connor when we worked so close together? The only plan I had at the moment was finding my phone and hoping it wasn't broken. There was an hour drive through some rural areas on the way home and I knew a phone was a good idea. No one knew where I was because you just don't say to your friends and family, "Hey, I'm going to kill my baby today would you like to come with me."

Getting out of the car I wasn't really concerned about the steady flow of tears still falling from my eyes. The curious looks of the people passing by were of no distress to me either. After searching for about twenty minutes I figured it was a lost cause. The best I could hope for was to not need it. Taking a deep breath I methodically walked back to my car. The drive home was uneventful. Maybe God was looking out for me. Jane's grandmother always said, "God looks out for babies and fools." There was no question as to which category I fell into.

I was trying not to think too hard, I quickly realized it made my stomach hurt, and when my stomach hurt it made me sick. Switching on a little instrumental jazz I focused solely on getting home without barfing all over the place. About half way through my trip my mind started to become a little uncluttered. Coming to terms with the truth that I wanted my child helped. I was sorry about what almost took place, but that made me want to hold on to the life growing inside me even more. Stress was the last thing I needed so change was inevitable for me. I wished I could talk to some of my friends about what was going on, but my friends were Connor's friends and it was ludicrous to think they would not feel some loyalty to him. I had been the last one in the circle of friends. I did not want to make them choose between us. No doubt about it I was scared. I cannot deny wondering what Tobias and Kelly would think about how I was managing my life. Johanna came to mind but I was sure she would rip Connor apart like nobody's business. By now I knew I should be about four month's gestation. All that time and I didn't know I was pregnant. How do you not know you are going to have a baby? How do you not know a life is growing inside you?

By the time I pulled into the parking lot of my apartment I knew what I had to do. I wasn't sure it was the correct decision, but I knew it was the only way. The next morning I made a doctor's appointment and was able to get a medical leave of absence from my job for the next thirty days. That at least would give me time enough to figure out what my next moves would be. Afterwards I purchased a new cell phone. Calling Jane was a must. The last message I heard from her was a threat to fly out the next day if she did not hear from me by 5pm. I almost laughed at her, 5pm. Why that time of all the other hours in the day. My voice mail was at its capacity. Connor, Johanna, Shirley, and even Michael were questioning my whereabouts. When I dialed Jane's number she did not bother to even say hello.

"Girl, where in the Sam Hill have you been? Got me worried half to death about you. You know better! If you didn't want to be bothered all you had to say was give me some space. I wasn't sure if Connor's family had tried to do something to you. You know people are crazy. Then I would have to come out there and whip their (bleep), oh Lord forgive me! Look at you, got me cursing! Have mercy to Jesus Han!"

Jane was upset. She did not use foul language. That would be me when I was upset enough. "I'm pregnant."

"You just do not treat your friends like that Hannah…you're what!"

The phone went silent for a second.

"Yesterday I went to have an abortion because I thought that was my only option."

"Oh Han. Han, why didn't you tell me?"

"I was scared. I knew you would support me, but I just don't have any answers right now Jane besides keeping my baby. Connor and I are over but our lives are so intertwined."

"How far along are you?"

"Sixteen weeks."

"That far?"

"Jane! With the stress of my job and all the things going on with my brother and then something happened when I took so many antibiotics during my sickness. My doctor kept saying it was normal every time I told him about my symptoms. Then I started doing some research on my own because I was certain it was my kidney again. I demanded he run some test but he refused. Anyway, I fired him and found a new physician. I told her about my hospital stay, the medications I'd taken over the three month period, and told her about the symptoms I was having. The first thing she did was order labs. The next day she called me with the news. She told me that my doctor should have told me to use an alternate form of birth control because some medications interfere with certain types of birth control pills."

"What did Connor have to say?"

"Talking to him is not in my immediate plans. He hurt me and I just want to move on with my life."

"How can you not talk to him when you have been inseparable the past two years?"

"I took a leave of absence. The doctor only gave me thirty days, but it is enough to figure out a plan."

"Great, you're coming here with me then. Robert has to go overseas for a few weeks anyway. Getting away will do you some good."

"Jane I don't know."

"I do. You will be ok. I'm going to be there with you every step of the way. When that baby comes I will be right there ready to welcome her."

"Her, who said anything about a girl?"

"You know I know these things Han."

"Oh boy, here we go. Are you sure Robert will be ok with this?"

"Girl I wish Robert would tell me one of my relatives couldn't come and visit me. He will be fine with it. He's been worried about me and his precious son being way out here by ourselves while he's gone. He was even thinking of asking his mother to come for a couple of weeks. I love my mother-in-law but that woman needs to stay home. At least now he won't have to worry. Besides, if she gives me one more parenting tip I may just plead temporary insanity."

"You are so bad."

"No, bad is her taking over my house. I can't cook it like she does, clean it like she would, or raise my son like I should. Now imagine her being here without Robert to referee. You need to come on so I won't have to go raging Cajun on her."

"I'll think about it, promise."

After I hung up with Jane I made a few calls to people that I knew would not stop bothering me until I did. Connor was not on that list. As promised I gave some thought to Jane's proposal. I had thirty days to come up with a game plan for the next phase of life for myself and my child. At the rate that my phone was going off and my door bell was ringing, I knew that was going to be impossible in my apartment. Driving down to San Antonio was not a consideration seeing as I felt awful more than I felt anything else.

What a day it had been. After I booked my flight for the following afternoon I had a sense of relief. Maybe things would eventually become alright again. That's what I thought until I foolishly listened to one of Connor's voice messages. After hearing his voice I cried myself to sleep.

When my plane landed in San Antonio I do not believe I have ever been so happy to see the ground. I prayed I would never have the misfortune of seeing any of those passengers again. It was bad enough I'd made a complete fool of myself having to use a barf bag every few minutes. I'd run a marathon getting to the restroom and put the icing on the cake by becoming light headed. Yes, I was pathetic and hating every moment of it. I am sure my cheeks became a little flushed when the elderly lady I was seated next to leaned over and whispered in my ear, "It gets better you'll see." I smiled and pretended to try and take a nap.

While waiting to get the all clear from the captain my emotions become bombarded with memories of the morning I left Brice's apartment. I'd circled the neighborhood twice wanting to stay and needing to leave at the same time. When I left that day I was pregnant and now returning I found myself in the same predicament. Sad it seems I was always running from someone or something. I was the last one to depart the plane. Somewhere between landing and exiting I'd been engulfed in an extreme heaviness.

"Han, Han, Han, over here!"

Seeing Jane waving like I was in a Mardi Gras parade in the midst of the crowd almost made me laugh. It was too comical to be embarrassing. Sometimes all you need is a touch from someone you know really loves you when you find yourself in a hole that you dug for yourself. That's how I felt when Jane threw her arms around me. All I could say was, "I've missed you so much Jane." The tears began to roll right there in the airport.

"Oh Han you and my little niece are going to be just fine. Do you hear, just fine?"

Shaking my head I acknowledged hearing her. My heart could not agree at the moment. She wiped my eyes and then took my hand and we walked arm in arm to claim my luggage. Had I not been so engrossed in myself I would have noticed her weight gain right then. I also would have given attention to the pretty chocolate skin being scarred and blemished. The beautiful hair that was never out of place was hidden under a wig; so not her. The 5'10 slender, confident person that would make any model become self-conscience no longer had the spunk that made all take notice. The most alarming thing was the bags under the big brown gorgeous eyes that drove men crazy.

Chapter 30

For the next three weeks Jane and I enjoyed being sisters again. We took the baby to the park, got ice cream, stayed up late and watched movies and talked. I continued to avoid my constant calls and text messages. Jane was just happy I was there. Motherhood was her pride and joy. She was a natural at it. Sometimes I watched her and Robert Junior or RJ as they called him. When he cried she knew exactly what to do. Often I wondered where that came from and if I would have it. What if I was a bad mother? What if my child didn't like me? What would I tell him about his father and his father's family? For God's sake what would I tell him about my own family? Honestly, I am certain it was this pattern of thinking that prompted me to pick up the phone the next time it rang or maybe I just wanted to hear his voice.

"Hello." Shocked delayed his answer momentarily.

"Renee?"

"What Connor" I said downright irritated just by the sound of his voice. He sounded tired. That did not stop me from being mean though.

"Renee, I am so sorry. Please forgive me. I've been worried sick. Where are you? Are you well? The office said you were on medical leave. I'm losing my mind, I can't sleep, I can't eat, and you are nowhere to be found. Please sweetheart, tell me what's going on."

His voice was that of pain. I did not care. There was no way he could ever hurt as much as I did.

"First of all Connor, I'm not your sweetheart. Remember I'm the little black whore you could find anywhere. Did I say it the way your father did? Stop calling me. If you wanted me so much, if you loved me so much, then it would not have taken you so long to figure all that out after that night."

"You are right Renee. I didn't stand up for you, for us, but that doesn't make me a bad person; just a stupid one. Please baby I will do anything to make it right, I want us."

His voice trailed off like he was trying to prevent breaking down.

"There is no us."

"Don't say that please don't say that. May I come by? I just want to make sure you're ok? Do you have pneumonia again?"

"Connor, I need to go."

"Tell him Hannah" Jane whispers. I vigorously waved my hand at Jane while telling her no vehemently using every version of sign language I could make up. After I turned a deaf ear to her she starts writing me notes. "He has a right to know." "He is the father." "He still loves you." "Forgive him" and other melodramatics of the like, but I ignored every one of them. Then the baby ganged up on me and starts to kick me with attitude at the same time. It was all I could do not to scold her and my little one. Connor didn't miss me. Connor did not love me. He loved having sex with me and I would be a liar if I didn't say I missed having him make me feel the way he did. Life would be grand if he was here rubbing my back when it ached. Rubbing my feet and going to my doctor's appointments with me, but I knew better than to put my faith in him again. He showed me who he was and I refused to pretend I did not see it.

"No please don't hang up. Please just let me talk to you face to face. Just once Renee can we meet and talk if coming to you isn't feasible?"

"That's not a good idea. No Connor. What's done is done."

"I was a fool. I listened to the wrong people. I was confused. I just had to get away for a while and think. It only took me two weeks to see my mistake, but by then you'd totally disappeared. I love you so much Renee. I need you baby. Please can we try again?"

"I have to go…goodbye."

When I ended the call I heard Connor still trying to say something but I'd had far too much. My stomach hurt, my head hurt, and all I wanted to do was pick up the phone and tell him to come and get me. Why was I so in love with him? Why did I need him so much? Why was I thinking about forgiving him? Jane must have read it all in my face.

"You can't tell your heart who to love Han."

Getting up from where I was seated in the kitchen I announced, "I'm going to rest for a while." Suddenly I no longer had an appetite. Of course my diversion did not work with her.

"You need to know it's alright to still love him Han. Something drew you to him. After guarding your heart for so long all those years your heart told you he was the one. Do you believe it was lying?"

"I'm going to take a nap. I'm exhausted."

"When you are ready to talk I am willing to listen."

"I know. Thanks Sis."

Chapter 31

My last week at Jane's started off very quiet and uneventful until Jane's in-laws suffered a tragedy. Robert's cousin was killed in a car accident. The two had been reared as brothers in the same home and were as close as any siblings could be. Robert's company was sending him home early to allow for travel and attendance to the funeral. Jane was insistent upon me accompanying them to Maryland but that was the last thing I wanted to do. Attend a funeral and be cooped up in a vehicle for several hours on end. All my attempts to get an early flight back to Tacoma were to no avail. So the only other choice was to stay out in the Hill Country all alone.

As I waved good-bye to them as they backed out of the driveway I had no clue what I was going to do in that big house for the next few days. Maybe I would accomplish what I set out to do in the first place. Come up with a plan. Answers still eluded me at this point and there wasn't much time left to figure something out. By now I definitely had a baby bump. A baby bump that squirmed and kicked and let me know my time was running out.

The first day or so I did nothing besides the usual; eat and slept. After feeling like I was going stir crazy the cravings for Mexican ice cream got the better of me. I grabbed the keys to Jane's car and hit Loop 410. I was on a mission. When I was in college our study groups always gathered around food. On the rare occasion I had money to buy something to eat it was always from an authentic Mexican restaurant. The same one every time. Never in my life would I think that I would be willing to hurt someone over ice cream and fajitas, but that was how I felt. Not wanting to be one of those pitiful people that ate alone I ordered out. Almost running to my car with my goodies wouldn't you know it, I ran right into another customer.

"Oh, sir, please excuse me." Embarrassed and hungry I wanted to keep it moving, but knew that would not have been proper. Looking up to acknowledge the gentleman I discovered it was no gentleman at all, but Brice Chandler! God had a sense of humor I was certain of it.

"Hannah Corel! My goodness, imagine seeing you after all this time!"

"Wow, Brice I am just as surprised as you are."

"How have you been? I thought you lived in Washington. At least that is what Jane told me the last time I spoke to her."

"I do. I'm only here for a few days" I said trying to shift my carry out to conceal my belly.

"My word it's great to see you. We must get together to talk."

When he said that he got this look on his face that mildly disturbed me. Drama was not what I wanted or needed. I'd managed to create enough of that already.

"Wish I could but I really need to get going" I replied walking through the door trying to get to the car. Wouldn't you know, he followed me outside.

"Here is my number. I never changed it, but I know you changed yours. What happen Han?"

"Don't call me that Brice. Things worked out the way they were supposed to be."

"Maybe. How have you been Hannah?"

Rubbing my belly I said, "As you can see I've grown." I proceeded to walk away leaving him with my flip remark.

"Looks good on you Han."

I wasn't prepared for his comeback. My preference would have been for him to be sarcastic, rude or anything besides polite. My hesitation was all he needed.

"May I buy you lunch while you're in town; for old times' sake? We could catch up."

"Next time Brice." I had no intention of having lunch with Brice next time or any other time. He'd been kind when I needed someone most and I couldn't return that kindness with meanness. I think perhaps I'd paid him well or maybe too much anyway. The only person I needed to be concerned with at this point in my life was my baby. "See you around Brice." With that I got in my vehicle and drove off. However, I did take the number and throw it in my purse. I just did not want to be rude.

"Good bye friend."

During the twenty mile drive I had some time to think. Think about Brice and Connor. I thought about my friends back in Washington and how much I missed them. I had time to think about the decisions I needed to make very soon. I couldn't stay in Jane and Robert's guest bedroom forever. My apartment was waiting and my job. I knew I still could not face anyone, not yet. When I arrived back at Jane's place I went straight to the guestroom and hid my head under the covers. Thinking had been a bad idea.

Maybe my mind was playing tricks on me, but there was such sadness in Brice's eyes. I knew what that felt like. He and I had never had any closure. My mind said that is the way he wanted it. The phone rings both ways and he never tried to contact me. At least that is what I'd thought. I could not leave myself out there so I changed my number and deactivated my social network pages. The past should be the past shouldn't it? That is what Jane's grandmother always said. Then she'd say, "If you stir in old kaka, it will stink." Then she would pick up her Bible and read it. She did not say kaka though.

Why I was having so many emotions about it now I could not tell? Jane and Robert had driven out only forty-eight hours ago and already I was bored, apprehensive and a nervous wreck. Country living was not for me, it was too quiet. It gave me too much time to think. Tobias Hunt taught me this, say what you need to say and do what you need to do because tomorrow is not promised to anyone.

Chapter 32

When I woke up in the middle of the night in pain like I'd never imagined I was mortified, petrified, and horrified all at once. I didn't know what labor felt like; I wasn't supposed to be feeling it. I was only five months pregnant. Jane and Robert were out of town burying his cousin and I was all alone. What should I do? I had no idea where the hospital was from this part of town. Maybe I could put it in the GPS or maybe I should call an ambulance. When another pain pelted me, I dialed the phone with shaking hands.

"Hello" the groggy voice on the other end answered.

Through tears I managed to get out, "Brice something's wrong."

"Han!" More alert and troubled he continues, "What's wrong? Where are you?"

"The baby, something's wrong with the baby. I don't remember how to get to the hospital and I don't know how to give the ambulance directions out here." Hysterical is how I sounded to my own ears. That and terrified would be a perfect description.

"I am already on my way. Just calm down I'm driving as fast as I can."

When we arrived at the hospital the pains were much worse than I could have imagined. After telling the nurse how far along I was everything changed. Upstairs I went to labor and delivery. I'd already reached my twentieth week of gestation and according to them the emergency room could no longer see patient's past that point.

It took several hours to get the contractions to slow and eventually stop, but Brice stayed right there with me. The doctors and nurses mistakenly referred to him as the father and I tried to correct them but he said just let it go. After going through a couple bags of IV fluids the head obstetrician came to speak to me. I could tell I wasn't going to like what he had to say.

"Whatever you are doing young lady you need to stop. I must be candid with you. If you do not get your stress levels under control you may lose your baby or have a very premature one with a small chance of survival. I am placing you on complete bed rest for the next four weeks. That means you only get up to use the restroom. No chores, no work, no traveling, and certainly no stress."

"Doctor you don't understand, I have to fly home and return to my job in Washington. I've already been on medical leave for the past thirty days. I have to work." I felt myself getting so worked up it made my stomach hurt again. That is when I realized what I had been feeling were contractions all this time."

"Which is more important to you Ms.? Your job or your baby, you choose."

My mind was racing along with my pulse.

When I was finally released Brice did not have to ask me if I was ready to leave. I felt great relief when I sat down in his Mustang. Then the flood gates opened up.

"Stop it Han. You are doing just what the doctor said not to do. Please calm down."

Ignoring him I just kept right on crying and looking out the window until I noticed he didn't take the exit to Jane's house.

"You missed the exit Brice."

"No, I didn't. You're not going back to Jane's alone Han. You can stay with me until they return in a couple days."

"That's not a good idea Brice."

"No, being sick and alone doesn't sound feasible to me Han."

"So now I'm a charity case? Take me back Brice."

"I'd call it more of a friend helping a friend. Remember that Han? Friendship, where people are honest with each other, help each other out, and forgive each other?"

"You wouldn't be saying that if you knew what I'd done."

"How can you judge what I would do if you never give me a chance?

Is that what's eating you Han? You know out of everything I miss about us I'd have to say it was our talks. When you had your defenses down. When you felt safe. When you felt loved."

"Stop Brice. I'm a bad person."

"Now that is hard to believe and also untrue. You are the strongest person I know."

"You wouldn't say that if you knew I killed your child."

"Excuse me."

"I had an abortion Brice. I aborted our child."

He was quiet for a long time. All I did was cry. Seem like that was all I did lately, cry. When we pulled into his garage he walked around to the passenger's side and opened the car door. When he took my hand to help me out of the car I looked into his eyes. I needed to see them. I needed to tell him face to face how sorry I was for making such a momentous mistake.

"I'm sorry Brice. Will you please forgive me Brice? If I had to do it over again I would make a better decision."

He looked at my face for a long time. Searching for something perhaps, I don't know. Unsure what to expect I knew I at least owed him the time he needed to express whatever he felt about the whole sordid mess.

"I'm sorry too. Sorry you didn't trust me enough to know I would be there for you and my child. Sorry you had to make such a decision on your own. Sorry you had to carry such a burden like that all by yourself. Sorry you still haven't forgiven yourself. Let's get you inside Han."

We didn't talk about it anymore. By the time we got into the house I went straight to the sofa and put my head back. Still crying I just wanted to go to sleep for a very long time.

"Are you hungry Han?"

"No."

"You need to take the medication the doctor prescribed."

"I know."

"Oh Han, things will work out. Sometimes you just have to take it one step at a time; one day at a time."

Shaking my head to let him know I was listening I continued to sit on his couch and cry.

He disappeared for a while and I was glad. I needed to process everything; bed rest, my career, my baby. When the doctor asked me if I wanted to know the sex of my baby I'd refused. I wanted to be surprised or maybe that would have made things all too real for me. I wasn't certain. The doctor was very clear about one thing. If I did not comply, he would have to place me in the hospital indefinitely.

All I wanted to do was put my head on a pillow and rest. It had been a long night. The pain started about three in the morning and it was now six in the evening. Since Brice had been insistent on me staying with him a couple of days I figured he couldn't mind me taking my shoes off and laying on his couch. The OB physician informed me that my iron was extremely low and that was a contributor to my being tired the way I had been for the past several weeks. According to him it was all a part of the ride for some women. Exhaustion had set in and sleep was inevitable.

When I woke up from my cat nap Brice was sitting on the floor next to the couch. Reluctant to move I laid there for a minute. Not much had changed in the past two and a half years. His house was just as I had last seen it. It still resembled someone just moving in. Minimal pictures on the wall, minimal decorations, but the flat screen and the gaming system were mounted. Just like a man.

"Hey sleepy head."

Unknown to me while I was critiquing Brice's home he was studying me.

"Are you hungry now?"

"No. Still a lot tired."

"Oh. You want to go and lay in bed then."

"That would work." Before I could get myself up he was taking me by the arm helping me get off the couch.

"I'm not an invalid Brice, just knocked up."

"I know you are with child Hannah but there is nothing wrong with a helping hand."

"With child Brice. Who says that? I'm not Mary. I had sex to get this baby ok. Good sex." He grimaced when I said it. There I was again being mean. The minute it came out of my mouth I regretted it. He never said anything else until I proceeded to enter the guest room.

"No you take my bed. That room doesn't have a bed in it anymore."

Feeling bad about my outburst I apologized, "I'm sorry Brice."

He still didn't say anything. I was beginning to feel like I was becoming Ms. Ann. Brice was loving, kind, dependable, and I was acting like he owed me something. I never asked or considered he had a job. It was a weekday and he'd spent it at the hospital with me after there had been no communication for over two years. Who in their right mind would do that except someone like Brice?

"You want something more comfortable to sleep in?"

"No I'll be ok. Thanks. I really appreciate you taking me to the hospital and staying with me today. I don't know what I would have done without you."

"Han I'll always be there for you" was what he said walking towards the door. For some reason I was full of more than drama. "Why? Why do you say you will always be there for me? We've both moved on with our lives. It's been so long since that week, since our college days, why do you say such things?"

"You're not prepared for what I have to say Han."

"You said you wanted to catch up that day. Here we are less than twenty-four hours later. Maybe somebody or something agrees with you."

"Something...Han? You need your rest." With that he closed the door. He was exasperated with me.

By this time I was now wide awake and voracious. I was starting to feel like I was bipolar or just plain crazy. Not wanting to force my company on him I sat on the bed just looking around. The furniture started to take on appearances of food. Chips and dip, tuna sandwiches, grapes and cheese; I really was losing it. Leaning back on the bed I closed my eyes. My stomach roared loud enough to make the baby kick. I knew there was not a chance of me lasting through the night. I felt so hungry it made me sick. Opening the door I attempted being as quiet as possible. I didn't know where Brice was but I knew the exact location of the kitchen.

The first thing I saw was a bunch of bananas. I grabbed two and went to town. I was looking through the pantry, banana in one hand, chips in the other and cookies in my mouth when Brice walked in. Embarrassed does not begin to describe how I felt.

He took one look at me and started laughing. "Yes, it is official. You are having a baby. Hannah Corel never ate junk food."

"I'm sorry for going through your things." Talking with food in my mouth I tried to be as apologetic as I could.

"Sit down. I will make you one of my famous omelets."

My eyes must have lit up. I know my heart fluttered a bit. He laughed at me again shaking his head this time.

"What would you like on it?"

"Everything" I said stuffing my mouth with chips.

Brice's memory was like a sponge. He cooked my egg on one side, and then flipped it over before he added the cheese, tomato, turkey, and peppers. My mouth was salivating I am sure. When he finished that omelet it took me less than three minutes to devour it. He watched like I was some freak show in the circus.

"Do you know how beautiful you are? Pregnancy looks good on you. Are you excited?"

Before I could answer my stomach began to feel like someone kicked me in it. The feeling was not new to me. Jumping from the bar stool I sprinted down the hall to the restroom praying I made it. Hearing Brice's footsteps right behind me I had no time to explain. He understood when he found me with my face in the toilet bowl puking my guts out. Before I could make another move Brice had a cool towel for my face. Exhausted I sat on the cold floor trying to recover. He wouldn't allow me to stay there. When he extended his hand to help me up I gladly took it.

"You ok Han?"

I shook my head but did not speak. The only thing I wanted to do was lay across the bed for a little while. Brice sat on the bed beside me. He didn't say anything and neither did I. Not when he began to gently rub my back or when he laid down beside me and took me in his arms. We must have stayed together like that for about an hour. Until the baby moved in a bad position and I grimaced.

"What's wrong? Do we need to go back to the hospital?"

"No I'm fine. The baby just can't find a comfortable position I guess."

"Is it moving around in there? How does it feel?"

I laughed at his hyperactive curiosity.

"I don't know; strange but beautiful?"

"I want to feel it. May I please?"

I took his hand and placed it on my stomach. Wouldn't you know it; the baby did not move a peep.

"I guess he or she is comfortable now because she isn't moving at all."

"You think it's a girl?"

"That's what Jane swears. I don't know."

"What would you like it to be?"

"Healthy. Normal. Loved."

He didn't move his hand and neither did I. Not long after that my stomach growled again, very loudly. Then my little bundle shifted inside me.

"She moved! I felt it Han! I could feel it."

His smile was as big as that of a child on Christmas morning that had received just what they wanted. Not sure if we were caught up in the moment, if I was being emotional again, or just stupid, but he kissed me and I kissed him back. He'd been my first; somehow I could never forget that. In the back of my mind I knew I'd never gotten over him either. No matter what I told myself.

"Let's go feed this little girl before she gets angry and kicks you again" he said playfully. What do you think you can handle?"

"I think you are asking the wrong person because that omelet was everything I have ever dreamed of."

"Maybe she just doesn't like eggs."

"She needs to learn to like something because I am tired of being hungry."

"So maybe you should just take it slow then. You really did not give that egg a chance you ate it so fast."

"Shut up Brice! You know they did not feed me in that hospital."

"What are you craving then?"

"Mexican food and all things peanut butter."

"What a combination," he says shaking his head.

"Don't judge me. Just feed me."

"That I can do. I will make you a peanut butter sandwich and you order take out, deal?"

"Deal."

After dinner we both fell asleep; me on the sofa and him on the floor right next to me.

Chapter 33

Brice whispered to me he had to leave for work sometime after dawn. I said ok and went right back to sleep. The previous day had been long, too long. I did not tell him but I was having some pains after I threw up. Being hospitalized so far away from the place I called home was frightening. Not that I did not know as much about San Antonio if not more than I did Tacoma, but I did not have a place to call home here. All my things were out west. I knew I could make it without a job, at least for a little while but where would I live? Jane and her husband needed their space and I needed mine as well. Having to be dependent on someone while I was on bed rest was a lot to ask of anyone. If my mother was alive I could go home. If I had a grandmother maybe I could go to her home, but I did not have those options.

When I heard the key in the door I was a little confused at first. Certain Brice was still at work my heart beat faster remembering my last sleep over and the altercation with his mother. That right now would be too much. It was no secret she didn't like me and now my being pregnant would just be fuel to her fire. Not knowing if I should pretend to be asleep or just face this monster head-on I braced myself. The way my emotions were working on overtime I was not sure how I was going to respond to China Chandler this time. Thinking better of getting upset and putting my baby at risk I decided to just keep my place and keep my tongue. It only took a second to figure out it was not the dreaded Mrs. Chandler but Brice. The cologne he wore gave him away.

"Hey sleepy head. I brought you some lunch."

"What are you doing here? You should be at work not worrying about me."

"No worries at all. I just wanted to check on you and make sure you were following doctor's orders, and fed the little princess of course."

"Or the prince."

"I think Jane may be on to something. She is dramatic already. That spells estrogen."

"So you still think you are a comedian? Now you add male chauvinist to your infamous list. That is so not funny."

"I thought you were your mother when I heard the key."

"My mother, oh no I would never have any privacy if I gave her a key. My father has a key for emergency purposes only because I know that is the only reason he would use it."

"So what's in the bag?"

"Your favorite, spicy chicken fajitas."

My mouth was already watering but I knew I must take care of my hygiene issues first. Why it didn't bother me to be walking around an old lover's apartment in one of his oversized shirts bare foot and pregnant with another man's baby was strange to me.

"Brice will you take me back to Jane's today? She said they would be returning soon. Besides I need some clothes. I can't exactly walk around here in your shirt for the next two days."

"And why not? You are barefoot and pregnant how much more perfect can that be?" he said teasing me yet again.

"Jerk!"

"Jane called me and asked me to keep you here until they arrived because she did not want you over doing it."

"You told her about the preterm labor?"

"Yes, I sure did. I knew you wouldn't listen except we ganged up on you."

"Some things never change."

"I guess not. I need to get back to the office but text me what you need and I will stop by the store and pick it up after work."

"No Brice. I already have clothes at Jane's place. That is a waste of money."

"Well, the way I see it you only have two options: text me what you

147

need or I try and figure it out myself. Either way I am going to the store after work my friend."

Anger is what I felt. Jane and Brice did not run my life. Picking up the pillow I aimed right at his head with all of my might. He closed the door before it got to him. My feelings of trepidation were returning. What was I going to do? My heart couldn't take it if something were to happen to my baby. Shirley was looking after my apartment for me. I'd sworn her to secrecy and so far she hadn't budged. Faxing my medical leave of absence was the next step. Being terminated from my job could become a reality for me but that was out of my hands. I needed my insurance to have this baby. I needed a job to take care of this baby. Childcare was a must and then there were all the things a baby needs to have. How could I even afford a baby? My inheritance was for the future. To insure I could buy a home when I found the perfect city to live. It was intended for emergency purposes only and not everyday living. It would never last that way.

My mind was in overdrive. The tears began to flow again. Panic was starting to set in. A river is what I'd cried by the time Brice walked through the door that afternoon. He immediately came and sat beside me and grabbed my hand. The devil in me wanted to snatch my hand away from him. Pity was something I did not desire.

"You're going to make yourself sick Han. Talk to me please. I'm still your friend Hannah, remember? I'm sure it's not as bad as you think. Whatever it is, it isn't worth putting your precious baby's life in jeopardy now is it?"

"You don't understand Brice."

"What that you're pregnant and alone. You're not the first Hannah Renee and you won't be the last. You have survived much worse."

"I just can't talk about it Brice."

"Talk about what? The baby or the baby's father?"

"It's complicated. There is so much to think about. My mind is just boggled."

"Let's make a deal. I get some tissues, you eat, and then we do some writing."

"Writing" I was confused.

"You write down everything you don't have an answer to and let's deal with it one thing at a time. Start with the most detrimental and work your way through the list. Do we have a deal?"

"I guess."

Dinner was not so appealing for me. My appetite came and went depending on the state of my emotions. Brice being the baby police I knew I had to at least put up a good pretense. After several minutes of pushing my food around on the plate I gave up.

"Maybe you'll feel better if we write down your anxieties now rather than later. Will you at least try for your baby's sake at least?"

"You hit below the belt but yes, I'll try." When he gave me the note cards I brooded over them for a few minutes. I knew what my problems were. I'd rehearsed them all afternoon. My problem was seeing how this could possibly help. If it were that simple psychology would be an obsolete profession.

"You ready?"

I understood that Brice was just trying to help me feel better but he was starting to work my nerves. So I picked up the pen to began his little exercise before I cursed him out. I didn't even use profanity often, but I was feeling like it at that moment. Labeling the first card number one, there was no doubt in my mind what it would say: health insurance. Babies were expensive and I was going to be a single parent. I needed insurance to have proper medical care before the baby and we would both need insurance after the baby. I needed to stay well to be able to take care of my child. That was the biggest thing at the moment if I lost my job. My number two was just as urgent as number one: a place to live if I couldn't get back to Tacoma right away. I did not want to be a burden to anyone. My number three was getting my child what he or she needed: car seat, crib, stroller, clothing, diapers, milk, bottles, and so much more. If I told Johanna I was sure my job and my friends would give me a baby shower but that meant having to deal with Connor. Deep down inside I was positive he would not want this child. He's stood right there when his father said such ugly racist things about me and he never spoke up or defended me. My child would never be put in that situation, not if I could help it. Somehow I believed Connor knew how his family felt. We were together a long time and yet I never met any of his friends outside our work place. Never met any of his family or hung out in any place that his Ivy League friends would be.

Maybe I used him as a pain killer and he used me for his own personal reasons as well. I'd deceived myself into thinking keeping us a secret was my idea. How wrong I was.

When I was done I gave the three cards to Brice. The gist of it all was: insurance, employment, and shelter. He stared at the cards going back and forth between the three.

"Do you trust me Han?"

With Brice I had to be honest, "More than anyone else I know Brice."

"Then I have a solution."

"Just what might that be?"

"Let's get married."

"How could you be joking when I am pouring my heart out to you Brice?"

"I'm serious. Let's get married."

"Huh, what are you crazy? What would make you say a thing like that?" At that moment I wasn't sure if I wanted to fight him or cry.

"Is there a chance of you getting back with the baby's father? Do you still love him?"

"Not in Hades. Connor and I are over. That is one of the few things I am sure of right now."

"Then let's get married. I have great health insurance that would cover you and the baby. I have a home already and if and when you chose to return to work childcare would not be a problem. My sister owns her own learning center."

"Don't you want to know anything about the baby's father?"

"Only if you wish to tell me and eventually I believe you will. As much as you try to deny it Han, I know we had something before you left. If you really didn't want to be here right now you wouldn't be. You could have called the ambulance and given them the address and they could have used GPS just like I did, but you chose to call me. You didn't have to take my number and you knew that restaurant was our spot in college. After your first altercation with Tobias you could have driven straight to Washington, gone to Jane and her family for refuge, but you came to me because you knew my arms would be wide open. You don't have to be afraid to let me love you anymore. Marry me and let's start over. You know I will be good to you. Don't you Hannah Renee Corel?"

"How would that be fair to you Brice? What about your family? What about the fact that this is another man's baby? What happens when you meet that special someone that makes your heart beat faster when she enters the room and you want to be with her more than anything, but wait, you'll already be married. Ludicrous, crass, dumb and stupid is what I call this. You deserve better Brice. Your heart is as big as an ocean and you are going to make some woman a great husband. You shouldn't throw your chances away."

"My life is my life Han and I want you in it. You make my heart skip a beat every time I see you, hear you laugh, watch you smile. I love you and I always have. Since the first day I saw you walk into the student center I've wanted you and only you. If my family can't accept that then that will be their loss. As far as the baby is concerned you know I would never ever do anything but love her…or him. I think you know that already deep down inside. Maybe this is a second chance for us. The greatest mistake I have ever made was waiting too long to contact you. I wanted you to realize you missed me and you loved me, but I know now that was a mistake. Sometimes you have to pursue what you want and not wait for it to come to you because maybe that person may not know how to find their way back home."

"That the sweetest thing anyone has ever wanted to do for me. Your heart is so kind. You deserve better Brice. I created this mess and I have to figure it out."

"We could be so good together Han. Tell me you don't still have feelings for me. Look at me and tell me that you haven't wondered what it would have been like if you had stayed here with me. One thing I know for certain is that you left because you were afraid. I get that. Say it Han, say you feel nothing at all for me and I will leave it alone."

He took my face in his hands turning my head towards him so I was forced to look him in the eyes. "Say it Han." I looked away. I couldn't say it. My heart ached and longed for Brice for so long after I left I had to fill it with something. I had moved on. That's what you have to do, move on or you stop and die.

"Marry me and let me take care of both of you."

I started to cry again. I was so confused and tired.

"Love I didn't mean to upset you. I just want you to be honest with yourself."

With that he pulled me close to him, kissed my tears and held me close. I put my head on his chest and listened to the rhythm of his breathing. "What about your mother Brice. She would never accept me or my child. I don't want to fight with anyone Brice. My entire life has been one altercation after another and I don't want to put my baby through that."

"You don't have to worry about that, promise. I will protect my family at all cost. Besides, I know my mother and eventually she will come around, she always does. Until then we will just live our lives and be happy doing it."

Chapter 34

When Brice dropped me off at Jane and Robert's I didn't know how I should be feeling. He turned to me and asked me to promise to at least think about his proposal. I promised him I would. What else could I do? He had once again rescued me and I owed him at least that much. Again when he kissed me I didn't pull away. My mind wanted to remember those times we shared and how good he felt to me and the way he treated me. I felt like my emotions had been placed in a disintegrator and I could not make sense of anything. How could you love two men at one time? Had I ever stopped loving Brice or just replaced him? Was it love or just desperation or was I trying to get back at Connor? Did I just use Brice and Connor to mask how messed up I really was or was I just running once more?

For a while I sat outside Jane's house in the rocking chair on her porch. There was something soothing about rocking back and forth for me. The warm spring sun felt good on my face. Although still cool, it felt invigorating to be outside getting some fresh air. Brice had been militant about me sticking to doctor's orders so my feet barely touched the floor, God forbid I went outside. The trees were waking up from their winter nap and stretching their branches in search of a new beginning. The curious birds peered over their nest into a world they had never seen before. Eager to get out and explore for themselves what they'd only heard their mother's sing about. Everything was coming alive with the zeal that only a new beginning could bring. I wanted that for my life and for my baby. A little of my sadness was starting to leave. I was going to be a mother and my heart was starting to embrace it.

After a couple of days of Jane acting like Nurse Millie my point was all too clear. No way could I be a house guest with her for three more weeks. She was driving me crazy. She checked on me so much I couldn't rest. She made me eat when I wasn't hungry, talk when I wanted to sleep, and asked way too many questions. Instead of her spending time with her husband she was spending it waiting on me hand and foot. I refuse to come between a man and his wife. Robert hadn't said anything but I know he was ready for me to leave. He was becoming less and less friendly towards me. When Jane wasn't around he made little remarks that let me know just how he felt.

Brice called or texted to check on us often. My guess is Connor got the picture because his calls and text had completely stopped. I heard nothing at all from him. So much for love. Shirley informed me in her, "As quiet as kept" manner that my place of employment was trying to terminate me. The only thing preventing them was the legal side of it all. Not disclosing what my medical condition was left a loophole and they were afraid to open the door for a law suit. Until then I would still be on sick leave and when that was exhausted my vacation days would be used.

I stayed with Jane through the weekend. I never mentioned Brice's proposal to her. My task was staying clear of Robert so that meant being in the room twenty-four seven sometimes. Even when he was at work because I never knew when he was going to randomly show up. He did that often; usually in the afternoons. I think that was because he knew Jane slept in. The baby did not sleep well at night and she was up with him a lot. Sometimes I wondered if he was checking up on Jane and her whereabouts. I'd noticed he did not like her spending time with anyone besides him. He had a problem with her talking too much on the phone. She visited too long with her family and he preferred she not work because her only duties were taking care of him and little RJ. She thought it was cute that he was jealous and it made her feel special. I had other thoughts about it which most likely ended with someone in jail or dead, but she would never take my word for it.

By that Tuesday I knew I had to do something. Sitting outside in the rocking chair that morning on March 10, I texted Brice just one word; "Yes." Then I thought about it and texted him right back because I did not want a lot of dialogue, just the peace of the moment. I sat rocking in that chair knowing I had just made the biggest decision I'd ever made. My life was changing and for the moment I just wanted to sit peacefully and think of nothing more than the clouds in the sky, the way the breeze swayed the grass, and the hummingbirds. "Brice we have to talk first, but not on the phone or through text. Pick me up after work please," that done; now it was time to talk to Jane.

It was still early. Some habits are just hard to break. As soon as I began to feel a little better my early morning routine was resuscitated. I couldn't work out at the gym but I still woke up at five am. After I heard Robert leave I made tea and sat in the sunroom and watched the sunrise. Dawn was a spectacular part of day that I was becoming to love. I was going to make breakfast for my sister and nephew. My baby may or may not allow me to eat any of it but I needed an ice breaker before I shared my plans with her. She loved French toast and that was what I was preparing, along with scrambled eggs, turkey bacon, and freshly squeezed orange juice. I was probably giving myself away but it helped keep me from being nervous about our talk.

As usual, it was the smell of food that aroused little RJ. That little boy loved to eat. Jane didn't have a choice but to get up once he was on the loose. When they made their grand entrance into the breakfast nook the table was set and breakfast was ready.

"Missy you are not supposed to be out of bed. Two words: bed rest!"

"Good morning to you too Jennifer. What a lovely day it is wouldn't you say."

"Morn din Tee Tee."

"Good morning RJ! How is my little man doing?" After planting a big kiss on his cheek I scooped him up and sat him at the table. I hope you are hungry because Aunt Hannah has something special just for you." He squealed when he saw the toast with the smiley face made with syrup and sugar.

I hadn't noticed Jane easing up behind me until she said, "What's up Missy. I know you and this spells trouble."

"See how you're acting. I am doing something nice and you just can't accept it."

"That may be true but I still know something is up."

"Can we just enjoy the food and the company please ma'am?" That is what we did. She didn't know but it was my last day as a house guest. It was the best time we'd spent together since they returned from the funeral. When we took RJ to the back yard to play Jane wasted no time getting to the point.

"Spill."

"Really, no foreplay or anything, just get right to it?"

She gave me her girl don't play with me look and I rolled my eyes at her. Sitting back in the lawn chair I continued to watch RJ play. Pretty soon this was going to be me. Running after a child, taking care of a husband, and a home, was all this right for me? Lost in thought somewhere my countenance must have displayed something not so pleasurable because Jane broke the silence.

"Han are you ok?"

"Brice and I are getting married." There it was out in the open. Knowing not to look at her I kept my eyes fixed on RJ who was having the time of his life playing in his sandbox. It wasn't that I was afraid of what she thought because my mind was made up. I really did not want to have a disagreement our last day together.

"When and where?"

Shocked I turned around to look at her. Her response was not what I expected. She was over protective to say the least. "That's all you have to say?" I was almost offended.

"You and Brice have had a thing since the first day you met. He dotes over you and you pretend you can't stand him. Yet you always managed to be in the same study groups, the same clubs, and have the same friends. I know you well enough to realize that out of all the people in the world you might have called when you went into preterm labor, you called him. Plus there was never any closure from your affair before you left for Washington."

"I'd hardly call it an affair Jane. We spent a week together."

"That's not who you are Hannah. You just don't sleep around. You just don't up and marry someone. You don't make rash decisions. That would be me."

"He's just helping me out until I can get on my feet since I will lose my health insurance with my job."

"No Han, it goes much deeper than that and you and I both know it.

Besides, you could do a whole lot worse than Brice. Anyway, didn't you tell me he was great in bed, huh, the sex does matter honey. Oh yes, it matters."

"You are so nasty."

"Do you love him?"

"How could I love two men at the same time?"

"Did you love Connor or just substitute him Han?"

This time it was my turn to shrug my shoulders.

"Anyway," she continues, "This means I get to have my best friend and sister back and help plan a wedding. It's a win win for me as long as you are happy and safe."

"Happiness is a fairy tale. I know Brice will make a good husband and father. He is a protector and he is loyal. He's happy having me anyway he can and that's fine with me. I have to look out for my baby and he or she needs stability and a father and he gives us both."

"Have you set a date?"

"No I just accepted his proposal this morning. We have to work out the details still. He's picking me up after work. I'm already packed and ready to go."

"So you're leaving me. I will miss you I can't lie about that."

"Stop it Jane. I will be across town and you're acting as though I 'm moving to Africa. Drama!" She was really sad about my leaving and that was such a mystery to me. That and so many other things about her and Robert's relationship. Who was I to judge though?

When Brice arrived late afternoon I was ready. After having a good long talk with myself that morning everything was now set in stone. I was going to marry him and make the most of the situation. On the drive to Brice's house I asked him if we could talk about everything after dinner and he thought it was a great idea.

Chapter 35

When we arrived at the house Brice escorted me to what had become my favorite spot in the house, the couch. He brought my bags in. Sitting on the sofa half watching television I didn't pay any attention to him when he came back until he was kneeled beside me and took my hand.

"Hannah Renee Corel-Waiters you are the best thing that has ever happened to me. Will you be my wife and make me the happiest man alive?"

He opened up a box that would have made any woman smile, it made me cry. "Oh Brice what are you doing. I already said yes."

"You deserve to have it done right Han. The ring makes it official. May I?"

I held out my hand and he slid the solitary diamond ring on my finger. It was just a tad big, but I didn't say anything. He definitely surprised me. I was now engaged.

"Brice what do you expect of me?"

"What do you mean?"

"What are the terms of our marriage? You're giving me what I need, but how do you expect me to satisfy your needs."

"I want a wife Han, in every sense of the word. I want a friend, a lover, and someone who believes in me and supports me. I want a family to come home to. Whether you decide to be a working mother, a student, or a stay at home mother is up to you. If you eventually want more children that would be great and if not I'm fine with that too. Can you handle that?"

"Will you love my child and your children the same if we had more children?"

"There is no mine and yours Han, it is ours. I plan to give that child everything I have including my last name. Please never make me a step-father; I plan to be daddy from start to finish."

Brice was a man of his word. If I knew nothing else I knew that. "What if your family makes a difference between the kids?"

"They will not be given that type of opportunity. When you are ready, I plan to speak to my family and I will address all of these issues. There are some things you don't know about me Han. My father has other children, two that were a part of his life before he and my mother ever met. The only time he saw them when they were growing up is when he had to sneak behind her back. She made a difference between them and me and my sisters and for that my father is resentful. That can never be our story. What she doesn't know is that it affected all of us. You should never have to choose what child you love. I needed those big brothers to look up to but she denied their very existence while I was growing up. As soon as I went to college I tracked them down."

"Does your mother know about it?"

"She knows we have contact with one another but I don't think she really knows how close we are."

"How close are you?"

"If no one else stands with me I know they will. I'd like them to stand with me when we are married if that's fine with you."

"So you want a wedding?"

"Don't you? I thought that was every woman's dream."

"Not mine."

"What do you want then?"

"Something very low profile, simple, justice of the peace type thing."

"Why is that? Don't you want your friends to come and celebrate you?"

"Less stress, I'm too fat, too expensive, and I don't have any friends in the area except Jane."

"You're not fat, you're beautiful. Is that the only reason?"

"What other reason might there be Brice?" What he was fishing for I don't know, but once again he was working my nerves.

Shrugging his shoulders he walked off into the bedroom leaving me sitting on the couch. I followed him. "What reasons do you think I have Brice" I reiterated.

"Nothing Han, just drop it."

"No Brice I won't drop it. You asked for a reason and I need to know what that reason is. If we don't talk about it now it will come up again so we may as well resolve the issue now."

"Are you ashamed of us Hannah?"

"What!? Ashamed, why on earth would you say something like that? That's absurd."

"If Connor comes back will you leave or are you committed to us."

"You have to believe me when I tell you things. You asked me to marry you and I said yes, what else do you want? I will be faithful to you, I will never intentionally hurt you, and I am not going anywhere. What else do you want to hear?"

"Did you ever love me? I mean head over heels, can't think about anything else, I have to hear his voice, and I can't live without him kind of thing? Please don't say what you think I want to hear."

"Yes. For the first year in Tacoma all I did was cry. For some strange reason I expected you to chase me. In the back of my mind I knew you would come one day, but that day never came." With that he kissed me and again I did not pull away.

"Let's file for our marriage license tomorrow. I don't want to wait."

"Brice are you sure this is what you want? Can you handle my independence Brice? My mood swings and my sadness? What about bills? How are we going to handle that? I have an apartment that is still under a contract for three more months. Then there is my car, it's paid for but how do I get it here along with my furniture and other personal belongings?"

"Right now Han all I want you to be concerned with is making sure we have a healthy baby and that means no worrying. First we get married, and then we have you placed on my insurance. I was thinking we should make the guest bedroom into a nursery."

"These are some big changes and so fast. You don't have to feel rushed because of the baby. I may qualify for some medical assistance for the baby. I don't want you to feel pressured or obligated."

"Are you backing out on me?"

"Marriage is hard enough all alone and we have some obstacles already coming into it. You know as well as I do your mother is not going to take this laying down. That stresses me out just thinking about it. I just want you to be sure that's all."

"I've never been so sure of anything in my life. My prayer is that one day I will make you the happiest woman on earth. Hannah you are marrying me, not my family, and I know we will be ok."

"What about the counseling requirements mandated by the state? You know I am not a churchgoer."

"My brother is a minister and the requirements can be satisfied doing online counseling. We can work at our own pace right from home and the test will print in his office. When we are finished he will complete the paperwork for us. The only thing he requires is that he meets with us twice before he signs the paperwork."

"Just how are we going to manage that?"

"He only lives an hour away and he is willing to come to us."

"Goodness, I guess you have it all figured out then. I wasn't aware you'd spoken to anyone about our plans."

"Haven't you talked to Jane about it?"

"Of course I did. She's my best friend."

"He's my oldest brother. I left work early today to go pick out the ring and I called him in route. Does that bother you?"

"What did he have to say?"

"He was concerned at first, but when he saw I was adamant he wished me well."

"Does he know about the baby?"

"He knows we are having a baby, yes."

My head was spinning. Everything was happening so fast. Sometimes I believed things would work out and then other times I was certain I would be a total failure at life. Today had been a great day health wise. Now I was tired and ready to go to bed. Tomorrow I was going to be one step closer to having a husband and what did I know about marriage?

"You still with me?"

"What makes you say that Brice?"

"You look so far away I was just wondering where you'd gone."

"I'm just tired. It's been a long day."

"You shouldn't overdo it Han. Why don't you go shower and get right to bed and I will find something to eat for us."

"Brice I'm not helpless, just pregnant. I will make some dinner for us and you go do whatever it is you do when you come home from work."

"Nope, doctor's orders. There will be plenty of opportunities for you to make me dinner. Right now your job is to keep that bundle of joy safe. So off you go."

My body must have been more exhausted than I knew. After my shower my only intentions were to lie in bed and wait for my dinner. When I woke up the only noise in the house was the low muffled sounds of the television. Brice was asleep next to me in the bed. He must have been tired, really tired because I called him twice and he never responded. The clock on the nightstand said one in the morning. Trying to ignore the pain I was feeling I shifted my weight under Brice's arm. Maybe I just needed to change my position. That wasn't the answer. The cramps in my lower abdomen continued to bother me. My heart was starting to become heavy again. Why couldn't I just have a normal pregnancy? All I could think of was the doctor's threats to place me in the hospital. I didn't want to stay in the hospital. I wanted my mother, I needed my mother. Johanna would do just fine too, but it wasn't fair to put her in the middle of my madness. Closing my eyes I did something I did not do often, pray. "God please allow me to carry my baby full term. Please let everything work out and please don't let me screw up Brice's life. He's a good person. Amen." The tears from my eyes must have fallen on Brice's arm without my knowing it and awaken him.

Worriedly he said, "Hey…what's wrong? Are you in pain?"

Shaking my head was the best I could do at that moment. Pain was doing martial arts in my back and abdomen. Immediately Brice was to his feet.

"Let's go. We're going to the hospital right now."

He did not get an argument from me. I didn't even bother to change from my pajamas. I threw on a jacket and we were off to the emergency room. Neither one of us said much on the way. I was too busy worrying. Who knows what was going on in Brice's head? I was petrified. It was a twenty minute drive and he held my hand the entire trip periodically squeezing it to reassure me. I think he was afraid too.

Why was the same doctor there as before? "Young lady I told you not to come back in here like this. What are you trying to do?"

The monitors confirmed I was having contractions. This was not a good thing. People were in and out of my room the remainder of the night or morning, however you saw it. By now I was terrified and starving. Going to bed with no dinner was not the smart thing to do. Seeing the look in Brice's face made me feel even worse. I didn't want to burden him, but he'd taken on the responsibility for me and my baby in every sense of the word. When the doctor came into the room I knew he did not have good news.

"Ms. Corel-Waiters we are going to have to admit you. Until we can get these contractions stopped I'm afraid you're going to have to be an inpatient."

My eyes immediately filled with tears. Brice was standing over me holding my hand. What was I going to do now? So many what ifs ran through my mind I wasn't able to process all of them.

The doctor went on, "We're going to do everything we can to keep this little one safe and sound until its time, but we need your cooperation. You my dear must stop stressing. Your blood pressure is too high, your iron too low, and the baby's birth weight is not where it should be. You've lost weight just since we saw you a week ago, that's not a good thing. Now I know all of this can be overwhelming, but I need you to think happy thoughts. In a few minutes we are going to be doing an ultrasound to determine the exact birth weight of the baby, amniotic fluid levels, and some other things that are important for us to know right now. During these tests we will be able to determine the sex of your baby. Would you like that information disclosed?"

"Yes, I want to know the sex of my baby." Having gone into labor twice already in such a short time I figured I'd better start preparing myself. Knowing the sex of my child would help me with that.

By the time the sun came up. I knew two things: I could not do this alone and I was having a little girl just like Jane said. Brice was elated. I had to force him to go to work the next day. He'd already taken off work before just a few days earlier. The way I convinced him was by telling him I was in good hands at the hospital. I would need him to be with me when I actually gave birth. So he needed to save his time. Then I lied and told him Jane would come and sit with me during the day. The truth is I had not been able to make contact with Jane as of yet, which was odd. Brice only worked half days on Friday so it shouldn't be so bad.

My stay at San Antonio Regional Hospital was three days and boy was I ready to go home. Brice came right after work each day and left when visiting hours ended at nine pm. I was so bored when he left. I was on the labor and delivery floor. Normally people came in, had their babies and left. That would not been a good thing for me. Yet I still had to hear other woman screaming, pushing, and families rejoicing all while praying my little girl would be full term, healthy and whole.

Dr. Jacobs was very stern before giving me my discharge orders. No sex, complete bed rest, take all my medications, and eat. My uterus was still closed and that was great news, but I needed to do everything in my power to make sure it remained that way. Since I was now considered a high risk pregnancy I would be required to see my doctor bi-weekly instead of monthly, which was a problem because my doctor was in Tacoma. The hospital gave me some referrals and sent me on my way.

When we pulled into the driveway that Saturday morning I couldn't have been happier to be out of the hospital. Being in that hospital bed gave me a chance to think about some things very seriously. I wanted my baby. I always did, even when I was in that abortion clinic that day. Maybe this was a second chance for Brice and I. There was no doubt he loved me and a girl could do worse. I was going to be a good wife to him, nothing less. Every day he stood right by my side and comforted me in any way he could. He supported me through it all and I wanted to give our marriage my all. At first I wasn't sure if he was just on some crusade to save little orphan Hannah but one day he left his phone at the hospital accidentally and yes, I went through it. I felt bad but I was still glad I did it. I read a text he sent his brother to pray for his fiancée and his baby girl. It said that he was scared for us both but he knew he had to be strong for us because we were his world. How crazy is that? What man does that? If he was willing to give his all for us and he got the least out of the deal I should be just as willing when I was getting the most from the deal. Brice helped me into the house and straight to the bedroom to put my feet up and comply with doctors' orders. There was no argument from me.

Chapter 36

The next day was Sunday and we both slept in. It wasn't until I got up to get something to drink from the kitchen that I noticed the guest room. Brice had completely emptied the room and painted the walls pink. He'd started working on the nursery. I sat on the floor in the room and cried. It was beautiful; such a soft soothing and peaceful color. Sitting in the middle of the floor crying is where he found me when he woke up.

"What's wrong Han? If you don't like it I'll change it. I wanted to surprise you."

"It's beautiful Brice," I said smiling through my tears.

Seeing his face light up was great. I am positive me and this little girl had worried him enough the past few days. He came and sat behind me on the floor and wrapped his arms around me. I leaned into him and the two of us sat there for a while until he broke the silence.

"What are we going to name her?"

"I haven't a clue Brice. We will come up with something."

"Yes we will," he said rubbing my stomach. It was a nice touch so I took my hand and placed it over his and closed my eyes for a moment. In my heart I was hoping for the best for my baby. My pleas were for her to have a much better life than I had and that she would be loved. I wanted her to be with people that accepted her regardless of how she looked, where she came from or how she got here. That was not even a remote possibility with Connor or his family so they would never know about her existence if I could help it.

After breakfast I watched Brice watch sports while dozing in and out of sleep. Being tired was still so much a part of who I had become. Feeling fat and lazy I tried not to think about things but my mind constantly wondered to life. Not just my life but Jane's and Johanna's came to mind in my worrying. There was still no return call from Jane and that concerned me a great deal. Not like her at all. Even in her busyness she found time to be there for others. She was always there for me. I knew it was time to grow up and I believed I was on my way, but I needed to know that she was doing fine. No matter how I attempted to dismiss it something just was not right with her and I would bet money on it. As far as Johanna was concerned, I just wanted to hear her voice. It is a common saying of Jane's grandmother that, "You never miss your water until your well runs dry." I longed to talk to Johanna. To hear her say things would be ok and that I would not be alone. She had become such a rock for me more than I actually knew up until now. Still, I was too frightened she would judge me about my decisions. Numerous times I dialed her number and ended the call before it connected. I'd answered her text messages often but then deleted them because fear did not permit me to hit send.

"Stop it Hannah Renee," Brice's gentle scolding ushered me back to reality. Sometimes it bothered me the fact that he knew me too well at times; parts of me anyway. There were still areas of my mind no one could handle; not even me.

"What Brice," I said wanting to be annoyed that he'd caught me red handed getting myself all worked up.

"Stop worrying. It isn't good for you and nor is it good for our little girl, so just stop. Tell you what Han, why don't you go online and find some baby furniture. Do you know if you want to do a theme or what type of baby bed you want, if you want a rocking chair or if you..."

"Wait a minute! You just told me to stop worrying and then you give me something to be overwhelmed about. I don't have a clue. This is all so new. We just found out the sex. Now we have to get furniture, along with a name, a marriage license, and a billion other things."

"Hey, slow down Han. We don't have to do everything today. Let's just start with you looking at baby furniture. It will take your mind off whatever was obviously troubling you a few minutes ago. One day at a time Han is all we are going to do for now."

He made a lot of sense but I guess I wanted to be devious. Finding furniture was a great idea but I noticed he said it was something I should do while he watched his precious game. Me being me decided to test him.

"Brice."

"Yes…may I help you the soon to be Mrs. Brice Anthony Chandler?"

"Shouldn't the father have something to do with all of this? I mean you should be helping me right? Instead of watching some game." I wanted to see if he would turn off the television he was glued to, plus, I wanted to see his response to the daddy thing. His answer shocked me.

"First of all I already know what I want my daughter to have." He took the computer and within a few seconds pulled up an account with an entire cart loaded with designer baby furniture. The most beautiful, elegant, yet durable I'd seen so far. The crib, changing table, glider, dresser, lamp, and bedding to match a princess theme. "She is my princess and you are my queen. Now if you want me to turn off the television, just say so. I love spending time with you and the game can be recorded, so what gives Han?"

Dumbfounded and a bit embarrassed I said, "When did you do all this Brice?"

"When I have a break at work and I can't get the two of you off my mind. I have already checked the safety ratings of the furniture, gotten a report on the company, and made sure there aren't any recalls. Have you ever wanted something so badly and it never seemed to be in your grasp and then one day it shows up at your door step? Han I am so in love with you and have been for a very long time. I never wanted anything the way I want us and I am going to do everything in my power to make you and our daughter happy because you've already made me the happiest man alive."

He was caught off guard when I threw my arms around his neck and laid my head on his shoulder. Being the cry baby I'd become I knew it was useless to fight back the tears. Scared this wouldn't last, shocked it was happening to someone like me, and determine to try for all three of us were just some of the emotions bottled inside me.

"Well, what will it be baby, TV or furniture shopping," he asked slightly turning his head to look into my face?

"Television Brice. There is no need to look for what we have already. I love what you found and that is what we will order. I will foot the bill for this one Brice. It's just right."

"You know that will never happen Han. If I am daddy I must do it all the way. I purchase our daughter's furniture and I take care of my family. You have to give me your word you will not interfere. That is all I ask Han. Let me be a true husband and a father. That is the only way it will work. I may not be living it right now but I believe what the Bible says about the man taking care of his family."

He was looking at me with sternness in his face that wasn't familiar to me at all. Like the bear that is standing between you and her cubs. The off limits kind of thing that makes it clear you will go no further so make a choice. So I did. I chose to do it Brice's way. "I promise." At that he switched on the television and I put my head in his lap and did a whole lot of nothing for the rest of the day.

Since Brice worked on a government installation he was off the next day because Monday was a holiday. Was I ever looking forward to him being at home with me. He wanted to do the on-line marriage counseling. It was a great idea for me. He and I were both over achievers so we looked forward to the challenge of getting three months' worth of courses completed in just two short weeks. It gave me something to do and that was therapeutic because it took my mind off the possibilities of me having a premature baby.

This was the real deal but the alarming thing about our first few sections of counseling is that we were compatible in almost everything. Go figure. Brice wasn't as disheveled about the answers as I was. He pointed out a few things I just had not considered in all my running back and forth. We both studied the same field. We both liked the same foods, restaurants, and loved a challenge. We both wanted families. We both valued people. We both wanted to make an impact in the world somehow. We were not frivolous in any sense of the word and we believed that God should be a part of every person's life although we had Him on the back burner for some reason. In my pain I had not seen that Brice wasn't without his share of pain and rejection, some of which I had caused myself.

By the time we were ready for bed I was completely and utterly worn out. Question after question after question, then homework, and communication exercises was almost more than I could handle. This was not the breeze I thought it was going to be. When we became lost or stagnant in the training Brice was quick to pick up the phone and call his brother. He put him on speaker and then we worked through the exercise. His brother always prayed first then we jumped into the counseling without reservation. This communication thing was work; especially since I was not good at it. Connor and I had mostly communicated through sex, this wasn't as easy. Even those times I'd tried to sex Brice up in my pregnant state he saw right through me and forced me to deal with the situation. Most times it angered me, made me feel stupid, and sometimes made me want to leave and say forget the whole thing, but in the end I appreciated it. No one had really stood up to me in the manner he did. Yet he reassured me not just with words but with his hand of support through everything. This whole counseling thing was making me confront some issues and get to the root of some behaviors. A part of me was way too tired of all the baggage anyway.

Chapter 37

When Brice's half-brother Ian pulled into the drive-way I immediately began to feel a little uncomfortable. For the past few weeks I'd stayed hidden from the world in the little brick house with the white shudders in the cul-de-sac. We'd spoken on the phone but to me it still wasn't real enough to produce any insecurity. A man of the cloth coming to counsel his half-brother and his expectant wife on the art of marriage made me feel a bit trepidatious. None of his family had come around since Brice announced our engagement. His sisters forwarded text messages, but didn't have much to say otherwise. They were trying to protect their mother and Brice was trying to protect me and the baby. In all the dreams I'd had of having a family, the husband that loved me and only me, the children and the extended family that would come with marriage; I never fathom it would start like this. Honestly, I understood that Brice's parents just wanted the best for him. I understood Brice was the wonderful person he was because they had done many things right. So I would not put my mouth on them and before I disrespected them I would stay away first. Jane's grandma always said, "There are three sides to every story, yours, theirs and the truth." Maybe one day my truth would be known.

Laughter almost spilled out when Ian walked through our front door. God really did have a sense of humor. He did not look like any Reverend I had ever seen. Dressed in blue jeans, a crew neck sweater and wearing a pair of sneakers he bore no resemblance to Brice or his father. Average height, medium build, green eyes, freckled faced and cinnamon hair would never have been my description, but there he stood. Never would I have guessed Brice's father had jungle fever. Love really was color blind. That had been a well-kept secret. Just like my own secret. Brice did not know that the little girl I was carrying may just be a red head like her father and her uncle Ian. He would love her anyway, but I wondered if I should say something. I was wondering about a few other things too. Was Mrs. China Chandler so upset about these two stepchildren because they were biracial? One thing I was beginning to see was there is no family without dysfunction. Those who deny it are just plain liars.

Right away Brice made the introduction, "Ian I'd like you to meet my fiancée, Hannah."

Rather eloquently he replied, "It's a pleasure Hannah. I've heard so much about you."

"Well don't believe any of it! He lies," I said.

Ian found that humorous and let out a chuckle and there it was, the DNA. He and Brice had the same laugh. Once you heard it you never forgot it. In college I use to instantly become angry when he said something comical and laughed at his own jokes and all the girls in our study group looked at him all starry eyed. Really, what line do you stand in to receive a sexy laugh in heaven? The two of them were so comfortable with one another it intrigued me. They bore no physical family resemblance, but throughout the next few hours I learned they were both so much alike. The same dry humor and a duplicate in their mannerism. There were similarities in television shows likes and dislikes; even the way they viewed world issues. How odd it was to me that you could be reared in an entirely different atmosphere and by different parents but still have so many likenesses. Pretending not to be listening while sitting at the kitchen table snacking while they caught up in the living I never realized just how much Brice knew about the Bible. He knew exactly what the man should do as the head of the household and what his responsibilities were as a husband, father, and provider. This side of him I knew nothing of because we did not talk about the Bible or God very often. Seeing him so at ease about the subject with his brother made me wonder about a few things. My having to wonder did not last long. We had a head-on collision with religion as soon as the counseling began.

"Where do you plan to worship?" was the question that started it all.

Before I could answer Brice announced, "The church my parents attend."

Looking at him rather offended I replied adamantly, "At home."

Ian not being moved by my outright disagreement continues his job. "I would like for each of you to expound on your answers starting with you first Hannah."

With attitude and all the pregnancy hormones I possessed I said, "No, Brice why don't you go first." He was not bothered by my defensive posture, the evil look I was giving him, nor did my attitude affect him in any way. He just opened his mouth and began speaking.

"Well, I have been doing a lot of thinking lately and I do not believe I should use God to my convenience. For the past few weeks I have asked Him for help more and more and I don't know why, but He has been there for me…for us Han and our baby. When your contractions wouldn't stop and I asked for His help they did. Every day when I leave for work I ask Him to protect the two of you here because I know you are here all alone and I worry about you. When I come home you and our little princess are doing well I know it is because of Him. I think that maybe I have to do better. Be thankful for all the good things. I want us Han. I want our family and I want our marriage to work. He can help us with that. Now I don't know of any other churches to attend, but I know we need to start and I just figured where I grew up would be at least a good place to begin."

"Your turn Hannah," Ian was in full minister's mode.

Again, my emotions were out of control. My defensive mode was completely and utterly blindsided by my soon to be husband's remarks. Getting my words together was difficult. It's not that I didn't know what I wanted to say. I was feeling very mushy about Brice's honesty. He deserved the same honesty, but I knew it would mean being more vulnerable. "I don't really know God except through the eyes or the lives of other people. I've waiver a lot about religion and about God. The God my mother served I think something in me longs for and most of the time I know He is real. I'm just not certain He wants me. The God of Ms. Ann I want nothing to do with. Only somehow they are the same God and I don't know how to comprehend or fathom that in my mind. There are times when I am angry with Him and times when I feel I should keep my distance because maybe He is angry with me. When I was with my legal guardian I used to write little notes to Him hoping somehow He would get me the answers I needed. One time I asked Him if I killed Ms. Ann if I would go to hell. I told Him I knew I would go to prison, but that was ok because I already lived in one and I was accustomed to that kind of life. That day I ended up going to see the Librarian and on her desk was a plaque with the Ten Commandments on it. One of them said, "Thou shalt not kill." I never forgot that. Possibly He might have heard me. Whether it was because I was desperate or so close to the edge who knows, but it taught me that when there was no other way out to go to Him. The right or wrong of it all I do not know. When you are at work or asleep I talk to Him and hope He is listening. I have blamed Him for so much, but I think maybe the only reason I have survived so much is because of Him. Like you I know I have used Him like a paper towel or the lining in the trash bag. Sometimes I did it in ignorance and other times with full knowledge."

When Brice grabs my hand and squeezed it my eyes fill with tears. Looking directly at him I continue speaking. "It's not that I don't want to try. It is just that I have been in a hostile environment all of my life. With the situation with your family I think it would be hard for me to begin a relationship with God among people that don't care for me. I need neutral ground Brice, can you understand that? I am willing, but rather than be placed in that type of situation I believe it would be better for me to talk to Him at home." Somehow I think we both forgot Minister Ian Cole was in the room.

Kissing me on the mouth he says, "Oh honey, I just want the best for us. I have looked up every scripture in the Bible about being a husband and a father just so I can do it correctly. I love you so much Han and I just want us to make it."

"I know you do baby and I promise to give us everything I have. I just don't have a lot to give."

Brice realized I called him by a pet name for the first time and grabbed me and drew me to him once again. "That's all I want." Seeing the passion in his eyes I kissed him this time. We had made a breakthrough and honestly at that moment I felt we might have a chance.

Ian chose that moment to end our session. "Great session you two. We can pick up here in our next meeting."

The counseling required that we have two separate sessions before our premarital requirements could be fulfilled. Not wanting to prolong the evitable day any longer Brice felt it best if Ian spent the night and we completed the training the following morning. Seeing the excitement in his eyes made it difficult for me to say no to him. I also wanted us to finish our counseling. Stagnant is where I had been for many weeks now; even before the sickness or the pregnancy. Moving forward is what I wanted and if that meant becoming Mrs. Brice Chandler I was becoming more and more comfortable with it.

Completely exhausted, Ian and Brice talked until the wee hours of the morning after dinner, but I took myself to bed. Just a little lighter and a lot closer to being married. When Brice woke me with breakfast in bed the following morning I dreaded being on bed rest more than ever. I desired to make him and his brother breakfast. I wanted to serve him and pamper him for a change but of course he wouldn't hear of it. Ian was the first family member to accept us, not without reservations, but he did open his arms to us. My yearning was to show some appreciation. It was Sunday morning and I felt awful about Ian missing out on his services to help us. Making an apology to him about it he assured me it was fine saying, "Sometimes the church has to go to those that can't come to it." He was extremely wise to be just thirty years old.

Midmorning we started the last of our counseling session. Things like money management, childrearing and disciple, resolving conflict, infidelity and outside friendships and so many other things were all tackled. Most of which we had already discussed in great detail. For some strange reason I wanted to come clean with Brice. Ian stressed honesty and being able to trust each other quite a bit. He said that we had to start out correctly to have a good foundation and that could only be built on truth. So I figured this would be the perfect time to tell him about my inheritance. If he wanted a way out then this would be it.

"Brice, there is something I haven't told you."

Not knowing what to do at the sudden change of atmosphere Ian says, "You two need some privacy so I'm going to step out of the room. Take all the time you need. We're pretty much done anyway."

Appreciative of the privacy and the respect I said a quick, "Thank you." My husband to be had not said one word. There was this look on his face that mirrored the panic in his heart. Wanting to put him at ease or at least let my news be a swift kill I did not prolong his agony. Moving closer to him I opened my mouth not knowing exactly how to tell him.

"Brice I haven't been honest with you."

"About what Han? Did you fib about being in love with Connor still?"

"No Brice. That's not it at all."

"Are you leaving again? Have you changed your mind about us?"

"I'm not leaving. Unless you want me to leave after you hear what I have to say."

"What could you possibly say that would make me want you to leave?"

"Well, it's not that I did something I just neglected to tell you a few things."

"Like what Han?"

"I have an inheritance. My mother left me an inheritance."

"But I thought you said Ms. Ann emptied out your trust fund."

"She did. Every single dime of it."

"I don't follow you Han."

"Do you remember Mr. Nelson? The man that helped me become a declared legal adult. He also helped me find my brother. As it turns out he was also my Mother's attorney and appointed by the courts to oversee my trust fund. When I graduated from college he attended my graduation ceremony. He gave me some of my mother's things. The Bible I keep under my pillow and some papers. That is when I found out about it. She had some money set aside for me that only I would have access to but not until I turned twenty-five or graduated from college. Since I graduated early I received my inheritance early. The only time I ever touched it was to purchase my car. For such a long time I never had enough. Then all of a sudden I had her letters and her Bible. They meant so much more to me than the money. I have actually been afraid to touch it and plus I have had a job and haven't needed to touch it. I guess if I received some kind of financial advice I could make it stretch, but I know it won't last forever. What I am really saying is that maybe if you helped me understand it all you don't have to marry me to take care of me. I could make it on my own."

"Is that what you what?"

175

He was hurt by my last statement and that was not my intention. "Brice I just want you to be sure of what you want. Your decisions concerning the baby and I need to be based on truth and now you have it, all of it. You are marrying me because you want to take care of us. I just want you to know that if I had some help, maybe I could be responsible for the two of us."

"See, that is where you are wrong Hannah. I am marrying you because I love you and have for a very long time. I don't care about any money. I care about you and our little girl. That's it."

He was agitated and I was annoyed. Getting up I waddled to our bedroom with my tail between my legs. My honesty thing hadn't gone so well. I wasn't looking for a way out. I was trying to give him one if he needed it. I was being honest in the case that he didn't need an escape route so that later down the road this wouldn't surface as a threat. Sometime later when Ian announced his departure I remained seated at our bedroom window. Hearing he and Brice talk I didn't have to guess what they were discussing. Still it did not matter. I continued to enjoy the scenery. The weather was beautiful. Everything was wide awake and completely thriving with life. The trees waved melodramatically. The birds played red rover from light pole to light pole. Children were riding bicycles and playing in the street. Joggers and walkers moved to the rhythm of music whether provided by Mother Nature or electronic devices. Sometimes accompanied by a stroller or dog, but moving right along smiling and laughing. I felt like I had been observing my life from a distance with little or no participation for a long time. Now I wanted to live it. I wanted to be a part of what happened to me and not allow others to choose for me. If I made a mistake, well at least I would have made it not someone else. When I'd first returned to San Antonio I deceived myself into thinking that Brice chose me. Now I had to admit that I chose him before he had a chance to think about it. I used his emotions and the love I knew he once had for me to reel him in and he willingly took the line. That was unfair and I could not, would not start our marriage in that way. Yes, I wanted to give us a try, but I knew I must put the ball back in his court so he alone could decide what he wanted to do with it. I wasn't a helpless little girl any longer. Sure I still had a lot of growing up to do but I knew I could take care of myself. Too many things had happened in my life and I survived. Being a single parent was just another one of them, but it by far wasn't the worst. Not even being unemployed was the most disastrous thing I could face, but never learning how to love myself so I could teach my daughter would be tragic and that wasn't going to happen. Yes I was an orphan but that didn't identify me. Yes I was mistreated but that could no longer define me. Only God could do that according to Johanna and I was becoming more and more interested in finding out just what He had to say about me every day.

The sunset and the street lights came on and the stars danced but still I sat. About an hour after Ian's departure Brice left too. Sitting in silence I did not worry about my life. If Brice was to be my husband then he would be my husband. Certain I did what was right and respected him enough not to take advantage of him, my heart was no longer heavy. Yes, I longed for the friend he'd become but I did not allow myself to think any further than that. Around 10 pm I heard the key in the door. I was still sitting in my chair when Brice walked in our bedroom.

"Hi Han."

"Hello."

"I texted you. Maybe you were busy."

"No. Just didn't feel like going in the other room to get my phone."

"Oh, are you feeling ok?"

"I'll make it."

"We'll make it Han."

For the first time since his return I looked up. He was in serious mode. I never knew if that was good or bad. Being considerate I allowed him time to explain so I sat and waited for him to expound.

"I'm not angry Han. At first I was really hurt. Hurt that after all we've been through together you were still trying to find ways to get out. I couldn't understand that for the life of me. Then it hit me. You don't want out. You're finally in. Kind of like the captain that throws all the dead weight from the ship to keep it from sinking. All unnecessary cargo is destroyed so the most precious, the passengers, may survive. Telling me about the money was your way of giving us a fresh start I believe. We're getting married Han and I can't wait to spend the rest of my life with you."

"Don't you want to know how much it is?"

"No. I am going to take care of us. Do you hear me? I want to provide for my family. I have been saving money myself. All along hoping and praying that I would be given this opportunity. We have to find our home now. One that we choose together which will include our dreams and the amenities you desire. In the neighborhood you desire with the square footage, color and whatever else your heart has ever longed for Han. Let me spoil you, pamper you, and love on you for the rest of our lives. That is all I want. Can you live with that?"

"Why do you love me Brice?"

"What's not to love? If I gave you a specific reason then what if something happens and that reason is no longer valid? I just do. From the very first time I saw you I knew you were the one for me. I had to take it slow because I also saw the pain in your eyes. We already know so much about one another whether you care to admit it or not. We spent a lot of time together in college Han. For the most part I know what makes you cry, sad, laugh, and what irritates the heck out of you. We have been together without you admitting it for a long time. So let's do it right this time. Again, can you live with that?"

"Yes Brice. I can and I will as long as you promise to be patient I promise to give us my all."

Before he helped me up from my chair and to the bed I swear the moon winked at me. My heart smiled. Just before going to bed that night Brice filled me in on his little outing. Apparently, he was at his parents' home filling them in on the details of his life. He invited them to the ceremony. If it made him happy then it made me happy. There were a couple of people I wanted there. Jane was one of them. I was beginning to worry about her. No doubt about it something was very wrong. My heart waited and secretly prayed for her and JR. It was the only thing I knew how to do.

Chapter 38

When my cell phone rang in the middle of the night I already knew why. Even so I needed to hear it for myself.

"Hello."

"Hi Han. I'm ok...we're ok."

"Where are you Jane? Where have you been? I've been so worried about you." Trying to get out of bed and not disturb Brice proved to be an epic fail. My baby bump was now a mountain and I had to move in shifts. Sliding over to the end, then shifting over a little, then a little more, and some more until at last I got to the edge. Just so I could swing the feet I had not seen in weeks over the bed and push myself up. Only to be able to sit on the edge of the bed because I was out of breath and too exhausted to stand up.

"Now that the earthquake is over where are you going Han?"

Everything in me wanted to do some bodily harm to Brice. His remark really hurt my feelings. Fat was something I never wanted to be. My self-esteem had always been low and that would only add to it. This baby was causing a war in my body and she was winning. Not being able to exercise I had gained so much weight. My small frame was trying to carry around one hundred and sixty pounds on a body that was used to one hundred and twenty pounds on a good day.

"Hello...can you hear me?"

Jane brought me back to reality. I decided not to talk to Brice and walked out of the bedroom. "I'm still here and yes I can hear you."

"Please forgive me for worrying you so much Han. How is my little girl doing?"

"She is fine. Her aunt I don't know about."

"This is the first time I've been able to call you. I've been in the country with my Aunt Ella and guess what, no phone service out there. She lives fifty miles in the middle of nothing and the only thing calling is the rooster."

"What…why. Why are you there Jane? I'm so not following you."

"Robert and I have officially split Han. I needed to get away to clear my head. Make some decisions."

"Sorry Jane."

"Don't be Han. I'm not. I should have done it a long time ago. I stayed thinking about what everyone else would say. I didn't want to be a failure and I didn't want to disappoint my family so I kept trying and trying. Then one day I woke up. They would not want me to be mistreated and if I needed them they would be more than willing to help me start over."

"Why didn't you tell me? We talk about everything Jane. You're my sister. You didn't have to go so far away I was right here."

"How fair would that have been to you and Brice? You are beginning a new life and you don't need any outside stress, drama, or interference. By the way how is Brice?"

"Great. Even on a bad day he's still wonderful. Sometimes I think it is too good to be true. I keep having this recurring dream that I answer the door one day and everything I have been given is taken away."

"Stop it Han! You stop right now. It is time for you to be happy and I believe you are. I can hear it in your voice. You're peaceful now. Embrace it and don't allow anyone or anything to take that away. Keep the power in your hands for your happiness. Do not give it away again. That is why my son is going through what he is suffering now because I made that choice. It is not worth it."

"What happened?'

"It is a long story and I promise I will tell it, but this isn't the time. Just wanted to let you know we were fine. Between you and Brice leaving e-mails I figured if I didn't make some type of contact you would have the FBI on my case next. When is the wedding? "

"Thursday, and you are right about that. You are my family Jane and I need you in my life now more than ever."

"I'll be there. Listen you had better get back to bed. I love you and I will see you on Thursday."

"Love you Jane. Kiss RJ for me."

When I got back into bed I cuddled up close to Brice. He welcomed me with open arms. Then whispered in my ear, "Sorry" and we both went back to sleep. My friend was well and that put us both at peace.

Chapter 39

Having never been a wife before I was unsure how our wedding night should be spent. Brice and I had not been intimate since we reconnected. Sex during pregnancy especially with me having complications was out of the question, doctor's orders. Having to wait to legally make me Mrs. Brice Chandler didn't seem to bother Brice. We talked a lot, cuddled even more, and yet I felt like I was really with him without the sex part of it. Sometimes we kissed and I know he struggled to keep it together, but he never complained. I actually looked forward to our nights together. All he wanted was my respect and eventually, my heart and that was enough for him. He was the kind of guy who gave his all. I'd always known that even back in college. If I chose to walk around the house butt naked with my hair uncombed it wouldn't bother him. He allowed me to be me. Whoever that was he was alright with it. That was great because I was still trying to figure out who I was although I was starting to have a glimpse of the woman I was supposed to be.

I was unrelenting about keeping my mother's name and again he had not argued. I told him it was all I had left of her. He said he understood. It was the only stipulation I had to our marriage deal. There would be no honeymoon and no time off for Brice because he wanted to be available just in case I got sick again and when the baby came. Our ceremony lasted all of ten minutes. Ten life changing minutes and I had a husband. The other Mr. & Mrs. Chandler were cordial. Whatever Brice told them it worked because Mrs. China was very quiet. I am unsure if seeing her stepsons, having her only son marry a pregnant woman none of them knew, or being threatened did the trick. Either way her silence was medicine for me. One day if my prayers were answered we would become friends. That day just hadn't come yet but I was willing to wait.

Jane stood with me snapping pictures every second of the ceremony. I threatened to accidentally step on her perfectly pedicure feet if she allowed any other living soul to see them. My stomach was doubled in size and the only dress I could fit was a long sundress and it was white of all colors. My swollen feet had to be stuffed in flats. After having Jane fuss with my hair all morning the wind had proven to be more powerful than the flat iron. By the time we got off the elevator to the fifth floor I was wishing it would all just end soon. The doctor had given me permission to be on my feet for no more than a couple hours a day, but today I was feeling like even that was too much.

When Brice said his vows I cried. It could have been hormones. He looked at me so lovingly, so sincere, so kind---I knew he meant every word of what he promised. That scared me so badly and yet it touched me so deeply my heart just opened up. When I reached up and wiped a tear from his face he grabbed my hand and kissed it. That made me even more emotional. So he kissed me and I didn't want him to stop. Jane cleared her throat and said, "Get a room," lightening the atmosphere and making us laugh.

Originally, Brice and I planned to go out to dinner with Jane, minus Robert and Brice's brothers, but I whispered in his ear and told him I was not feeling well. One look at me and he put me in the car and spoke to the others. After that we headed home and I was happy just to be able to put my feet up. Anything else was exasperating. This little girl was taking a toll on my body. Whoever said pregnancy was beautiful told a lie. The life that comes from pregnancy was nothing short of a miracle, but the process my body was going through to get this little one here was painful and that was trying to put it nicely. My face looked like I ate a cantaloupe and my feet resembled loaves of bread. Breathing was difficult; especially at night and boy did I have a temper. Sleep was evasive and I was always hungry or using the bathroom. Brice didn't even bother using the restroom in the master bedroom anymore. He just went down the hall. It was a mystery to me how he even functioned at work. Every time I moved so did he---checking to see if I was ok. This happened numerous times during the night, but he never complained. My doctor's appointments were now once a week and he took me to each one. Going into my seventh month I was petrified. We would not be able to take Lamaze classes and that made me a little sad. It would require me to be on my feet too much. How would I know what to do and what not to do constantly bombarded my mind.

Our wedding night was uneventful. We ordered take out and fell asleep watching television. Brice had work the next day. He was doing the paperwork to add me to his insurance. Basically he only had to sign and date. One of his friends worked in that department and we'd already completed everything we could beforehand. That way I wouldn't be required to do a lot of running around.

The next morning when he kissed me good-bye he said, "See you at lunch Mrs. Chandler." Maybe that was when panic set in. Mrs. Chandler. What had I done? Had we done the right thing for us, the baby? The diamond ring on my finger didn't make me feel any better. That morning I reasoned and rationalized with the reality of happily ever after for me and concluded life held no such possibilities. When Brice came home for lunch I made small talk and pretended everything was fine. Depression was kicking my big fat behind. Crying was how I spent my afternoon until I just couldn't take it anymore and picked up the phone.

"Hello…Oh Lord have mercy baby girl. The Lord answers prayers. I've been worried sick about you."

That was all it took for me to burst into tears again.

"Oh angel it's ok. You just cry until you feel better but I know things have to work out for you. Remember the words the preacher spoke that day. Well, God doesn't lie so I have to believe whatever is going on with you, my baby girl will be just fine. Just allow me be there for you. It's alright to let someone love you angel. It's ok to trust someone other than yourself. My shoulders are here for you."

"No, I don't know if things will work out. You have no idea some of the things I've done."

"Have you murdered anyone?"

"No…God no!"

"Have you taken someone's husband?"

"Certainly not Johanna."

"Have you stolen from someone or robbed anyone?"

Getting frustrated I answered, "No! Why are you asking me all these crazy questions?"

"Because those are the types of people you will find in the Bible. And guess what God still loved them and accepted them into His Kingdom. Talk to me baby girl."

"I don't even know where to begin."

"Understand that I have been counseling people for a long time and I have heard just about everything. Just start from the beginning. Why did you leave?"

"Actually I only planned to be gone for a short while. I needed to think…to try and figure things out. But then I didn't feel good again and the doctor here wouldn't release me."

"Are you feeling better now? Did you have pneumonia again?"

"No, I got married though; yesterday."

"You did? Who did you marry?"

"Brice is his name. We went to college together. When I came to Washington I was running from him I guess. He wanted a relationship and I…"

"You were scared?"

"Oh Johanna, I've messed things up so badly."

"Do you still love Connor?"

My tears started again. "No, I don't think so. Oh I don't know. When I got to Tacoma I longed for Brice so much I thought my heart would break. Connor helped me with that but I don't think he and I would have worked out anyway. His family never knew about me all that time. Did you know his family members were racist? His Dad said that I was only good to sleep with, not to marry. He never stood up for me once. He let his father humiliate me and say all kinds of things about me and he never defended me or us for that matter. He hurt me Johanna."

"So you ran from Brice to Connor and then back to Brice. Running away never helps. Just ask Elijah and Jonah. Now running to…running to God never failed, just ask the woman with the issue of blood, the blind man on the side of the road, and you could ask me."

"Since I don't know them I'll go with you. Besides at this point in my life I know God doesn't want to hear anything from me."

"Really? So why does He wake me in the middle of the night to have me pray for you?"

"Is it God or you just worrying? I know God's not a fan of mine."

"What makes you so certain of such things?"

"Just look at my life. My mother loved Him and prayed to Him all the time but I haven't been able to reach Him."

"When was the last time you tried?"

"At night…when Brice is sleeping. I don't want to hurt him Johanna. He is such a good person. He loves me. Maybe I don't deserve that kind of love."

"Is that why you left the first time?"

"Yes, mostly."

"What if we prayed about it together? Is there something else?"

"Yes." I was quiet for a long time.

"Whatever it is God already knows so you won't surprise Him. As long as He knows and still loves you, anyone else shouldn't matter, including me."

"Summer. I want her to be healthy and normal and not come early."

"Summer…who's Summer?"

She was confused. That made two of us.

"Well, it doesn't matter. We will pray for Summer and your marriage."

"Summer is my unborn baby. I'm pregnant. That's why I left. I couldn't face Connor or you. So I took some time off, only once I got here I began to have complications with the pregnancy. If I tried to go back I would risk my baby's life. I've been on bed rest ever since."

Waiting for her to scold me or hang up in my face or even yell I held my breath.

"Oh angel I am so sorry you've had to carry all this alone. I want Summer to be healthy and to not come until it's time too so I can spoil her rotten when she gets here. I'm going to be a grandmother," she said and I knew she was weeping. I'd never known Johanna to shed one tear.

Now I was sobbing rather loudly. Liberated is what I felt more than anything else. It felt good talking to someone about everything. Brice knew some things, Jane knew parts, and Connor knew pieces, but no one had knowledge of most of me. The next thing Johanna said made me know maybe God was listening because I had not said anything to anyone about my secret prayers.

"When is your due date because I must take some personal time off so I can hold your hand while you push and help you when she comes home?"

Answering her was out of the question for the moment. My emotions were out of control. This time I knew it wasn't all the hormones from the pregnancy but all the built up anxiety from the last several months.

"August 1st, but I don't know if she will wait. I'm scared Johanna."

"I know you are but we just have to pray and believe that Summer, Renee, and Brice are all in God's hands and that is the best place in the world you can be."

"Connor doesn't know about the baby. Just one more thing is more than I could handle right now."

"Let's just get you through this and I am sure when it is time you will have the strength to make the right decision concerning Connor. Until then, my only concern is you and that little granddaughter of mine. I love you Renee and maybe you might not understand all of this now but someday you will. God brought you to me not because you needed me so much but because I needed you."

What she said was beyond me but all that mattered was that she would be with me when the baby was born. I wanted her there, I needed her there and I had silently prayed that she come and now she was. We must have talked for hours. When my battery was low I plugged the phone into the charger and we continued to talk.

When Brice came home from work that evening I was sleeping like a baby on his side of the bed. His pillow smelled like his cologne and for some reason I missed him that day more than any of the others. He must have been tired himself because he eased next to me trying his best not to disturb me. When his breathing slowed and I knew he was comfortable I took his arm and placed it around me.

"Did I wake you baby?"

"I'm glad you're home Brice."

The look he gave me was one of surprise and pleasure.

"Mrs. Chandler I missed you too. I have some great news."

"You do? What is it?"

187

"Our health insurance will pay for a certified Lamaze instructor to give us classes at home since you are on bed rest."

Letting out a squeal I almost jumped up and down on the bed until Brice stopped me.

"Han! You had better not!"

When he caught me by the arm to steady me and my big baby bump I planted a big kiss on his mouth, then his ear, then his chest.

"Han stop you know we can't..."

"Brice I want to. If you're gentle I know it will be fine." Ignoring his protest I moved my hands over his body, caressing and massaging his spots.

"No Han. We can't risk it."

"We'll be careful Brice."

"No, doctor's orders. There is no way I want either of us to have any regrets when it comes to this little princess." He kissed my belly bump and took me into his arms trying to get his breathing under some control. I listened trying my best not to feel rejected.

"Is it because I'm fat Brice? Do you think I'm unattractive?"

Turning over to look me in the eyes he spoke, "You are the most beautiful, sexiest, strongest, wisest woman I know and I am so proud to be your husband. I want you Han and I dream of the day when we are able to consummate our marriage, but right now this little girl is our priority. She is depending on us and we cannot let her down."

For a while neither of us said anything. He misinterpreted my silence for attitude but I was just thinking how lucky I was to be with such a strong man. Then I remembered.

"Summer."

"What about summer Han?"

"Summer Anna is what I want to name her."

"Summer Anna Chandler," he mouthed in pure pride. "It's perfect. How did you come up with it?"

"Well, it was the first day of summer when we said, "I do" and your middle name is Anthony and I thought she should have a part of you. So Anna was what came to mind. If you don't like it we can find something else."

"I love you Hannah Renee Corel-Waiters Chandler and I love you baby Anna."

"You sure we can't Brice?"

"I'm sure. We will have endless nights to make up for lost time once our daughter is born. Now we have a baby to grow and a nursery to complete."

"Brice."

"Yes Love."

"I need to tell you about my god-mother, Johanna."

Chapter 40

Johanna checked on me every day from then on and I was sure to answer her phone calls and text messages. We surf the net while talking, she cooked while talking, and she prayed, a lot. You know the kind of prayer that just sneaks up on you and finds its way into the conversation. For example one day we were talking and I said something like, "I just don't know if I'm cut out for this housewife thing," you know just thinking out loud while she stirred in her pots. Out of the blue she just goes to God on me like I asked her and says, "Lord help Renee be the kind of wife you desire, a virtuous woman, let her be like Sarah calling her husband Lord." Now I never met Sarah, but I think some of that stuff she asked I wanted to take it back, but how do you do that? Or when I said something negative about Brice she just interrupted the conversation with, "Lord thank you that Hannah loves Brice and respects him and he loves her like Christ loves the church." Then go on with the conversation like she hadn't just had a prayer pause. That was Johanna.

From the day Brice refused to be lured into temptation when I tried to seduce him, I had a new found respect for him. Weak men always turned me off. Backbones were a vital necessity and I could not deal with a man who didn't have one. Each day I made it a point to let Brice know in some way or another how much I appreciated the sacrifice he was making for me and the baby. That was tough for me because being on bed rest meant I couldn't cook, clean, or even do laundry and that said dependence for me. Since the age of twelve I'd done everything for myself. Even if I must figure it out as I went, I had taken care of me since my mother's death. Those who wanted to help I was afraid to let them in and those who would

190

not take no for an answer I found some way of repaying them. Trusting people was hard for me but people like Jane, Brice, and Johanna were living proof that good people did exist. You cannot do life alone is the lesson I was living at the moment. You must love, learn how to receive love, and give yourself permission to be loved.

Pacing the floor back and forth my mind raced from one tragedy to the next. Something must have gone wrong. The trip to the airport was thirty minutes one way. So that was an hour's travel time. Johanna's flight was on schedule because I checked it three times. They should have been back by now. Three hours had passed and nothing. Brice's phone was going straight to voicemail and my nerves were on edge. Where could they be? Leaving my post for a moment I decided to make sure I hadn't forgotten anything in our nursery/guest room. The nursery was complete. Summer had a five in one top of the line crib, a rocking chair for our special moments and a twin size bed that would allow Johanna to have a place to sleep while she was visiting. We'd found a nightstand and matching dresser at a great price too. All that was missing now was Summer and of course, Johanna.

Summer had been behaving herself for the past six weeks and finally my doctor had taken me off bed rest. Drill sergeant Brice Chandler could no longer make me stay in bed and there were no words to describe how I felt. My doctor said if she comes, she comes and that is exactly what I wanted her to do…break out of solitary confinement. My uterus had dilated two centimeters at my last visit so we were both hopeful and scared. Well maybe I was the only frightened one, but having Johanna with me made it all the better.

"Han! Han, where are you!"

Brice's voice was music to my ears. They were back and I was so excited I could not contain it. Running down the hall from the nursery I felt like it was Christmas and Santa had just come down the chimney. She was here, my Johanna was here and I was truly happy about it. Standing in our living room was my Johanna with her arms wide open and I ran right into them.

"Renee, oh Renee! Look at my baby girl. You're beautiful!"

She gave the best hugs. Tears flowed freely down my cheeks and I didn't care. She held on to me tightly and I was happy to stay right there. She rubbed my hair and repeatedly kissed my forehead and I still wouldn't move. Sometimes you just need a mother and for me God had sent me Johanna to fill in for my own mother who I knew was in heaven looking down on me. Grateful was how I felt.

"My angel. Let me get a good look at you."

No is what I wanted to say. Moving from her arms was the last thing I wanted to do. Instead I held on to her a little tighter. She wasn't used to me showing a lot of affection and knew if I was holding on to her there was a reason for it. All I wanted was to stay right there. Sometimes you don't know how hungry you are until you get your meal and then your body reminds you that you have actually been starving way too long. Love starved is how my heart had been for so long. Now being connected to someone who had so much love to give and express I wanted nothing else. Brice stood by watching us together. His thoughts weren't expressed, but after a minute or two he walked away and took Johanna's things to the nursery. After he didn't return right away I knew something was up with him, but I would deal with that later. For now being someone's daughter is what my heart longed for and I was beginning to believe Johanna when she said she and I were all a part of God's plan. Several minutes later I lifted my head from Johanna's shoulder and she wiped my tears with her handkerchief and kissed me on the cheek and said, "Now, my precious daughter, go greet your husband and I will be right here when you return." Listening to her, something I was still learning to do, I made my way to the bedroom.

When I got there he was standing in the window looking out. It was a beautiful summer day and the light breeze swayed the magnolia tree in front of our bedroom window. Left out is how I'm positive Brice felt. When he came home from work he scarcely got a Hi sometimes, let alone a hug and a kiss. He never said anything. He was a giver and that was all he knew how to do. It was beyond his nature to be selfish. Really, I wanted to be a good wife and friend to him but how would I know such things except I be taught. Willing to learn I was but I needed help loving and embracing my new roles, duties, and responsibilities.

When I entered the room he didn't move from his position. I knew he heard me open and close the door. From behind his posture looked worn. Still in slacks, shirt and tie from leaving work early to pick up Johanna from the airport, I admired his choice of clothing and his physique. He was a professional and he took not only his job, but life seriously. My heart strings tugged at me when I thought about what he had sacrificed for me. His mother had not spoken to him since our wedding day. His father, not wanting to cause trouble, only called to check on him when he was alone or if his mother was at church. His sisters didn't want to upset their mother and had decided to stay out of it. They were a close knit family and I know he missed them immensely, but he never complained or acted resentful towards me or the baby. While his back was still to me I put my arms around him and held on to him as tight as my baby mountain would allow. He grabbed my hands and held them to his chest. We stood like that for a long time. Until I began to plant featherlike kisses on his back. For Brice little was much and I knew it. He turned around to face me and I looked into his eyes and it nearly broke my heart. Pain is what I saw and for the first time since we had reconciled; I wanted to make him better. Putting both my hands on his face I pulled him to me and kissed him like he'd been away on a trip somewhere and I was happy to see him at last. When he attempted to stop me I pressed in even harder and begin unbuttoning his shirt.

"Han…we can't…" his breathing was heavy and his voice raspy.

Answering him, "Yes, we can. The doctor said so." I did not stop loving on him. I knew he needed to be loved. Again he tried to deter me, but I was persistent and eventually he gave in to me and then he took the lead. That is what I wanted. He picked me up and took me to the bed. He kissed me softly at first almost teasing as his hands found places I forgot I had. He knew more about my body than I did and he had forgotten nothing in the almost three years since we'd made love. He took his time and awakened everything in me I thought was dead. For the first time in a long time I forgot everything and everyone but the two of us. My body responded to his every touch and he was careful to appease my every need. Forgetting about Johanna in the other room he muffled my screams of pleasure by kissing me repeatedly. Everything in me screamed for Brice and he answered every call until all of me was satisfied into silence.

"Did I hurt you," he asked. Wanting to answer I stayed close to him with my eyes closed in the peace of the moment. Two things had become a reality for me in the last hour: Brice was my husband and he was who and what I wanted and my heart had never stopped loving him. He knew it I'm sure. As I lay in the quietness of our bedroom my heart yearned to talk to God in that moment. If I could just have one moment with Him I would ask Him to show me how to be a good wife and mother and how to straighten out the mess I'd made of my life. I would ask Him if it was true what Johanna told me about Him having a plan for my life. Did He really want me to be happy? Was He really listening if I spoke to Him or if He would abandon me like everybody else if I reached out to Him? Tears rolled down my face.

"What's wrong Mrs. Chandler?" Brice whispered.

Finding my voice I answered, "Nothing Mr. Chandler, nothing at all."

By the time we reentered the living room Johanna had an entire meal prepared. I was feeling happy. A little scared to admit it but a strange feeling was coming over me and I was hoping it lasted. My heart pleaded for it to last.

Chapter 41

Each day Johanna and I went out for short periods of shopping. She had seriously gone overboard shopping for baby Summer. She wasn't born yet and had a bigger wardrobe than her parents. When Brice came home the three of us sat at the dining room table and had a big lavish dinner. He'd taken to Johanna and she took to him almost instantly. Most liked Johanna, but I could tell there was something special developing between the two of them. I secretly wondered if it had anything to do with the deteriorated relationship between him and his mother. They conversed as much as she and I did. That made me happy.

After dinner Johanna always retired to the guestroom/nursery. She said it was her God time but I knew she was giving me time with my husband. She was sure to groom me every opportunity she had on being a good wife. I accepted all the help she gave to me. There was much for me to learn and I wasn't afraid to admit it. She had never been reluctant about giving advice and this was no different. Even to the point of my in-laws. "Now baby girl, God put families together for a reason. Although things are strained right now with his family you make sure you don't add to it. When Mother's Day, Father's Day, Birthdays and Anniversaries come you make sure you buy the cards for him to send. The same with Thanksgiving and Christmas; you get the cards and make gift suggestions. Leave a crack in the door just in case someone doesn't have the strength to turn the door knob. Be to them what they won't be to you. The relationship you desire to have with them you show it or sow it and God will fix it for you. You understand me?" Yes Ma'am was always my answer to her.

Johanna was not about to miss church for the entire time she was visiting. So she went on-line and made some calls and the following Sunday we, Me, Brice, and Johanna were in True Life Church. Johanna obviously did not get the memo about visitors' etiquette because she was acting like she was there when they poured the foundation to the church. Shouting all over the people's church, yelling back at the preacher, and worst of all having way too much to say when the visitors were asked to stand. She made my husband stand up for his pregnant wife because she had just been released from bed rest. If that wasn't good enough she not only introduced herself but all three of us. "This is my baby Hannah, her husband Brice and my first grandchild, Summer. They need a church home with a good family to look after them when I have to return to Washington." If I would not have looked like the good-year blimp I most definitely would have put my finger up and waddled out of that church. Brice thought it was hilarious but I did not share his amusement. I wasn't upset just a little bit embarrassed. An embarrassment I would not trade for anything in the world.

We were out on one of our shopping frenzies riding the escalator in the mall when my water broke. At first I was mortified because I thought I was using the bathroom on myself. Thinking Summer had kicked me one time too hard and bam, urine was running down my leg. Johanna started screaming with excitement, "It's time baby girl, it's time—your water just broke." My previous shame was immediately replaced with terror. "Oh God, I don't know if I am ready for this, please help me through this. Help me be prepared. Help me be a good mommy. Teach me how to raise my baby God," was all I kept repeating. Not caring if my voice was audible.

"You'll do just find baby girl."

"I want my husband Mommy. I want Brice," I managed through a contraction. Not realizing I'd called Johanna Mommy for the first time, but she caught it though.

"He's on the way baby. He's meeting us at the hospital."

How he did it I will never know, but when we pulled into the emergency section of the hospital my husband was waiting for us. He was pacing up and down the entrance to the hospital. God was I glad to see him. Upon seeing us he grabbed a wheelchair and sprinted to the car.

"Oh Brice, I'm so afraid." My mind was a mess. Our Lamaze classes had never happened. The paperwork was lost and then had to be resubmitted and then the in-home instructor was overbooked. What am I supposed to do was coursing through my mind.

With such emotion and confidence in his voice he answered, "God is with us and we will be just fine. Now let's go have our daughter." He then scooped me up from that car and put me in the wheel chair and got me to the fifth floor in record time. Johanna was right behind us after parking the car.

Yes, I was in active labor my doctor confirmed. The pains in my back made a believer out of me without him having to add his expertise. My cervix had dilated five centimeters. I was half way there. That epidural was everything I imagined it to be until it wore off because I was dilating too slowly and I was too far along to have another one. It got real in that delivery room. The pain I felt was like no other. Hour after hour and Summer just refused to come. I was perturbed, distraught, exhausted, and frustrated. I was also thirsty but was sick and tired of ice chips. Brice and Johanna tried to console me as best they could but I reached a zone where I just wanted her to come and nothing else and no one else would do. Crying, moaning, and pleading for it to stop was all I could do. Longing to hold my little baby was what my heart ached to do and needed like the oxygen mask I was being forced to wear. There were moments she caused an uproar on the monitors and then I would cause those same moments. Everyone has a breaking point and I reached mine around that fourteenth hour. Throwing the cool towel Johanna placed on my head across the room, knocking the ice chips from Jane's hand, yelling at Brice who was so patient, and then just shutting down. I think I died several deaths during my sixteen hours of labor. To the pain I'd carried so long. To the rejection I'd made mine far too long and to the little girl that now must be a mother, wife, and daughter. Mostly to the unforgiveness I'd carried for all the people who hurt me so badly. My birthing my daughter freed me from those people so that I could love the people that mattered, my family. When Brice grabbed my hand and held me praying in my ear for God to "Help my wife and child. Give her the strength and allow Summer to come so the pain will stop." I literally felt strength come into my body. It was unexplainable but I felt a presence in the room that I was not familiar with or use to. Peace, hope and love surrounded me. Brice and I had conversations about God but never had we prayed together before. It worked.

At last with Johanna on one leg, Brice on the other, and Jane at my head and holding my hand, Summer Anna-Joy Chandler was born weighing 9 pounds 15 ounces and 21 inches long. Joy really was in the room. She was perfect, just perfect with her hazel eyes and curly light brown hair. When I saw Brice hold his little girl for the first time crying like a baby yet being the strong man he was I knew without a doubt that my heart belonged to him and only him. I also knew that God really did answer prayers. Brice was the one that added Joy to our little girl's name after Johanna and because of the happiness that she was bringing to all of our lives. I was elated and so was Mommy. I had my family just like the preacher man said that day in the church. Both of Brice's half-brothers sent flowers congratulating us on our new arrival. That was special for me. One of his sisters, Kayla sent a gift card to the baby store and that shocked me. The rest of the family remained silent, but silence was the last thing we had in our home.

The next three weeks were a whirlwind of sleepless nights, diapers, swollen breasts, and lots of tears. Tears of joy. My heart was overjoyed I had a bloodline that would continue. My mother would be happy I just knew it and that alone made me ecstatic. Brice only took a couple of days off work in conjunction with the weekend. That took everything to convince him. Johanna would be with me for the next three weeks so there was no need for both of them to be there. It made more sense for him to take leave when she went back to Washington. Reluctantly he agreed, but every day when he came home that little girl belonged to no one else but him. He carried her around with him everywhere he went. There was nothing we could do to stop him. He said he needed to make up for lost time when he was being forced to go to work. Seeing him with her was more than my heart could stand. He rocked her to sleep, sang to her, and insisted I express milk in a bottle so he could feed her too. Johanna would not allow me to do anything at all in the house. She cooked, cleaned, and watched the baby for me to have naps daily. Joy, as we decided to call her was her pride and joy. She was already in her will and stitched in her heart. When it was time for her to leave I cried all day and so did little Joy. That was a difficult day for everyone including Brice. It was definitely a bittersweet. None of us wanted her to leave. The only good thing about it was that I was able to give her the key to my apartment and she was going to store my furniture in her garage and turn in my keys with the special power of attorney I'd given to her. She would keep my car at her place until my husband and I decided what we should do about it. My job never terminated me but I decided to resign as soon as I'd used up the remainder of my leave. There was nothing for me at Terrofare International any longer and I was ready to move forward with my life.

Chapter 42

Jane was building her life again. She'd found an apartment not far from our home not wanting to be isolated any longer. She had not wanted to stay in their house because she had experienced too much pain there. Still gathering bits and pieces I gave her the time she needed to heal. Eventually I learned infidelity and abuse had played a major role in their split. Later she admitted she knew he was not right for her all along, but her family was crazy about him so she decided to ignore all the warning signs. All I wanted was for her and RJ to be safe and happy. She always listened to my problems, gave me advice, and loved me no matter what. Now it was my turn. I loved having her close again. She was the overprotective aunt, sister and friend I longed for all my life. She was bossy, opinionated, loud at times, loving, caring, and would fight to the death for you. I just wanted her to learn to fight for herself again.

Deciding to be a stay at home Mom, for the moment anyway, I planned menus, re-decorated our home, cooked, cleaned, and Jane and I took daily walks. Getting back to my pre-pregnancy weight was a top priority. Not wanting Joy in any type of childcare facility my husband ordered me a treadmill. If I couldn't get outside I walked a couple miles on the treadmill each day. Johanna had become the video phone stalker of a grandmother. She had to see her "Joy" at least daily and I found it all amusing. Her life was changing as well. She was thinking about retiring. So many changes took place during the merger it was almost like she did not have a choice. I knew it was selfish but I secretly prayed she would come back for a very long vacation.

Jane went with me to my six week postpartum appointment. She watched the baby while I saw the doctor. Leaving my little Joy with anyone was out of the question. I loved being a mother and I was falling more and more in love with being a wife. For so long Brice had chased me but after my doctor's appointment I was going to turn that around. He was a great husband, best friend, and outstanding father, and he needed to hear it from me. My appointment went well. Besides still having some pregnancy weight and being two cup sizes larger all went great. I made sure birth control was not an issue before leaving. If we decided to have another child we would most assuredly plan it. It was time I enjoyed being a newlywed. After my appointment we stopped by the mall so I could get a special outfit for a special night. Lingerie, candles, strawberries, cool whip, massaging oils and a few other unmentionable were on my list.

"You are so nasty!" Jane teased.

"Honey tonight when I put this little girl to bed I'm going to see if I can't bring some joy to Mr. Brice Anthony Chandler's heart."

"What! I know that is right," Jane high fives me.

After shopping Jane came home with me and helped me get my house in order. Joy had so much stuff it was literally everywhere. So we did some rearranging. She helped me put the storage containers I'd purchased to good use. Next I stripped our bed linen and replaced it with the new comforter set I purchased. Then I set up our bathroom and transformed it into a spa. Lastly, I made a simple dinner that I knew Brice loved. I couldn't wait for my husband to come home. It really wasn't about the sex, not all of it anyway. I wanted my husband to know he was appreciated, loved, and that I was committed to our family. Jane visited for a little while longer then made her exit around mid afternoon. When Brice put his key in the door I had music playing softly and a few candles burning. He saw it in my eyes and I saw it in his, still I wanted to wait. He needed to be pampered. It was hard for me to pull back from our greeting but I did. While he spent time with Joy I made his favorite beverage. Feeling his eyes on me and the little outfit I was wearing I strutted my stuff even the more. He never liked to eat dinner right away so I served him an appetizer; chocolate covered strawberries. When I gave him the dish he reached out and grabbed my hand and pulled me to him. He didn't say anything. There was no need. Taking a sleeping Joy from his arms I took her to the nursery and put her in the crib. Then I went across the hall to our bedroom and started the bath water. Proceeding to go back to the living room I turned around and ran right into Brice.

"Don't make me wait any longer. Everything is beautiful but it's been such a long time."

He grabbed me and kissed me and all my ideas and plans went right out of the window. All I had time to do was turn off the running water. "All I want is you Han. All I've ever wanted was you." His voice was very low and deep. He took matters into his own hands and my plans were abandoned. He had always known how to love me, but today it was different. He was even more attentive in every way possible. Everything inside of me came alive and responded to him to the point that I screamed out, "I love you so much Brice!" That was like pouring gasoline on an already blazing fire. I felt like everything in the past was being consumed so it could finally be just me and my husband. For the first time in our marriage only the two of us would matter. When it was all over I cried. He held me tightly.

When our daughter turned eight weeks old Brice announced that we were going to church and I agreed. He wanted our daughter to be dedicated to God and I knew he was right again. His brothers were coming, Mommy was coming, Jane and RJ would be there, and I hoped his parents and siblings would come. Remembering what Johanna taught me I'd sent invitations out to each of them praying for a response. I even sent an invitation to Mr. Nelson because when I did not know it he had been looking out for my welfare. Brice was out of control. He had a professional photographer and a videographer at the dedication. Joy's dress had been hand made in Italy and shipped special delivery by one of his college roommates who now worked there. Reservations had been made for everyone to have a celebration dinner afterwards at his expense. I just didn't know what to say about him and all of his carrying on. Mommy insisted I leave him alone. I couldn't agree to that but I allowed him his happiness for the moment.

The morning of the dedication before going to the car I returned to our bedroom and got on my knees. I needed to talk to God before I left the house. It was urgent. "Lord I don't know what this day will hold, but I place it in your hands. I even ask you to take my life if it is something you still want. I realize I've made many mistakes but I want what good there is left of me to be yours. I place my husband and my daughter in your hands and I ask that whatever we face from this day forward we face it together in you. Amen." When I got up Brice was standing in the doorway. Obviously he'd left Mommy and the baby in the car.

"You're an awesome woman Mrs. Chandler."

Chapter 43

When we arrived at the church the god-parents, Ian and Jane were standing in the parking lot talking. Excitement was in the air and for once I was not afraid to be happy and show it. I could not wait to get in that church. When altar call was given I planned to be the first one there to give thanks to God for all he had done in my life and to make my profession public. Unlike most services the baby dedication ceremony was done at the end. Normally that would have bothered me, but not today. I was too busy enjoying the service. When I looked down the row and saw my husband standing beside me, Ian and Nick next to him, Jane and Johanna and RJ sitting beside them and on the row behind us were his parents and his sisters I was so overjoyed I cried the entire service. It was the first time in my life I worshiped God with a family; my family. When the other Mrs. Chandler asked to hold little Joy everything that preacher said to me came back in a flash. Brice's sister Rebecca and I shared a moment when we realized we were wearing the exact same dress, hers in blue and mine in green. "You have great taste my dear" she whispered as we all walked down to the altar for the ceremony. I smiled and said, "Great minds fashion alike."

The pastor was just about to begin the dedication when Brice interrupted him. "Brother Brice do you have something to say?" The preacher gave him the floor. I was confused and so was everyone else.

"Yes sir we are here to dedicate our daughter Joy today, but I realized I need to dedicate myself first. I want to give myself to the Lord so I can teach my daughter about Him. What do I need to do pastor?"

The entire church literally went up in praise. I dropped to my knees and lifted up my hands to heaven and shouted, "Me too! I want Him in my life too!" I lost it, but in a different way. All the stuff I had been carrying for so many years I gave to God when I lifted my hands to Him and I said, "Take it, I just want you." It took a long time for the church to calm down. Brice's parents, Johanna and his brothers were dancing right along with half the congregation. When the preacher got himself together because he had fallen to his knees right beside us; he lead us through the sinner's prayer. I not only had a family now but I had a God that loved me and lived in me. My life was perfect.

The ringing doorbell puzzled me a bit. We weren't expecting anyone. It had been a wonderful, but long day. When all the family finally left I was just as happy to see them go. I was anxious to talk to my husband about the day and our new relationship with God and his family. He and I were both happy. Johanna was on her plane, the in-laws were gone but not without the promise to visit again soon, I was tired and so was my crying baby girl. When I opened the door, screaming baby in my arms feeling flustered from sleep deprivation and my dwindling efforts to console her. No one and nothing could have prepared me for that moment. Reaching for the door I used it to steady myself.

"What are you doing here?! Why would you come here! Why couldn't you just let me have my life?"

When she opened her mouth I literally covered my ear with my free hand. There was nothing in this world I wanted to hear Ms. Ann say. Except why hell was throwing people back? She was supposed to be dead, not standing in front of my home.

"Hannah I know you hate me but please I have to speak to you."

"Brice!!!!!!!!!!! Brice!!!!!"

Running to the room in only a towel, 357 magnum in hand Brice I am sure did not know what situation he was running into.

"Make her leave Brice! She shouldn't be at my home. I don't want her here!"

"Please, oh please Hannah, just let me say what I have to say and I swear I will never bother you again," she pleaded.

"No, I don't want to hear anything you have to say. I heard enough, remember. You said enough to me. All your evil words, your mistreatment and your lies, but I made it. I made it anyway so you can just rot in hell

Ms. Ann because I don't need you in my life and I don't want you in my life. You should have never been given a child. Some people shouldn't have children!"

"But I did Hannah. I had you. I gave birth to you. You are my daughter and I just want to say how sorry I am for giving you up for adoption, for mistreating you, and for not telling you the truth."

I have heard people talk about the hand of God. How at times they knew it was Him that carried them or held them in moments of devastation. I was in one of those moments. Something in me knew she was telling the truth as much as I hated to hear it. She hated me too much not to know me. Some things just did not add up from my childhood. Plus she had two different sets of birth certificates waving them around.

"Please, please Hannah just let me explain," she cried.

My hatred was trying to resurface but my kicking crying baby forced me to do everything in my power to never let it back in again. Brice attempted to take the baby but I held on to her. My hands needed to be occupied or I just didn't know what I would do. When I refused to let go he asked me what I wanted to do. I stepped aside and motioned for her to come in. As much as I did not want to hear her I knew I must so I could have my life.

Once I comforted my baby we sat in silence. Not Brice. He was in protective mode still. Leaving the room just long enough to throw on a jogging suit he stood behind the chair Joy and I were seated in. Judging by the budge in his pocket I was positive he was still packing. "You are supposed to be dead," I spewed at her. It hurt and I wish I could say I was glad I hurt her, but that need to get even I discovered was no longer there.

"True. At least that is what I thought until I made peace with God and figured out the only thing killing me was guilt."

"Don't talk about God to me please." It may have sounded rude but I meant it. Seeing God through her eyes was not an image I wanted in my head ever again. I had found Him for myself and I wanted our relationship to be a right one.

"Alright Hannah."

"Why are you here? How did you find me?"

"Jonathan."

"Mr. Nelson told you where I lived?" That was hard for me to believe.

"No, not exactly. He recently passed away.

Hearing that hurt. Brice knew it and put his hand on my shoulder. Mr. Nelson had been a wonderful person. I was sorry I had not kept in touch with him. "Go on" I told her.

"Because he was your mother's attorney and also the executive over her estate when he died some of that paperwork was forwarded to me. Since I had been your guardian and the office could not find you. One of those pieces of mail was the letter you sent inviting him to your daughter's dedication ceremony. I read the letter. For years now I have been searching for you and I just knew it was an answer to my prayers."

"So God wanted you to go through someone else's mail?" I said sarcastically.

She was quick to reply, "I think Jonathan would have wanted you to know the truth. Anyway I immediately drove to San Antonio. I was too afraid to approach you at the church so I sat in the back."

"The devil would be afraid of God. Now that I can believe."

Ignoring my remarks she continued, "When I was dying I wanted to apologize out of guilt. Then I had a real encounter with God and I just wanted to make things right with you because you did not deserve to be treated the way I treated you. Out of respect you deserved to at least know the entire story I have never been brave enough to tell you. Your mother was my best friend. Kind, loving, and would do anything for me. One year I came to visit her and well things happened. When I found out I was pregnant I knew I couldn't be anyone's mother. I was too selfish to love anyone and she and I both knew it. She told me she would take you as her own and no one would ever have to know. It was perfect. Those yearly visits were her way of getting me to come to terms with my past, but I did not want to and then she suddenly died. Unknown to me she made me your legal guardian. She felt like you should know the truth when it was time, but to me you were just a reminder of my stupidity. What I had tried to bury and forget just would not go away. No one knew about you except your mother. I just couldn't handle it. The entire time you were with me I abused prescription medication to cope. They didn't make me better just more depressed and even meaner. There is no excuse for what I did. You deserved better and I know it. I was wrong and I ask your forgiveness. No, I do not deserve it and I am certain I have no right to ask for it. When I told your father about you he denied ever knowing me and mocked me around town. When you were born you looked just like him and still do and I took my hatred for him and made you the recipient of it."

"So my entire life has been a lie. Is Hannah even my real name?"

"No I believe you are living the life you are supposed to have. As a matter of fact I am certain of it, minus me of course. Here is a copy of your original birth certificate and a copy of your adoptive one. Your name was always Hannah. Your mother named you. She always said you were the child that she asked God to give her. She was your mother and she loved you more than anything. She only wanted the best for you and I know she is smiling down on you now. Believe it or not you are more like her than anyone else."

My head hurt and I just wanted to fall out in the floor. The birth certificates confirmed everything she said. What was I supposed to do with all this information? How was I supposed to handle it? My heart ached so badly I wanted to scream. How could they all lie to me? Why would they deceive me in this way? When I got up I wasn't sure why but when my legs took me to the door and I heard myself say, "Leave please" I soon found out. She walked out without saying another word. Giving Brice little Joy I walked to the bathroom, locked the door, and opened the medicine cabnet.